THE POWER
OF
MINDFORCE

6034-MILL

THE POWER OF MINDFORCE

Birth of a Hero

V.J. Miller, Sr.

6034-MILL

To order additional copies of this book, contact:
Xlibris Corporation
1-888-795-4274
www.Xlibris.com
Orders@Xlibris.com

CONTENTS

PROLOGUE

Not of her own free will, she stood there by the pot-bellied stove in a hunters cabin in the Pocono Mountains of Pennsylvania.

Standing at the stove, sweat gathered in increasing beads upon her forehead and cheeks. Running down her face in various rivulets to gather at the tip of her chin where they amassed into glistening droplets. Droplets that rhythmically fell to the blistering surface of the stove; there hissing their displeasure and hers.

Occasionally she would dab at the increasing moisture with the cuff of her bulky wool turtleneck; a most adequate barrier against the wintry weather without, but, in the confines of the Spartan cabin it proved an oppressive sauna. She was damp along her flesh constantly. But for Ray and Lyle, she would have peeled it off without hesitation, but she could not; she had nothing on beneath, and she had nothing else to wear. Even so, a few more days confined here she might do it anyway and take her chances.

Sheila DiAngelo had been hitchhiking north on the Schuylkill Expressway when two men, Ray and Lyle, driving in a battered old green pickup, with the doors half falling off, stopped to give her a lift. Being a raw February day, and since beggars can't be choosers, she climbed aboard.

She'd strode with her thumb out in the misty rain for over an hour; cursing everyone that passed her by. Now was not the time to be particular. Sitting between the two men, neither seeming to have bathed recently, the air was ripe. It was just as well the heater didn't work.

After driving for about an hour in that drafty rattletrap, all agreed they should stop somewhere for coffee.

Ray pulled his six feet of crew-cutted gaunt out from behind the wheel and stretched while Lyle, some twenty-five pounds heavier and two inches shorter got out to pump the gas. His longish hair had the tendency to fall in his face at will causing him to ever be pushing it aside. Neither had shaved in days.

If Ray hadn't bought that paper at the truck stop, like as not Sheila wouldn't be where she now found herself.

Sheila was a runaway. Just not your typical adolescent run of the mill type runaway. No, Sheila was over twenty-one; sporting the finest college education. Coming from a well to do family; coddled and pampered most of her formative years. Even so, she found it unbearable to put up with her father's incessant over-protectiveness. After enduring all she would, she blew up in his face and stormed out the door. Head strong? Definitely. With a tendency to leap before she looked; this was the short definition of Sheila.

Her picture graced the front page only because Momma wanted to know where she was and if she was okay.

Ray, being the smarter of the two, but not by any measurable amount, recognized Sheila's picture. He knew of the DiAngelo family, and that there might be a buck or three in it for Lyle and himself. But they'd have to be careful. Ray and Lyle weren't exactly unknown to the law.

When they were on the road again, Ray ordered Lyle to check Sheila's belongings. She'd taken little, wishing to move fast and light. But she wasn't altogether incompetent. She'd had the good sense to take $750 from her room before she left, though now it wasn't hers anymore. All her protesting and a failed attempt at shoving Lyle out the rickety door availed her nothing.

Her money in his pocket, Ray showed her the paper. He explained to Lyle in the simplest terms he could muster, that they had a gold mine here; and if they played their cards right they'd get very rich, very fast. But they needed time to plan. Lyle knew of a place in the Pocono Mountains where they could hide out. It was secluded, and no one would be there this time of year.

Three days later, here she was again. At the pot bellied stove in the corner of the tiny cabin. Cooking yet again another meal for her captors.

"What's holdin' up dinner woman?" Ray griped in his usual manner while he sat cleaning his nails with his hunting knife.

"Hold your water," shot back Sheila. "It's coming."

Lyle, who felt he was the more suave and sophisticated of the duo, sat on the lone cot picking his nose; pondering if he should sample it or just flick it on the floor. "I'll help her," he said. "She just needs some incentive."

Rising from the cot he ambled over toward Sheila. Placing his eager hands around her waist he whispered in her ear. "We both know what you need. Don't we honey?"

From the stew pot she lifted a spoonful of the boiling liquid and poured it onto Lyle's hands about her midsection.

While Lyle yelped, leaped back and shoved his burning fingers in his mouth, Ray damn near pissed himself from laughing so hard.

Whirling around, Sheila waved the large wooden spoon in Lyle's face. "Keep your grubby paws to yourself, slime! Or you'll be wearing this upside your ear."

"Whoa! Chill out woman," bitched Lyle; sucking on his rapidly blistering fingers.

Jamming the spoon into the stew pot, Sheila stalked across the room, folded her arms in disgust then plopped down on the bunk. "If I hadn't been hitching you wouldn't have me for a hostage. . . . I may cook and clean for you, but no way will I be your plaything. And furthermore—"

Crashing glass from the window behind her cut short her tirade. Bursting through over her head hurtled a strangely garbed figure.

Clad in skintight burnt orange spandex, sporting a high collared cape and hood, the stranger rolled in the air, landing lightly upon his feet. Upon his hood, over and around his eye sockets, and emblazoned on his chest she saw a large letter "M".

Ducking down on the bunk, pulling her head in under her arms, Sheila avoided the shattering glass flying over her head.

Lyle the lover, not the fighter, froze in a catatonic stupor against the door.

Ray on the other hand, leaped out of his chair; knocking it over. Reaching behind his back for the 9mm Ruger he'd bought from the Mob supplier with Sheila's money, he got off two quick shots at the stranger when he whirled around to face them. If this was a rescue . . . it was going to be short lived.

Ray gaped dumbfounded when the slugs found their mark in the middle of the strangers chest, then merely bounced off, rattling around the floor at the strangers feet. The stranger was not unaffected as a distressed "OW!" came through the mask, his hands leaping up to rub the sore spot.

Assuming the stranger wore a bulletproof vest, Ray prepared to fire again; he never got the chance.

Raising his right hand, the stranger gestured in Ray's direction. Slowly, then ever more violently the gun began to vibrate in Ray's grasp to a point where he could no longer hold on to it. When it slipped from his fingertips it defied the law of gravity. Instead of clattering to the floor it flew to the strangers open hand where he promptly crushed it in his grasp as easily as you'd squeeze a blob of buttered taffy.

As if on cue, Lyle found the use of his muscles. His right hand flashed to the hilt of the survival knife at his waist. Determined to disembowel the intruder, Lyle lunged at the stranger. With the howl of a prehistoric hunter erupting from his throat, he attempted to plunge eight inches of tempered steel deep into the intruder's chest. Wasted effort. The blade only bent to the side.

This attempt in futility, with what transpired in the last few seconds, and being the he-man he was, Lyle took the only recourse open . . . he fainted. He was as much a fighter as he was a lover.

On the other hand, Ray being the smarter of the two knew exactly what to do—and he did it without hesitation. He ran like a scalded dog for the door.

He leapt barely two steps onto the porch when the stranger

jerked him back by the collar. A four-knuckle sedative sent Ray to meet Lyle in lullaby land.

After lowering Ray gently to the floor the stranger grabbed a poker from the stove; bending it easily as one might a licorice stick about the ankles of the two kidnapers; ensuring they wouldn't be going anywhere prematurely. Then he turned to the girl.

The first thing Sheila was aware of was that she had gotten up from the bunk and now cowered in the corner.

"Sheila."

He knew her. But how? She frowned.

Eyes darting, she trembled while the stranger casually strode toward her. Keeping her distance while attempting to forestall his approach, she backpedaled around the tiny cabin.

"S-Stay away. Don't you come near me."

Coming ever nearer she backed up ever more quickly. Her mind raced through all manner of dread. Heart pounding in her ears, the backs of her calves caressed the edge of the bunk when he halted before her. Reflexes brought her right hand up to the chest of this what ever he was, giving him a stiff arm in an attempt to keep him at some measure of distance.

Frenzied nerves stretched to the limit she found her courage again, voicing her displeasure. "Look You! I've had enough. First these two slime . . . and now you. What's this friggin world com—"

"Leave," he cut her off in a firm tone. "Someone will meet you down the trail." That said, the stranger turned his back and strode toward the open door. "Now I must go," he said over his shoulder.

Stepping lively the few steps to the doorway, Sheila gaped while the stranger strode regally, his cape flowing in the light breeze, to the edge of the porch where he leaped into the air . . . and kept going; of all things.

"Wait!" cried Sheila from the edge of the porch. "Who the hell are you?"

Under the clear full moon, Sheila stood transfixed while the mystery man flew into the distance; bathed in its light.

"What the hell was that?" she mumbled, returning into the cabin.

Realization, that she was free and what the hell was she hanging around for, had her coat and purse in her grasp. Stepping quickly out the door, tiptoeing across the ice and snow she yanked on her coat and hurried along the trail, slipping and sliding all the while.

Stealing repeated glances over her shoulder, fearing Ray or Lyle might somehow be chasing her; she neglected to stay aware of her footing. Careening around a bend her feet chose to position themselves over her head. Sliding across the trail she ended in a heap in the snow-laden ditch.

Almost simultaneously a firm grasp had her by the upper arm. Silhouetted in the moonlight a large trench coat and fedora lifted her easily from the slush.

Chest heaving, heart pounding, she yelped and struggled to pull away. "No No. Lemme go! Lemme go!" But the grasp of the trench coat proved too strong.

Then it spoke firm and assuring, "Sheila . . . Sheila. I'm a private detective. Calm down. Your mother Rita sent me to find you. Everything's all right now."

"Mother?" Something in the voice or the mention of her mother's name brought her into focus. "Mother sent you?"

"Yes."

"Who, are you?"

"Name's Jason, Jason Parks. Now let's get you home."

"But . . . what about Ray and Lyle."

"Who?"

"The men, back there . . . in the cabin."

"Forget about them. I'll call the Sheriff on the way."

Excited, she begins to babble. "Did you see him?"

"Who?

"The weirdo. . . . The, the whatever in the orange tights."

"Are you okay? Did they force any drugs on you?"

"No. No. He . . . or it crashed in there; clubbed Ray and Lyle then flew off into the Moon.

"Yeah, right," said Jason while he turned his rugged features with the mustache and three-day stubble into the radiance of the moon, and grinned broadly. "C'mon. My car's just down the trail."

"You don't believe me."

"We'll talk about it later. Now let's go."

Stepping quickly the hundred yards to Jason's car went smoothly; with nary a slip or slide.

"This piece of junk is it?" she said in disbelief.

Tucked in an opening between a boulder and a fir tree sat Jason's car. A mud covered, peeling, navy blue 67 Mustang sporting rusted out quarter panels, crooked driver side door and a large ding in the left rear fender—and the vinyl top wasn't too healthy either.

"Hey. It gets me there and brings me back."

"How? On the back of a tow truck."

"Watch it. You wanna walk back to Philly."

"It might be safer."

"Get in."

Despite its looks and its instilling of trepidation, the 'Stangs engine fired instantly to life. A few revs on the pedal for effect torqued the cars body. A gentle shift into the first of four speeds and a practiced press on the gas while releasing the clutch bolted the car from its seclusion; quickly down the lane.

* * * *

CHAPTER ONE

She Wants What?

Jason's car bounced, body parts creaking, into the entrance to the DiAngelo estate. The drive had taken just over an hour with a short pause for a pit stop at a dinky little filling station up in the mountains. From there he'd called her parents; telling them they could relax and that they'd be there shortly.

Jason's car had the habit of running on for several seconds after the ignition had been shut off; it didn't break the pattern this time either. Barely stopped, Sheila was out of her seat; hurrying to embrace her parents waiting in robe and slippers between the mounds of snow around the front door.

Anthony rung the hell out of Jason's hand, thanking him profusely. Invited inside, Jason stayed as brief an interval as he deemed discrete, then excused himself to allow this reunion to proceed in private.

The sun tinged the horizon dark crimson when Jason turned the key to his agency door. It being closer than his apartment, and since he felt no need to sleep, he went there to celebrate his good fortune.

The agency looked exactly like something out of the Maltese Falcon with its 40's style inner and outer offices, sporting frosted glass from waist level to ceiling between the offices and the hall. Only, Sam Spade was an infinitely better housekeeper. Unkempt and cluttered would be an act of kindness in describing the setup.

After fumbling with the keys he let himself in and went straight to his inner office; never pausing an instant in the practiced ritual of withdrawing the last vestiges of a drooping cigarette from the corner of his mouth and stubbing it out in the overflowing ashtray on the corner of the receptionist's desk. Ashes lying in a neat circle like a halo about the receptacle.

The desk harbored no receptionist because he never had the funds to employ one. No, it sat there, a shrine to the futility of junk mail and every unpaid bill he hoped would get lost in some other realm, never to be seen again.

His private office, only so because the previous tenant had chosen to have it painted on the glass door wasn't much different from the other. Except here at least one could see some portion of the desktop.

Hanging his hat and coat on the clothes tree just inside the door, he lit up another Marlboro. After firing up the coffee pot he sat in his chair, plopped his crossed size twelves onto the radiator beneath the window, where, inscribed in reverse was painted PARK'S DETECTIVE AGENCY in a slight arc, blowing smoke rings.

Jason dabbled in the business of finding missing people. But it only paid well when the clients were rich. Anthony DiAngelo fit the category nicely. The Landlord would be pleased.

Rising from his perch he grabbed his mug and filled it from the tarnished, dented old pot and filled it halfway with the dark steaming brew. From his desk drawer he lifts a half empty bottle of *Old Grand Dad* and tops off the level of the mug. Taking a swig from the bottle, swishing it around like mouthwash, it goes down bland as water. Disappointed, he sets the bottle firmly on the desk. He'd made a mental note to seek out a better brand of hooch.

Standing at the window he downs the mixture in gulps. While the coppery rays of the new dawn wash over his taught face he stares out over the awakening snow covered city. This was the first Saturday morning he could remember in years that he wasn't on his way home to crash and sleep it off, and, strangely enough, it felt good for a change.

Monday morning continued the trend set on Sunday. The weather had become unusually warm and sunny, causing the recent snowfall to recede at an accelerated pace.

True to his own ritual, Jason, unkempt and still unshaven, paused at the corner newsstand to pick up a copy of the Philadelphia Inquirer before climbing the stairs to his second floor office. The elevator worked, but the stairs were usually devoid of people, and it passed the time.

Checking his answering machine, there was nothing there for the fifth day in a row.

"Ahhh. The start of another busy day." He smirks and shrugs, tossing the paper on his desk.

On the front page is the story of the return of Sheila DiAngelo to her very relieved parents by a local P.I., *Bert* Parks. Great! That'll certainly get him a lot of new clients. He thought of calling the paper, then set the receiver back in the cradle. What good would a correction, buried in the back, do anyway? The *hell* with it.

Flipping the paper over to the back an obscure article catches his eye while he lights up another smoke. The filler reported no progress on the mysterious sonic boom last Friday evening, nor on the reports of a UFO and unaccountable radar blips at the airport, or if the two were connected. Jason smiles broadly, but his attention is directed to the opening of his front door.

Dropping the paper he steps to his office door and pauses. Back to him, stands a luscious young thing. Tall, even statuesque, you might say, with long black hair done in tight curls that looked as if it had recently been permed. Built like a brick shithouse, with every brick exactly where it belonged. She sported a snug, short-skirted business suit, with long shapely legs that went all the way down to her dainty feet, set in the highest pair of black stiletto sling backs he'd ever seen. So, naturally, he was aroused.

She stands absorbed, inspecting Jason's many citations and plaques for bravery and dedication to duty from the NYPD.

Leaning on the doorjamb, Jason drinks her in appreciatively.

"Can I help you, Sheila?"

She turns half around at the waist; a curious grin on her face. "How did you know it was me?"

There is the minutest of pauses while Jason's eyes divert from the inviting jade green of hers. "Hey. I'm a detective."

She turns completely around and strolls toward Jason. "But, I look altogether different."

"Yesss. I see," he says, unable to help but notice the way her breasts strain at their confinement. "Now, how can I help you?"

She sneers disdainfully at the half smoked cigarette hanging from Jason's lips.

"It's not so much what you can do for me, but rather what we can do for each other."

"Oh? And just how is that?"

She nonchalantly plucks the cigarette from Jason's mouth and stubs it out in the ashtray. Jason, mildly annoyed, remains silent.

"You remember our talk on that long drive home Saturday morning?"

"We covered quite a bit of ground. You wanna narrow it down a bit."

Sheila sits back seductively on the corner of the receptionist's desk and crosses her long legs. "You said that . . . "

While Jason gazed at the expanse of leg before him, the memory of forgotten idle conversation came drifting back. He recalled he did ask her about herself.

She went on about her childhood: born into a rich family, she was the last of four children and the only girl.

Being the only one she became Daddy's little girl; even into adulthood. He lavished all kinds of presents on her. There wasn't anything she wanted that he wouldn't get for her, and she took full advantage of it.

She went through all the phases while growing up.

As a little girl she was a brat to say the least. She was Daddy's little snitch to boot. Her three brothers couldn't get away with anything when she was around. She told all she knew to any adult who would take the time to listen to her. Even when they didn't want to.

She lingered in the tomboy stage. Wanting to play all the sports the boys in the neighborhood played, and truth to tell, she was quite good at them. There were many local boys she bested with her prowess even her brothers. Which she especially enjoyed. Naturally, they never wanted her around.

Eventually, in her late teens, she discovered boys. The wild flower became the spectacular rose. She dated frequently; Daddy never approved of any of them. They were all after his money as far as he was concerned, a bunch of social climbers.

Her brothers agreed with their Father. After all, he had all the money. They did everything in their power to shelter her from the inferior strata. They even enjoyed throwing a few of them off the grounds bodily. No wonder she developed a rebellious nature.

In the early years she enjoyed the attention, using it to her own ends. She got all the best of everything if she whined just so. If one of her brothers didn't exactly please her, she could get Daddy to punish him.

Like maturity oft times will; all things change. The attention lavished on her that she loved, began to smother her instead.

She'd gotten above average grades in high school; she couldn't wait to graduate and go away to college; her sights set on UCLA. When all her pleading, threatening and cajoling Daddy came to naught, she played her trump card: *Mother*. The one person she learned early on that could change Daddy's mind.

Southern California has a different way of observing the world. Two and a half years of it brought her maturity into full flower.

Mid way through her Junior year she decided she'd had enough. She wanted something different, something better from life. Thus, she came home to inform her parents of her decision. That then was what the quarrel was about. He was paying for her education and wasn't going to throw his good money down the drain.

She told him to more or less kiss off. Grabbing some money from her room she stalked out the door. She stayed with a friend for a few days while she let her parents stew before she made her decision. She'd hitchhike around the country while she made her way back to L.A. She had friends there who'd help her get a fresh start. She never got very far.

Her life up to speed, she questioned Jason about himself. He'd allowed her the short version, neglecting to fill in the reasons why he was asked to leave New York. He idly told her he was so inundated with neglected paperwork that he sure could use a good sec—re . . . tary . . . Uh-Ohhhh! Jason was abruptly plucked out of his flashback.

" . . . you were sorely in need of a secretary. And so. Here I am."

"What? You? I don't think so. Besides, it was just a wish. I can't afford a secretary right now."

"Now hold on Jason. I'm no idle rich kid with no brains. I know my way around an office."

"But—"

"No buts. I know I can handle a typewriter better than you. And from the looks of these files, I can do that better."

"Sorry. I can't afford you."

Sheila, not to be denied, blurts out before she thinks. "Well if you worked a little more often you'd have the money."

Jason's lips tighten to a thin line; he roils within but keeps his temper. "That's it. Don't let the door hit you in the butt on your way out."

Breaking off the interview, Jason turns his back and stalks off into his office. Her hackles up, Sheila is hot on his heels. Firm strides bring him behind his desk; she pulls up in front, placing her hands on the cluttered desk.

"Don't get your shorts in a knot. I only told the truth."

Jason sits and reaches for his pack of smokes. Sheila shoots him a nasty glare. Discretion the better part of valor, he tosses the pack aside for the moment.

"What makes you think you can handle the job?"

"Two and a half years of Business Management at UCLA. I can handle the job."

"What about your parents?"

"What about them?"

"Won't they be upset?"

"About what?"

"Won't it bother them that you're working at such a, common job?"

Sheila leaned in close, looking him straight in the eye. "I've had a long talk with Mother and Dad. We all decided I should do what I really wanted for a change. Daddy still protested some, but Mother said she'd handle him. She agreed with me that I should be out on my own, earning my own money. I've even found my own apartment already."

No longer able to contain it, Jason lights up another cigarette. "So why pick on me?"

Because you need help," she said while glancing around. "You gotta improve your image. Shave a little more often. And you need to get rid of that cigarette!" Whereupon she plucked it from his mouth and stubbed it out in the ashtray with authority. "That's a nasty habit that can only do you no good!"

"Old habits die hard," was his weak defense. "But, I'll try to do my best to kick it . . . someday."

Her being a good talker had little to do with Jason's decision. The sincerity he felt from her ultimately nudged him to relent and at least give her a shot.

"What the hell. When would you like to start?"

A smug air about her she said succinctly. "From the looks of this place I'd better get right in on it today."

"Okay," he said, leading her to her office. "Here's your desk . . . your chair . . . and here's your typewriter. I think it needs a new ribbon."

"You better let me handle that. So. What's my first assignment Boss?"

Jason points to a hodge-podge clutter of papers on top of the filing cabinet and on the corner of her desk. "Search through, collate and file all of these."

Sheila's shoulders droop, her lip curling up. "I have but two questions. Where's the coffee pot? And where's the front end loader? . . ."

Across town in a posh apartment, a pair of gloved hands removes a foreboding black hood from its stand and places it about the owner's head. Nothing can be seen of the man's head save a pair of penetrating slate gray eyes. This simple act began the case the would bring Jason nearer to the Grim Reaper then anyone should care to be . . .

* * * *

CHAPTER TWO

The Crime Czar

The short, lean, hooded man, turns from the mirror to face two other men in the room.

"Gentlemen. Today brings the dawn of a new era in Philadelphia. Today we begin taking over the Rackets in this city from the assholes who think they're in charge. As I discussed with you in previous weeks, we'll start by taking over all the bookie joints and grabbing their bagmen off the streets. After getting as many of the bozos as we can to see it our way and join us, we move on to phase two. That being to move in on the dope pushers and pimps. Under cover of the ensuing turmoil, while they're chasing their tails, we move on to phase three.

That's when the lawyers take over. They've been working for months finding loopholes where I might take over the legitimate businesses they run to launder their ill-gotten money."

"But Boss. Isn't that a pretty tall order?" says Alfie Tulio. Your typical Sicilian stereotype. Your greasy haired, slick it down, love 'em and leave 'em type. His cold, cruel dark eyes mirrored his deep-seated hatred of most anything.

"Yes it is. But that's why I had you two recruit all those men to infiltrate the places we're moving on today.

"What about the Big Syndicate, Boss?" says Freddy Lester. A short, thin, quiet type. His hollow green eyes echoing his willingness to follow; never to lead. A fence sitter who could be dangerous. "You never told us, when you recruited us two, how you were going to handle them. They take a pretty large cut outta the Rackets."

"I'd like to know how you're going to handle that myself," says Alfie.

"That my good man is the real gem in this whole operation. About a year ago I had my lawyers contact their representatives in New York. Basically, what my lawyers laid before them was an offer for a bet."

"A bet?" says Alfie.

"Yes. A bet."

"But, what kinda bet could you possibly interest them in that they'd take you up on?" says Freddy.

"Just this. The City of Philadelphia, and all its rackets, against my life."

The inside of a coffin just before the mourners gather could not be any more quiet than the silence that fell over the room. Alfie is the first to find his tongue.

"Doesn't sound like a good deal to me. What's in it for them?"

"Just this. They get to keep their integrity, and the knowledge that their security system is working properly if I lose. Plus they get to do with me as they please."

"And If you win?" asks Alfie.

"I get to run all the Rackets in the city," gloats the Crime Czar like an adolescent with his first car.

"But what exactly was the bet?" says an uneasy Alfie.

"Simple in its wording actually. I bet them I could take over the city in six months."

Alfie and Freddy, who were standing at the time, decide they need to sit after all. The magnitude of this revelation greatly shook their senses. Each eases around to look at the other; wondering if they haven't thrown in with a mad man.

There were rules in this business; once you were in there was only one way out . . . and it didn't include retirement benefits.

"You're gonna have to bump off a lotta guys at the top to pull it off," says Freddy, wiping his brow.

"Uh uh. Part of the appeal of it is that I could throw their people out with a minimum of bloodshed. If they wanted to kill them later, well, that was their prerogative. And I wouldn't sick the cops on any of their people. I'd just make it inconvenient for them to remain in town."

"You've done some pretty risky things since I've known you," says Alfie. "But this. . . . Why?"

"All my life I've had just about everything handed to me. There was no challenge. Nothing I could get into that money couldn't fix."

"Sounds good to me," says Alfie.

"You never had a father like mine."

"I never had a father."

"Well mine always wanted perfection. I was always under his thumb. Even when I tried to join his business. . . . This will be my graduation. When I pull this off, I'll be better than him."

"Ain't you biting off too much to chew?" says Alfie.

"That's why I have the two of you to help me swallow it. . . . Now, any more questions?"

"Yeah Boss. Why the hood?" says Freddy.

"Only you two and the Syndicate leaders know who I am. Not even my lawyers know. You two know my family is quite wealthy and influential in this town. You also know I plan to lead some of the raids personally. So I need to disguise my face. It wouldn't do well for that information to get out to the general public, or the people running this town. I don't want my comings and goings hampered."

"But you've got plenty of money and influence now," says Alfie, trying to fathom this lunatics reasoning.

"Not enough! And not fast enough in coming. More control is what I'm after. That even more than money."

Pausing to compose himself, the hooded man continues. "You two have known me from the clubs we frequented. If anything, it's your fault I made the bet."

"How do you figure that?" says Alfie.

"You knew I was a big gambler. You led me to Quigley's where I came in contact with the Mobs."

"But—"

"No buts. I knew you two were a couple of cheap hoods looking for the big-time. When I propositioned you, you couldn't sign up fast enough."

"Okay. . . . Okay. You know we're in with you all the way, Boss. But, you know, and we know, that the Syndicate isn't going to let you walk all over their action here," says Alfie. "They're not crazy y-know."

"That's the simplicity of it all," the hooded man replies, pacing the floor. "Those . . . fat cats, up in their ivory towers are so pompous and arrogant, so sure of themselves, they don't think I have a snowballs chance in Hell of pulling it off."

Turning and jabbing a rigid finger northward, the hooded man yells. "They as much as told me, that if I can take it I can keep it! The fools. . . . Oh sure—they know I'll make a few scores and they'll plug the leaks afterward. But their fucking pride will never let them believe that I can throw out all their people here. They pride themselves on who they hire."

"But they gotta tell their people what's going down if they ask for help," says Alfie.

"They can't. That's the proviso in the bet. They don't inform their people what's going down and I'll show them just how stupid are the people they have running this city."

"And you trust them?" says Freddy.

"For now. Why not? They don't have anything to lose by my testing their people. But I'll show them. I'll humiliate their people so badly, they'll look like second rate bag men."

"Then what, Boss?" says Alfie.

"Then they'll either have to sneak out of town like the rats they are or they'll blow their brains out before the Syndicate can get out a contract on them. They don't like failures on their payroll. Especially in important positions."

"Can you pull it off in six months?" says Alfie.

"It's now been three months since the big shots accepted my wager. In that time, your men have been put in place. Since then, and in the time prior, my lawyers have been going over every lease and contract in the city. They've informed me that they have discovered sufficient leverage that I might take over. They've been setting the stage to undermine all their businesses. We even know which officials are being paid off. There are now three months with which to complete the bet."

"Three months. I don't see how we can pull it off in so short a time," says Alfie.

"We'll do it," gloats the hooded man clenching a gloved fist. "We'll grab them by the throat and choke the living shit out of them. We'll take over here, then we'll assault those pompous, arrogant fools in their ivory tower. They'll be sorry they had any dealings with the *Crime Czar!*" and he slams a gloved fist on the table before him.

The two hoods survey each other's faces; each knowing instinctively what the other believes—that they are indeed in league with a psychotic.

With some effort, Freddy screws up his courage, or just his lousy timing. "What if something goes wrong?"

"What!. . . . What can possibly go wrong! I've thought of everything. . . . And what I haven't, my lawyers have. We've planned for everything. Nothing. I repeat, nothing, can possibly go wrong . . ."

I guess the Crime Czar never heard about a little guy named . . . *Murphy!*

* * * *

CHAPTER THREE

Skirmish

The phone nagged in Jason's office. Reflex had his hand about to raise the receiver from its cradle before he remembered—he had a secretary now.

Jason briefly cocked an ear while Sheila, the official phone answerer, took the point. Filing, typing reports and telling people Jason was indisposed if he so chose were her domain now.

Being a private investigator would be a whole lot easier, if more expensive. His savings were gone; that's why he turned to his Old Grand Dad for help. Trouble was, after a half dozen shots he came to expect a decent buzz—today—nothing.

The fee he'd gotten from her parents had already gone to pay a lot of old debts; leaving the new ones to hang in limbo. Plus he had one more salary. Right now he could use a customer—the person on the phone wasn't it.

Tossing back his tenth shot, Sheila stood disapprovingly in the doorway.

"Jason."

"Yes Sheila. What did he want?"

"He wanted to. . . . Wait. How did you know it was a he?"

Hesitating, Jason scrolls through his mind; leaving Sheila hanging ever so briefly. "Why . . . I accidentally picked up the phone in here out of reflex . . . and before I put it back down I heard a man's voice."

Nodding, but uncertain, Sheila informs. "Well, that was the Police Commissioner. Seems those two that held me for ransom, that the costumed guy left tied up in the cabin, were wanted for assault and robbery in Virginia; as well as escaping from the prison in Rahway. He wanted to thank you for calling the local Sheriff to say where they could be found."

"My pleasure," he said, screwing the cap on his partner. "Anything to help the boys in blue of our fair city."

"I know. That's what I told him," a sly grin on her face.

"Very funny."

"There was a small reward for information leading to their capture . . . and since no one believes the costumed guy exists, they're giving the money to you."

"Small reward huh. How small?"

"$1500. They'll be sending it over by the end of the week."

"Great. Now I can cover the rest of the rent and come up with your pay this week."

The sarcasm bounced off her like bullets off a battleship. Her lip curled in a wry grin meaning she was unimpressed.

"You always drink so early in the day?"

She pulled no punches.

"Only when I'm sitting down."

It fell on unreceptive ears.

"With all the booze and cigarettes you consume, you shouldn't have to come up with the rent much longer," she said while she backed out the door.

Ouch! He knew she meant that with a vengeance. Prompting him to follow her to her desk to say something real intelligent.

"What did you mean by that?"

"You don't know?"

"Pretend I'm stupid. Inform me."

A moment of silence preceded her collecting her thoughts.

"I, had you checked out."

"Checked out?"

"Lt. Carlson filled me in on your background."

"What'd he tell you?"

"Enough. . . . He told me how you worked together in New York. And . . . why you left."

"Why I was abandoned you mean! A knife in the gut couldn't have hurt as much as having your life exposed by who you believed to be a friend."

"Sure. Sure. Every drunks lament."

Caught off guard, his response was delayed, and lame.

"Thanks! Thanks a lot!" Sulking into his office, he slammed the door. Four rapid-fire shots later, she entered. Even through his anger, he sensed remorse.

"Jason. . . . Look, I'm sorry."

"Sorry I'm a drunk!" he snapped. "Or sorry you work for one."

"I deserved that. . . . You see . . . it's just that sometimes my mouth runs away with me."

"Touché. . . . So, why did you want to work here?"

"Because I'm not convinced you're as bad as your publicity."

"Or . . . maybe I'm another cause to champion."

"Pardon me?"

"I had you checked out too. I know all about you . . . and UCLA."

Shifting her weight to her right hip, her head tilted to the left, she postured as if trying to fathom what he knew. Resentment, suspicion, anger revolved around in her mind; finally stopping on compassion.

"So . . . why did you hire me?"

He let her wonder just long enough to become uncomfortable. Speaking just before she was about to re-ask. "Because . . . I'm not convinced you're as bad as your publicity," he punctuated with a rigid finger.

"Touché."

This little skirmish over, there was nothing left to do.

"Now. Shall we finish our reports."

"You're the Boss," she said, closing the door behind her.

She meant well, as most did; on this he was clear. He just didn't care for the pep talks.

Half a fifth in ninety minutes—and nothing—neither a buzz, nor the usual giddy feeling. Something nagged at the back of his mind but he pushed it aside, immersing himself in his work.

You can't forget the training the Army and the Police Academy gives you. Action, adventure and danger became non-existent since he'd gone private. How dull he allowed his life to become.

Finding missing persons kept him one step up from the poor house. While some satisfaction could be gleaned from joyful faces when you return a loved one. More so when it's a lost or kidnapped child of worried, frustrated parents. He'd settled . . . settled for the occasional warm feeling at the close of less and less frequent cases; from a career on one long spiral into the depths.

His rapport with the Police stood two steps below pitiful. Being a former cop gone to ruin left a sour taste with them. Part of him understood where they were coming from; but mostly his anger festered like a sore picked at with dirty fingers because he'd been tossed aside with little regard for an accomplished career.

They could have all their red tape; all their restrictions placed on them by society; hindering their effectiveness.

When they couldn't do their job quickly enough to suit society, everyone cried cover-up; demanding an investigation while flinging a volley of obscenities.

An air of indifference pervaded between Jason and the law, though they did steer the occasional customer his way. Likely out of sympathy, pity or guilt; the situation depended. Mostly because of serious manpower shortages. Let *him* do all the legwork looking for some missing person. Self-preservation, and an unnatural hunger for booze kept him from sending them packing.

"Earth to Jason!" Sheila said firmly when she tried again to get his attention. Lost so deeply in thought, he'd been oblivious to her call.

"I'm sorry Sheila. What was it you were saying?"

"I was wondering, do you think that costumed guy will ever show himself again?"

Jason was introspective. "You, Ray and Lyle were the only ones who saw him; and from what I understand, they refused to talk about it."

"I'd like to know how he knew I was in trouble."

"Your guess is as good as mine."

"I sure hope I run into him again sometime."

"How's that?"

"Because I'd like to thank him properly."

"I wish you luck," said Jason while he lit another cigarette and was instantly accosted verbally by Sheila.

"Uh uh mister. You may want to turn your lungs to hamburger but I don't need the second hand smoke."

Dutifully if reluctantly he stubbed it out. "Okay okay it's out already. Christ. I thought I hired a secretary not a nagging stepmother."

"And don't you forget it."

Along the riverfront near the Ben Franklyn Bridge a sleek black limousine with windows tinted so dark seeing inside was impossible, parks in a back alley. Seated in the back is the Crime Czar; his two accomplices sit facing him.

"All right gentlemen. The time to begin taking over the city has come. For better or worse there's no turning back. Are all the men in position Alfie?"

"We're all set."

"I trust all your men have been informed that there is to be no unnecessary killing."

"They've been informed there will be severe penalties for breaking the rules Boss," he says, tapping the pistol under his coat.

"Good. I can't convince dead men that they'd be better off under my protection working for me. Okay Freddy, give the order to move in.

Brief terse commands into a walkie-talkie and the wheels of a criminal takeover are set in motion.

Around the city the same scenario is simultaneously played out.

A door to a basement office is thrust open. The location of one of many bookie joints in the city.

Several men step in quickly. Heavily armed and demanding those inside put up their hands and prepare to be taken over.

Guns are reached for from all angles by those employed in the joint. They've been around too long and they know that the Big Shots in charge don't want to hear you went down without a fight. Better to die instantly, here and now by a bullet in the head, then by some excruciatingly slow and painful death that could come later from those Big Shots.

Record books and cash boxes are reached for to no avail. Cut short by those infiltrators secretly in league with the Crime Czar. Abruptly, the hostilities end as swiftly as they began. The takeover so swift and thorough it seems scarcely a heartbeat of time has elapsed.

Runners and bagmen all over the city are abducted and dragged into waiting cars; spirited away to some central waiting area. A little traveled warehouse section of the suburbs to be dealt with later.

At the bookie joint all is secure. Through the still open door steps the Crime Czar; slowly smoothing the fingers of his gloved hands.

"Gentlemen. Today begins a new order in this city. I and my army of men are taking over the Rackets all over town. This joint, its records and cash and all the others around the city now belong to me."

"And who the hell are you?" shouts one man who is instantly shut up by a backhand to the face.

"Now now. Gentlemen please. There is no need for further violence. . . . For your information I call myself the Crime Czar. And I'm here with a proposition for all of you."

"What could you possibly have to say that we'd want to hear?" says another, trying to free himself from the goon restraining him.

"Simply this. You have the choice of joining me and my organization; thus coming under the protection of my vast army."

"Or?"

"Or . . . you are free to leave and return to that fool who likes to call himself *Mr. Big.* But . . . remember this. This is a onetime offer. It won't be extended to any of you ever again. If you don't join me now don't try to join me later after I throw that fool Mr. Big out of the city. You won't be welcome. . . . Now gentlemen. . . . It's your choice."

The men huddle together. Amid much whispering and accusing the pros and cons of the deal are weighed. Mute cursing, chastising and threats are lavished.

Growing ever impatient the Crime Czar chimes in. "Come, come gentlemen. What is your answer?"

Of the five men, one decides he will have no part of the deal. He'd been with the organization too long, preferring to take his chances with them.

"Well go quickly then. . . . But don't ever try to come back."

The man remarks just before he exits the door. "You'll never get away with it."

"But I already have my good man . . . I already have. The fool just doesn't know it yet."

The Crime Czar focuses on the remaining men. "You've seen what's happened here today. The same has happened in all the rest of your places. Excuse me. My places, around the city. If any of you is thinking he will change his mind later . . . forget it! You'll be watched closely until your loyalty is assured. The penalty for turning traitor is too severe to think about."

Silence blankets the room like a shroud. Had they made the right choice? Or should they have hurried out and tried to find honest employment? It was too late for doubts.

Then there was that little guy named *Murphy.* He reared his pointy little head a lot sooner than the Crime Czar could have imagined.

What he and his raiders couldn't know is that one joint, in the north end of the city, was also on the list to be raided by the local constabulary on the same day. The police had their own infiltrator working along side the Crime Czar's man. Neither knowing of nor suspecting the other.

First to hit the joint were the Crime Czar's men; entering from the north side of the building.

The Police converged from the south in preparation to surrounding the building.

A single gunshot from within thrust both sides into a rout. Fearing the deal gone sour, both sides closed in and opened fire; escalating into a fierce, confused gun battle.

Of necessity, the Crime Czar's men and those who ran the bookie joint joined forces to fight the common enemy.

While this transpired a frail little man enters an opulent office high and aloof in the center of the city. Hurried steps bring him before the desk of the Syndicates representative in this town; the man who likes to call himself, *Mr. Big*.

How such an alias should be interpreted is unclear for he isn't very tall. To meet him on the street you'd probably call him shorty. A balding man, big in one respect—he looked twice the weight he should be for his height. Someone who should lay off the gooey pastries and chow down at the salad bar.

Stereotypically, with most little men with power, he succumbed to a Napoleonic complex; a short man drunk with power. Someone used to being obeyed because he's got the muscle behind him to back it up.

Glancing up from his desk this sudden intrusion has him half annoyed.

"Well. What is it?"

"Sir. Our bookie joints around the city are being raided."

"What!" he bit off.

"Y-Yes Sir. And there are reports that our bag men are being picked up all over."

"These cops have gone too far! Get that Judge on the phone. He can start earning the payoffs we give him."

"But Sir. The cops have nothing to do with it."

"What are you babbling about?"

"It's not the cops. It's some organization run by some guy in a hood calling himself the Crime Czar," bubbles out of the shaking man. "We've had reports from our people that were raided that he says he's going to take over the Rackets and throw you out."

The frail man winces when Mr. Big hurls his bulk to his feet in a rage, slamming his pudgy fist on his ornate antique desk. "And how did these people get away to even come to tell us this?"

"The Crime Czar let them go," says the thin man cringing; trying to keep from stammering. "He offered them a deal . . . Sir"

"Deal? What deal?"

"They could join his new organization . . . or they could leave in peace . . . Sir."

Face contorted, the wheels grind slowly; faced with this conundrum. Eventually he comes to his conclusion.

"You've got to be out of your mind, and so must they, if they think I'm going to believe a cock-a-maimy excuse like that! Take them out and have them all shot."

"I wouldn't do that Sir."

"Oh. You wouldn't would you. And just why not may I ask?"

"Many of our men are joining the Crime Czar. He's offered them a deal they couldn't refuse. Word has it that they've been disenchanted with how you've been running things for some time. If we go killing off who's left, we won't have anybody."

The fat little man slumps back like he'd been smacked in the face with a brick. Eyes dart in all directions, searching for an answer. While the wheels spin his secretary enters with a telegram.

Holding the envelopes contents with both hands he reads the message thereon.

For scant seconds, the frail man was certain his employer's head was going to explode.

Eyes bulging nearly out of their sockets, Mr. Big's face, ears and neck glowed a bright crimson hue. If pressed to tell, you'd swear you saw fire emitting from his nostrils and steam escaping from his ears.

Hands shaking in utter rage, Mr. Big rises slowly from his chair and roars. "THIS, IS, WAR! . . . Send out every available man we have! I want this, this Crime Czar bastard found and brought to me. . . . Alive!" His voice nearly strangling, he squeezes the telegram into a ball in his pudgy fist. "I want to see what mad man would be so fucking crazy to even attempt a ridiculous scheme like this," he rants, flinging the crumpled telegram at the thin little man; who, after juggling it a few times, manages to secure it in his grasp while he backs toward the open door.

"He's signed his own death warrant! No one treats me this way and gets away with it!"

The fat man raves on while the frail servant exits, closing the door carefully behind him. Pausing outside the door he unfolds the crumpled telegram.

"Oh, my, God," escapes his lips in a hushed tone. The message short and to the point.

"TODAY WAS JUST A TASTE OF WHAT'S TO COME. MOVE OUT, OR BE THROWN OUT!"
regards,
THE CRIME CZAR! . . .

* * * *

Standing at his office window, Jason sipped a cup of coffee for a change, while sneaking a smoke. Good Lord! He'd become a secret smoker again. Not since his father caught him at the age of thirteen, smoking in the bathroom, had he done this. After a talking to that nearly peeled the paper from the wall he promised never to do it again; keeping that promise until his tour in 'Nam.

As luck would have it, Sheila chose that time to burst into his office. Spying the smoking butt in his hand she stood in the doorway arms crossed. After giving a glare that should curdle milk, while tapping her high-heeled shoe on the oak floor, he dutifully, and silently, deposited the butt in the ashtray. "Turn on the radio to the police band!" she said.

"What's up?" he said while he tuned the radio to the proper frequency.

"There's a shoot-out going on between the Police and a bunch of gangsters at a bookie joint on the north end. I heard a news flash on my T.V."

Having found the right frequency on the short wave, the ensuing conversation between the officers on the scene and their superiors corroborated Sheila's words.

One of the detectives who infiltrated the place had managed to escape during the confusion. He talked about some bozo calling himself the Crime Czar or something, attempting to take over the Rackets here.

"What do you think of that?" Sheila wanted to know.

"The Police have an enormous amount of experience in these situations. They can handle it. As for this Crime Czar . . . he's probably just some lunatic out to make a name for himself."

"Yeah. You're probably right," she said, backing toward the door. Jason wasn't as sure of his words. Something foreboding nagged at the back of his mind.

When he'd been a cop in New York he'd seen plenty of shoot-outs like this; not all went down easy. Too often people got either hurt . . . or killed, some of them his fellow officers. Occasionally, the curious or the seriously unlucky bystander met the same fate.

Jason wanted to do something . . . but it wasn't his place. Still, he couldn't prevent his emotions from rising. He wanted to turn off the radio, but the part of him that was still cop wouldn't allow it. He sat absorbed in the play by play.

Part of him wanted to help; part of him didn't give a shit for the cop's chances.

Then, something proposed on the radio sat him bolt upright in his chair.

"You stupid fucking bastards," slipped out harshly. "Don't do it."

Torn no longer, adrenalin rising high, he grabbed his hat and coat and rushed from his office. "Mind the store," he said while hurrying past Sheila's desk.

"You gonna be somewhere I can reach you?"

"Not likely. Later."

In the hall he needed the quickest way out of the building. One of the offices on the alley side of the building was empty. It was as good a place as any.

The locked door gave with very little effort. Thrusting up the old sash he stole a quick glance into the alley. Devoid of prying eyes . . . he threw himself out the window . . . and instead of falling to his death on the brick paving, rose sharply and steadily into the sky. Flying at such a pace that if anyone had looked to the sky all they would see is a blur.

Instants later he landed firmly on his apartment building roof; flung open the access door and raced down the stairs.

Bursting into his apartment he flew straight to the trash compactor. Ripping open the bag he jerked out a crumpled burnt orange costume.

"Christ. Don't let me be late," he swore while shucking his street clothes.

Climbing into the crude costume he flew to the window: opened it, looked to see if the coast was clear; then launched himself out into the afternoon air.

With the speed he achieved, only a matter of seconds elapsed until he arrived on the scene. While on the way he tried to recall all his police training in such matters he was about to involve himself.

Hovering at 500 feet he paused to reconnoiter the battle going on below. This was no time to run in all brash and cocksure like he had when he rescued Sheila. He'd been lucky that time; this situation called for serious intent not blind luck.

Enhanced visual powers brought the tiniest detail to his ken.

The Police held their own but made no headway either. The thugs clung to a heavily fortified area. They could be stalemated for hours or days. But at what cost in men and munitions.

Enhanced hearing tuned in on the police radio, of officers conferring with their superiors. What he heard evoked the urge to puke. The bastards were really going to do it. For the good of all, *Mindforce* must take a hand in things.

Some of the thugs took positions out in the alleyway exchanging gunfire with the police. Too cramped an area for the SWAT team to make an assault without huge losses.

The logical thing to do was land in the alley behind the hoods. While the police kept them busy at the front he would attack from the rear.

Landing behind two gangsters crouching behind a dumpster: he grabbed them by the collar, conked their heads together before they knew what hit them, destroyed their guns and flung them into the dumpster; then made onto the next man.

Standing to the left he tapped the hood on the right shoulder. Being normal, the hood turned that way; seeing nothing he jerked his head back to the left. Whether he saw it coming before the lights went out was a moot point. He rested quietly. Three down; number four coming up.

Combat juices flowing, the fourth man found himself yanked up by the belt, spun about over the costumed man's head so fast that when he was set back down he was too dizzy to even find his own feet.

By this time, both police and criminal knew something was amiss.

DANGER flashed across Mindforce's mind. Whirling round to a rifle trained on his back. A gesture and the weapon flew from the dumbfounded hood to his outstretched hand. It twisted easily into a pretzel. The hood gaped and ran but was set upon before he could take a single step.

"Get your fucking paws off of me!" groused the hood while his attacker spread the bars of a guardrail about a basement entrance, shoved in the hood's head, then quickly closed the bars. He'd stay put for a while.

When Mindforce stood to continue his disassembly of their ranks, *DANGER* flashed once again.

Three hoods turned their attention from the slowly advancing police and took out their fury on the costumed man, firing simultaneously. Three 9mm slugs thumped on his chest. They stung like hornets before clattering to the brick laid alley.

Forestalling any further attempts he raised his hands, whipping the guns from their grasp. Each man, gaping at the other, got laid low by his own weapon whirling above then dropped swiftly on their own noggins.

Kneeling to collect their guns, the avenger, concentrating fully on them, fails to sense the approach of one huge goon. Six feet, eight inches of massive shoulders and powerful arms. All muscle and no fat the Goliath weighed well over three hundred pounds.

Grabbed in a full nelson, he jerked the costumed man at least a foot off the ground; applying the raw power of his massive frame to the back of Mindforce's neck. Probably used to killing with his bare hands.

Grabbed unawares, long dormant reflexes kicked in. The full measure of Army combat training locked into gear.

Hanging like a limp rag from the huge man's grasp, forgotten superhuman strength forced the avenger's arms down to his sides; releasing the goon's hold, horribly dislocating both shoulders in the process. Arms hanging limply at his sides, the pain evoked a howl that would have sickened the strongest of combat veterans. A crushing left elbow shattered three ribs followed by a swift right hand that grasped the back of the goons head. Before he knew it he'd flung the brute thirty feet to the mouth of the alley, fracturing both his legs. Mercifully, he didn't stay conscious long.

Stunned by what he'd done, the thought that he may have destroyed another human being, he stood dumbstruck, staring at his outstretched hands.

The scene had an immediate affect on the remaining hoods. They stood demoralized while Mindforce kicked in the side door to the joint; allowing the SWAT team to pour in; surrendering in short order to overwhelming pressure.

A sniper on a nearby roof damn near swallowed his tongue

when Mindforce appeared in his scope before him. His mouth hung limply as Mindforce hovered with naught but fifty feet of air between boot and pavement.

Dropping his weapon he ran like a scalded dog. Circling around, Mindforce was in his face in a heartbeat, allowing the sniper to crash into him.

"Going somewhere?"

"What the hell are you?"

"I'm still trying to figure that out."

"Huh?"

"Let's go."

Taking the sniper by the collar he pushed the shaken hood back to the parapet.

"What the hell are you doing? . . . You're not going to push me over?"

"Don't worry. I won't let go."

"You're nuts!"

"You don't know the half of it," he said while he stepped over the edge and took them to the street.

Shaken and confused, he humbly turned himself over to police custody.

From a safe distance the Crime Czar squirmed while Mindforce made mincemeat of his troops. Upon seeing the huge goon he intended to use for his enforcer destroyed, he ordered his driver to retreat.

"I'm gonna find out who that costumed motherfucker is and make him wish he'd kept his nose outta my business!" he vowed while the limo sped away. Nobody was going to stand in his way on his ascent to the top of the heap . . .

Hesitant, unsure how to react to the unbelievable, a policeman steps up to Mindforce while he extracts the gangsters head from the iron bars. "Thanks pal. Whoever you are."

An alerted television crew waiting by rushed in now that the battle was over.

Zeroing in on Mindforce standing in the intersection talking to the police, the reporters move in swiftly. They can smell an award winning news story a mile away.

"Hey you. You in the orange tights," shouts one. "We'd like to talk to you."

His job done; a possible tragedy averted, he was not about to be cross-examined by the media. Hands trembling, throat dry, the swirling mass of conflicting emotions clawed at his sanity. He had to get out of there.

Eyes darting, head swiveling about, the only way out was straight up. Up between the circling police helicopters, past the hovering news copters. If they got any footage during his departure, he didn't give a shit. Escape was the sole driving force.

He was sick. Sick because he'd nearly killed another human being . . . again. . . . He felt a long binge coming on.

* * * *

CHAPTER FOUR

Aftermath

The sun had retreated well below the horizon when Mindforce returned to the parking garage where he kept his car. His big ears telling him no one was present, he sped in.

Stripping off the costume, he heaved it into the trunk then put on his spare suit.

About to slam the trunk lid down in anger he remembered his increased strength. Not needing a huge repair bill he punched out one of the steel columns instead, leaving a large dent in the flange.

"How'd it go?" said Sheila when he entered his agency.

"Don't ask," he shot back; walking straight through to his office. Depositing himself in his chair he yanked open the desk drawer, removing a fifth of Old Grand Dad and a single glass.

"What's wrong?" said Sheila from the doorway.

The shot came first. "I don't wanna talk about it." Then another quick shot of the piss water.

"What could be so bad you have to drink yourself into a stupor?"

"None of your damn business! Why don't you go home?"

"You pay me by the week remember; not by the hour. So I'll go when I damn well please."

Another fast shot went down like water. "So go give me a reason to pay you."

She was pissed, though she did her best to hide it. "Anything you say, Boss," she bit off, backing out the door.

"And close the door behind you."

Jason sulked while he stared at the night scenes; downing shot after shot; feeling sorry for himself. After twenty minutes and half again as many shots he was still stone cold sober. He feared thinking of what he was sure was the cause.

Time eventually affords calm and he felt he should apologize to Sheila. With some trepidation, he opened the door.

"You're still upright," she said when she saw him. "Will wonders never cease? Or did you just run out of booze?"

His snide remark got suppressed when his eye caught the TV on her desk. On it the evening news. They played a videotape of his escapades of that afternoon. The pit of his stomach churned while he watched the replay of the large goon being flung from the alley. Then watched himself fly off into the distant sky.

"Whoever this costumed vigilante is," added the commentator, "he waded through the criminal lines in a brutal show of force that brought one man nearly to his death. That man is in intensive care at this time . . ."

Not getting an answer, Sheila turned to Jason, then the film clip, then to Jason again.

"Jason? Are you there?"

"I'm sorry Sheila. What were you saying?"

"I just wondered what you thought of him. He wasn't as brutal when he rescued me as they make him out. What do you think?"

Collecting his thoughts, the truth seemed the best answer; even if it did sound like an excuse. "Obviously, this fella must have just acquired these powers; otherwise we'd have heard of him sooner. He must not be used to the strength he's got. It was probably just a mistake."

She rolled it around in her mind for a few seconds. He knew the answer before she said it. "I agree."

"But he should have minded his own business."

"Why? If he's got the means to be a positive force . . ."

"Because people as a whole are afraid of what they don't understand. Now that he's been branded as dangerous by the media he doesn't stand a chance. If he's smart, we'll never see him again."

"But the world needs heroes to look up to."

"In fantasy worlds maybe—this is reality."

"I don't care what they say. I'm for him."

Jason's reply was cut off by Police Commissioner Jake Parman, who'd been at the scene; his comments did little for Jason's self esteem.

"We had the situation under control," he began. "We were prepared to make our final assault when the mystery man disrupted their forces. He was lucky he wasn't killed. And even luckier he didn't kill someone else. While the Police Dept. welcomes any support we can get from the populace, we cannot tolerate any form of vigilantism. All I can say to this man is that he refrain from any further action and allow the police to do what we're paid to do."

Jason didn't like Jake Parman; and now he liked him even less. They didn't have an ounce of control there. If he hadn't stepped in when he did the news would be reporting a lot more death and destruction right now. He was fuming and could feel Sheila's confusion at his reaction.

"What is it?"

"He's a liar! From what I saw . . ." He shut up before his anger could get him into any more trouble. Without another word, he retreated to his office . . . and the bottle in it. Sheila close on his heels.

"What did you mean? What could you have seen?"

"Nothing! It just occurred to me they were taking credit they didn't deserve just to save themselves from a lot of embarrassment." Another useless shot went down his neck.

"Jason. Have you ever thought of getting some help?"

"You mean AA?"

"Yes. Why not?"

"When they promise me they can rid me of my memories, then I'll think about it."

"You mean Carmen?"

Carmen. . . . After all these years, her memory haunted him to this day. It still seemed like only yesterday. Only the abyss of alcohol could blot out the horror and anguish he carried like a monkey on his back ever since that night. That, and work. . . . But there never was enough work because he was usually too drunk to accept any.

"Vince told you about her too, huh."

"He went over it briefly, but I'd like to hear your side of it."

"It's none of your business," he snapped, pouring the next shot.

Abruptly, she snatched the bottle from his hand, sloshing a portion of its contents on the desk. "The answers aren't in here either!"

"Go home Sheila," he said while dabbing at the spill.

"But . . ."

"Look! I want to be left alone."

They glare at each other for several heartbeats. Pissed, though still concerned, she calmly placed the bottle gently on the desk. "Okay . . . drink yourself into oblivion." Firm steps take her back to her office. Grabbing her coat in a huff, she heads for the outer door.

Shamed speechless, Jason hangs his head.

Pausing, Sheila calls back from the front door, near tears. "Just make sure you call yourself a cab! I wouldn't want you to kill someone else with your car!" She slammed the outer door.

Alone, he wallowed in self-pity. Who needed her? . . . Or anyone else for that matter. Tomorrow he'd get rid of her.

Minute by minute, shot by shot, cigarette upon cigarette, an hour passed—two. Bottle after bottle—nothing. The sweet oblivion of alcohol never came to claim him. There was a truth in here his conscious mind refused to grasp, or even come near. He tried to concentrate only on pleasant thoughts—but his failures always found their way in.

He didn't want to think; afraid to face his life. But he could do nothing but *think*. All the pain he'd suffered; all the pain he'd inflicted, all the pain he would continue to suffer stood before him like the *Grim Reaper*. Laughing. Laughing at this poor stupid motherfucker who'd dropped to the depths of despair.

He'd swallowed over a gallon of booze and was steady as a rock. Clear of eye and faculty. He could deny it no longer. These powers were truly a curse—rendering him *immune* to alcohol and all its effects. He felt damned by God to suffer his own consciousness for as long as they lasted.

Frustration mounted gradually; erupting in a frantic fever pitch. "NOOOOOOOOOO! IT'S NOT FAIR! It's not fair! It's not fair. Not fair. Not fair . . ."

Clutching at his head he throws it back in angry hysteria. Then in a childlike tantrum he swipes everything off the desk; smashing all against the wall. Shattering every liquor bottle. Even one that was half empty.

"WHY! WHY! WHY WON'"T YOU LEAVE ME IN PEACE!" He rants, pulling at his hair while loose items rise and swirl around the room with a life of their own.

His chest heaved convulsively while he sucked in volumes of air between each heavy bout of sobs. Burying his face in his palms, still sobbing, he slides from his chair to his knees. Books fall from the shelves, framed pictures and citations lift from the wall to join in the swirling dance.

Shortly the sobs subside. As they do the whirling objects subside in tune; settling gently to the surfaces of the desk, files and shelves. Soon all is quiet. Jason lifts his head from his hands meekly; his face sodden with tears.

"Oh God. Please. Please help me."

Emotionally spent, he drags himself to his feet; lifts his coat and hat from the tree and shuffles out of the office, just barely latching the door. A meek shadow.

He stood staring blankly at the trunk of his car; knowing what lay within. The curse he'd thrust upon himself in a weak moment of childish delight. If he could get drunk he wouldn't care. The urge welled up inside him to rip off the trunk deck and tear the costume into the tiniest shreds; sanity prevailed. He could destroy it later at home.

Instead of going straight home he opted for the long way around via the Parkway. With the windows rolled down to let the cold night air roar past his face; he couldn't feel the cold anyway. Driving had a calming effect; it was hard to think of anything while concentrating on the road ahead. Even so, the news commentator's words still crept into his consciousness. The brutality tag was way off base. He'd had no intention of causing anyone harm. But, after all, they were trying to kill every officer there.

The human psyche remained ever the mystery. They demand the criminal element eliminated from their environment. But if you use too much force the bleeding hearts cry brutality; and call him a vigilante. To some extent it was true but it wasn't the whole story.

A vigilante sets himself up as judge, jury and executioner. This wasn't his view of super-heroing. He didn't want to supplant the law; just clear a path for it to do a better job. With the loss of the fewest lives on both sides.

Doubt piled upon doubt whether he had done the right thing. Having been a cop didn't give him the right to play cop.

Flashing lights in the distance interrupted his pity party.

Traffic stood at a standstill; there was no going forward or back. Killing the engine he prepared himself for a long wait. Instinctively, his enhanced senses tuned in on the events up ahead. The smell of gasoline, the frantic talk of the police, the cries of distress sought him out; ignoring it failed as an option.

Curiosity got him out of his car. Care for another human had him standing on the hood.

His binocular vision thrust him into the scene. A hundred and fifty yards up ahead a tractor-trailer loaded with scrap iron had jack-knifed, flipped over on its side and hit a bus. Both vehicles then slid across the road, pinning a Chevy Nova against a bridge abutment.

The police were frantic in their attempt to reach the little car to see if anyone was still alive. But getting past the wreck of the truck and its heavy load was impossible.

It was happening all over again. For the second time this day Jason was caught up in a situation of extreme need where his help could be invaluable. He attempted to go but the words of the news commentator screamed in his brain. He didn't need the torment again. They'd have to go it alone while he played the helpless citizen.

Then he heard it. . . . The frantic wail of an infant.

Even his heart wasn't that hard. He couldn't pretend to be helpless any longer when a life so young was about to be cut short. Fuck the press! He'd deal with them later.

Most of the cars behind him were empty because their occupants had long since strolled forward to do their share of rubbernecking.

Grabbing his costume from the trunk he vaulted the guardrail; down the embankment into the bushes.

He'd never made a faster change of clothes.

Alighting amidst the carnage he spoke to the nearest officer. "Is there any way I can help?"

He looked over Mindforce curiously. "Unless you can lift that truck off the car you'd better just get back with the crowd."

Mindforce froze, listening. The infant's whimpers continued from the wreck; along with two other heartbeats—one slowing by the second. "Those people in there are still alive. When I lift the truck get in there and get them out."

The officer caught his arm. "Wait. How do you know they're alive?"

"Just trust me. Now. Let's see what I can do with this truck."

What *could* he do. The officer was as desperate as anyone else to get them out. There was nothing to lose.

Mindforce sought a place to get a firm grip. He knew not how many tons of steel were on the truck; he'd never attempted to lift anything this heavy. Doubt was not an option here; he had to try.

Waves of doubt crashed over him; emanating from the crowd

when they realized what he intended to do. Muscles bulged and strained at the spandex costume when he put his entire body into lifting the truck. The strain was enormous; he'd never known such agony. Every fiber of his body screamed as if it were on fire.

The crowd gasped when the truck began to give to his insistence. Ever so slowly it rose off the ground while the twisted heap of iron screeched its disapproval. He'd forced it nearly six inches off the surface while the antsy EMTs stood at the ready. But for all his effort, he could raise it no farther; he'd reached his limit. Forced to stop, he had to set it down; his entire body screaming in agony. The screeching groaning metal drowned out by the moans of despair from the crowd.

He'd failed again; not only them, but himself. The look of dismay from the many accusing faces was more than he wanted to bear. Some even jeered. Some hero he was . . . and he felt they were right. His emotions overloaded, about to shatter.

"That's all right," said an officer. "Ya did the best ya could."

"No I haven't . . . yet," he gasped. "Lemme catch my breath. I gotta get those people outta there! Don't you smell that gasoline?"

"Why don'tcha just wait for the crane?"

"Bullshit!"

What he had in mind was insane; he just hoped it'd work. It had to work! Else the couple in the car didn't have a chance. The proper equipment was still several minutes away.

He'd attempt to combine his levitation power with his increased strength. Together, they just might do the trick. There was everything to gain if he succeeded—and everything to lose if he failed.

He said a silent prayer while the emergency people backed off to give him room. No one dared try to stop him. They were equally anxious for it to work.

At the wreckage he grabbed hold of the truck, the waves of doubt washed over him again. He'd not allow their influence to spoil his concentration. He'd shut them out, focusing all his being solely on the task at hand. His levitation power strained to the limit he then combined it with his superhuman strength.

At first nothing happened. He was in too deep to quit now. Forcing himself to shut out every other sensory input, he concentrated ever harder.

Maybe it was his concentration—or maybe it was the faint whimper of the infant; either way his supreme effort increased by several factors. The tonnage literally jumped off the surface; so much he nearly lost it. But he was not home free yet. It required all his concentration just to keep it balanced and aloft. He couldn't quit until he had a safe place to set it down. Flashbulbs crackled all about, invading on his concentration, tearing at his will. It came down in a screeching, braying mangle of scrap after the officer shouted the all clear. His tortured legs let go, crumpling to his knees; sucking in huge quantities of air.

Now that it was safe the police and EMTs scurried in to check on the cars occupants. Still sucking hard, Mindforce was right on their heels; ignoring the advise of one Tech. to have some oxygen first.

Through the twisted metal and splintered glass he lifted the unhurt child from her car seat. Exposed to the crisp cold air she began to wail to the relief of all around.

The mother, on the passenger side, lay unconscious as did her husband. Apart from minor cuts and contusions she was fine. Her husband was another matter; he lay pinned under the crumpled dashboard. His leg partially severed below the knee; blood flowed profusely. He'd not live to see the rescue vehicles that would soon arrive. Mindforce did not hesitate; long unused training coming to the fore.

Into the opening that had been the windshield he stood on the floorboard after peeling off the roof. Onlookers gaped in astonishment when he stuck his forearms under the dash, braced his feet and put his back into it. The metal bellowed its displeasure when it gave way like so much taffy.

"See to the woman," he barked, "while I get this man out."

Finely tuned training by the emergency crew had them on the move in a coordinated fashion.

Uncertain, Mindforce suspected the man might have broken ribs as well. There was no time to lose. Grabbing the child's blanket from the back he tied it tightly around the near severed leg. Grabbing the cervical collar from the EMT he carefully placed it about the man's neck.

"Can you handle her? I've got to get this man to the hospital now!" Nodding reflexively they watched in awe. Not wishing to inflict further injury, Mindforce lifted the man out supported solely by his levitation power; giving every inch equal support. Cradling the man he rose rapidly into the sky then zipped away.

Less than a minute later he burst into the ER barking for assistance. The confused physician listened intently to what Mindforce believed was wrong. Then put his own training to work barking orders to his assistants.

Leaving quickly, Mindforce returned to the wreck where they were just placing the woman on a stretcher.

Standing amid the carnage an officer approached. "How is she?" said Mindforce.

"She's gonna be all right. She was conscious when you pulled her husband out. I think she'd like to talk to you."

When he knelt by her stretcher she began to talk, but the sight of the amount of blood on his costume horrified her.

"MY GOD!" she screamed, trying to get up. "Is he all right?"

"He's in good hands," said Mindforce in that eerie calm tone. "I'm sure we got him out in time."

Much to his surprise, her frantic outburst rapidly spiraled down into serenity. At first he was afraid for her well being until an assured nod from the EMT confirmed she was okay; though he did not know why.

"Bless you," she said, placing a trembling hand beside his head. Tears staining her face.

Removing his gauntlet, he held her hand all the way to the ambulance.

"If not for you fella, I don't know that we coulda gotten those people out alive," said a much grateful and relieved officer when the ambulance pulled away. "I don't care what that bozo on TV said about ya. You're all right in my book."

No one could have said more to lift his spirits, evoking a broad grin under his hood.

While he leaned against the overturned bus catching his breath he spied the approach of a TV news van to the scene. It was time to find his car. He'd be the topic of the news for a second time today. Hopefully, the eleven o'clock report would see him in a more favorable light.

* * * *

CHAPTER FIVE

Vivian James

Tuesday dawned particularly warm and sunny. The snow having melted and dried up put Jason in an exceptionally good mood.

The muscle he'd pulled on the previous evening had totally healed while he slept. Such things had been happening since the accident.

Up early, before the sun itself, he took his costume from the sink where he'd left it to soak, and hung it up to dry. Why he didn't throw it away again he had no clue.

Why did he keep torturing himself with this indecision? Superheroes don't exist. They're a figment of some writer's imagination, and the people in those universes are totally unreal. Why he was here beat the shit out of him.

A pot of boiling caffeine proved no more stimulating than the gallon of booze he'd inhaled the night before. The thought of having to cope with his life alone gave him something else to dread; now with a life more complicated than ever. Sheila's suggestion was not an option right now . . . or maybe ever.

The morning news touched on his heroic effort last evening. Confused, they could not decide if he was friend or foe—and who was he? Jason hadn't a clue and wasn't sure he even cared.

He cursed Vince. Damn him! If he hadn't sent Rita DiAngelo to his office he wouldn't be faced with all these questions.

He heard typing when he neared the door to his agency. He was early for a change—Sheila was earlier.

He entered to icy silence. She never looked up from her typing when he crossed the room past her. He opened his mouth to say something, but it seemed futile. She refused to give any notice when he opened the door to his office.

It was spotless—and he was incredulous. The office was a shambles when he left it. London after the Blitz had not looked that bad. He backed out to look at Sheila. She still gave no notice.

After hanging his hat and coat on the hook he sat behind his immaculate desk. Allowed to stew for five minutes, Sheila eventually strode in on determined steps; a mug of coffee in her grasp, her expression firm.

"You must have really tied one on last night," she said, setting the mug before him.

"What's this?"

"Coffee. Or had you forgotten?"

She wasn't very pleased, and he was loathe to think she cleaned up out of the goodness of her heart.

Sheila, I . . ."

"If you're going to trash your office on a regular basis I'll be expecting an increase in pay."

"You didn't have to do this."

"Damn straight! And you didn't have to drink yourself crazy either."

She didn't know the half of it.

"Here."

"What's this?"

"Exactly what it looks like. It's a listing of all the local AA chapters."

"I don't want this."

"You've needed this for too long," she said, tapping a sharp index finger on the list.

He stalled, sipping the coffee while he contemplated. She was right but he wasn't ready; nor did he wish to acknowledge she knew best. Pride y-know.

"I can only promise I'll think about it."

"Don't think too long. And don't ignore it either."

"Why are you doing this?"

"Why? Shouldn't I?"

He had no answer. How could he? He had no idea why he chose to be a costumed hero.

"Thanks for tidying up."

Her eyes rolled back at the absurdity of the word tidy, then focused on his. "Just don't do it again," she said, then let herself out without another word.

She had a knack for making people feel guilty. The trip he was on was a long one.

The coffee went down in short sips. Not because he felt the heat, just from habit. While he fingered the AA list he felt uncertain of the validity of any past or future decisions.

He'd finished his coffee by the time Sheila returned to his office. She laid the morning paper before him. Across the headline in bold print: "MYSTERY MAN SAVES YOUNG COUPLE FROM FIERY DEATH IN AUTO ACCIDENT!"

The article below, though favorable, carried a hint of caution. After what had been said about him on the early news the previous day he opted not to hang around to be interviewed. Once the young couple was safe he returned to his car and beat it out of there.

It went on to say: This man can't be the danger to the public that was earlier reported. The reporter just wished he'd hung around to explain himself; closing with, thank you. Whoever you are.

"See. I told you he was a hero," said Sheila.

"I had no doubts."

"Oh. By the way. You got a phone call from a prospective client last night. In all the excitement I forgot to tell you."

"Who was it?"

"She said her name was Vivian."

"No last name?"

"No. She just said that she knew you from New York and that you'd know who she was."

"Did she leave a number?"

"No she didn't"

"Well, I guess if it was important she'll call back."

Nodding, she left Jason to his thoughts. Once out of sight he reached for a cigarette.

"No smoking in there," came his conscience from the outer office.

Now he was certain he'd hired a witch. Even with his enhanced *Esper* powers he couldn't read minds. Oh well. He threw the smokes in the desk drawer and promised the witch he'd be a good boy.

Sitting and gazing out at the ever-thickening air pollution he went through his mental file of all the people he knew from New York.

The only Vivian he knew was Vivian James. They'd had something going for a while when he'd been a rookie cop.

They met at graduation from the Police Academy. His roommate was her cousin who introduced them after the ceremonies. A real looker she was, he didn't hesitate to ask her for a date.

They hit it off real well for about six months until an old flame of hers, Rick James, blew back into town. He'd been away on business; she thought for good. But now he was back.

Wining and dining her again, flashing his money around, buying her expensive presents and taking her to all the best places. No one really knew how he earned his money. He gave the impression of being on the up and up, but somehow, Jason just had a bad feeling about the man.

With his rookie policeman's salary Jason couldn't keep up with Rick's flash and dance. Soon he was all but forgotten. Vivian thrived on life in the fast lane; Jason was just too slow for her pace.

Three months later he received an invitation to their wedding. That they'd tie the not seemed inevitable. Jason sent a wedding gift but begged off from attending; saying duty had to take precedence. A lie because he couldn't bear to see her marry the guy.

He warned her Rick was no good. But since his only proof was a gut feeling, it fell on deaf ears. She as much as told him he was full of it. She loved the guy and would marry Rick no matter what anyone else thought.

Jason chalked it up to a character flaw on her part and bowed out of the way.

Before a year was out she and Rick had a little boy. Tommy they called him. Jason calculated he'd be about ten by now.

Last he'd heard, She and Rick had gotten a divorce before Tommy was a year old. Rick wasn't the father type. He had no use for women with kids.

Rick went about his business, what ever it was. And Vivian? The city just seemed to swallow up her and Tommy. Jason never heard from them again.

Leaning in the doorway, Sheila's light rapping on the jamb pulled Jason thoughts back to the present.

"Jason. There's a woman here to see you."

Before he could ask who it was the woman brushed past Sheila, totally ignoring her. She stepped quickly to the desk, eyes pleading.

It was Vivian. Ten years older but still a looker. She was drawn from lack of sleep; her apprehension hung upon her like a lead shroud.

"Jason, I need your help," she blurted out.

"What's the matter Vivian?" he said, rising to his feet.

She started to speak, halting to glance fearfully at Sheila, then to Jason uncertain. Sheila caught on quickly.

"Well, I've got work to do. If you need me Jason I'll be right out here."

He nodded and she backed out, quietly closing the door.

"Jason! It's my son!" she spouted rapid fire.

Tommy? What's the problem?"

"He—he didn't come home from school last Friday," she said. The fear coming across in waves to Jason's senses.

"Did you call the police?"

"Yes. Yes. Yes I did."

"And what did they say?"

"You know what they said! They just told me to wait because

they couldn't do anything for me right away. They said something about manpower shortages and some other things!" She said thorough gathering tears, wringing her hands nervously.

Being a former cop, Jason knew the drill. They'd put it on the list and would get to it when they could along with all the other missing persons reports.

He knew the standard questions in regards to missing persons and runaways; and he knew all her answers must have been no. Otherwise she wouldn't be here trying to hire him. So he didn't bother to repeat them.

Experience told him when it came to missing persons, the greater majority of adults were missing because they chose to be. For what ever reasons.

Children were another story: Sure, they'd go away for a few hours, forget what time it was, forget to call home and show up some time before bed. If not it was because they were either kidnapped or ran away.

Jason could understand her not wanting to wait for the police to find the time to look For Tommy. He could understand her wanting a private detective to take her case. But there were many excellent P.I.s in the New York area. Why come all this way to hire him.

"Because you were the best there was in New York."

"That was a long time ago. New York has too many bad memories for me."

"I know. I called yesterday, but your secretary said she didn't know where you were or when you'd be back. This morning I just couldn't take it anymore. So I got on the first plane to Philadelphia. . . . Please find my Tommy for me Jason. I know something bad has happened."

"Let me make a few phone calls. I'll get back to you this afternoon."

Her eyes pleaded when she got up to leave. He couldn't look at her without feeling guilty. He knew he could never return to that city and that he'd have to turn her down. He'd ease his conscience by fixing her up with a reputable P.I. he knew there.

After seeing Vivian out he went of reflex to the bottom drawer of his desk. It was empty. He forgot he sucked it all down last night. He slammed the drawer when he realized it wouldn't have helped anyway.

Vivian dredged up a horde of memories he'd managed to suppress. Who was he kidding? He never could shake them. They shadowed him his every step.

The pity session about to kick into high gear got stalled when Sheila returned.

"Here," she said, placing a memo in his hand, then turned to leave.

"What's this?"

"A reservation for two on the one o'clock shuttle to New York."

"I'm not going to New York," he said, dropping the memo in the wastebasket.

"Just go home and pack."

"Why?"

"You wanna wear those same clothes all the time you're there?"

"Perhaps I didn't make myself clear. I'm not going to New York."

"You have to. You're taking your client home."

"What client?"

"You're going to look for Tommy."

"I never told Vivian . . ."

"I know. I did."

"You had no right . . ."

"You need the money. And you need to stop running away from the past."

"I'm not running from anything."

"Yes you are; every time you stick your head in a bottle."

She had him . . . and from the reading he sensed from her, she knew it too.

"It's time you went back and faced all those demons."

"I still don't like it."

"You can bitch about it while you're packing."

Practically ordering him to have a good time, she said she'd hold down the fort.

Reluctantly, though secretly grateful for the push, Jason went home to pack while Sheila took Vivian out for coffee and some girl talk.

On the short plane ride to New York, Vivian clued Jason in on Tommy's friends, where he usually hung out, where he went to school and the like.

Jason took the opportunity to ask about Rick. The tension emanating from her was thick enough to spread; he'd hit a sore spot. Almost afraid of what he was about to hear he nearly withdrew the question. He listened intently to the tale of Rick James.

Nothing could compare with the happiness she felt the first months after the wedding. Every night Rick was home was a party. He took her everywhere, showed her off to all his friends, made her the center of attention; and the lovemaking was out of this world. When the Doctor told her she was expecting she was on top of the world.

Rick was out of town on business; it would be three days before she could tell him the good news.

When he returned home she ran right to him and blurted out the happy news. He recoiled like someone had dropped scalding coffee in his lap.

Afterwards, Rick changed. Slowly at first then ever more dramatically.

Rick's disinterest in Vivian grew in direct proportion to her belly. The less he took her anywhere the more she believed he was seeing someone else; but she couldn't be sure.

After Tommy's birth Rick sorta changed. The idea of having a son seemed to make a difference to him. He lavished them with all sorts of presents.

Before long Vivian had her figure back and Rick resumed wining and dining her.

A mother now, she had many new responsibilities. She didn't always want to leave Tommy with a sitter; and Rick never wanted to stay home. The crying of the baby and having to share time with Vivian drove Rick out for good.

He'd come to visit infrequently; giving her large amounts of money to support Tommy and herself. They never wanted for anything.

"What kind of work is Rick in?"

"I-I never found out what he did. When I asked . . . he just told me to mind my own business; just shut up and enjoy the wide."

Jason's *Esper* sense lit up big time. That was an out and out lie. She was aware of Rick's occupation but didn't dare tell anyone. He didn't press it any further, but the cop in him was determined to find out how Rick made his money; it couldn't be from honest effort.

"How did Tommy and Rick get along?"

"There wasn't much of a relationship there. Oh, Tommy knew Rick was his father, but they didn't act like they were related. He was never there when Tommy needed a father's guidance. If the boy ever wanted anything Rick just tossed him the money and told him to buy whatever he wanted."

The plane entered it's landing pattern and the flight attendant gave her final instructions; prompting Vivian to change the subject.

"So what about you and Sheila? Anything there?"

"Strictly employer/employee. Nothing else."

"I don't know. She talked like you and this new guy who rescued her from some kidnapers were her personal property."

"You must have misunderstood her. She's just grateful to us for rescuing her. In a few weeks it'll wear off."

Vivian nodded in mock agreement; like she really felt he believed all he'd just said. Somewhere inside, Jason's doubts lingered about Sheila's feelings . . . and just how far she'd try to go with them.

A damp, gray, New York greeted them when they deplaned.

The late afternoon sky glowered ominously; there was a nip in the air.

Jason's mixed feelings about returning here were compounded by an increasing sense of foreboding. He couldn't shake the feeling he was in for deep trouble . . .

* * * *

CHAPTER SIX

The Big Apple

By the time they reached Vivian's apartment it was too late to check out Tommy's school to see if they knew anything. Instead, Jason chose to roam the old neighborhood in hopes of coming across any of Tommy's friends.

Vivian offered the comforts of her apartment, asking him to stay there until he found Tommy. He declined; saying he didn't know what his comings and goings might be. It could be at any hour of the day or night. She took his excuse, but that wasn't the whole reason.

Calling ahead from his apartment in Philly, Jason set up a reservation in a nearby hotel. True, he didn't know what hours he'd be keeping, but for some reason, he brought along his costume. It wouldn't do well if she were to accidentally discover it, making for some embarrassing questions. It all boiled down to privacy. Mindforce might have to go into action. Whether he did or not he wanted to be prepared.

Walking the familiar streets there was a sameness yet an uncanny strangeness to the city. It felt like the city didn't want him there. It growled at him; nipping at his ass like a nasty pit bull. He suffered from DT's it seemed without the pleasure of a decent drunk. He quivered inside, approaching an emotional overload.

He had to snap out of it. Inadvertently he'd been absorbing the emotions of the crowd around him. Knowing this made it easier to shut them out.

Thirty minutes later He found himself in the one spot he'd

avoided since that night. His minds eye could still see the pool of blood. Oh Carmen. Why did you have to be there that night? Why did he step on that bottle? Why? Why? Why? ·

He'd been on loan to Homicide from his post at Missing Persons because of the ever-present manpower shortages.

He'd gotten lucky; the perp practically fell into his lap that night. But he'd been spotted and the perp fled on foot; Jason giving chase while calling it in. Shots were fired; flying wildly on the empty street. Jason pulled his own weapon, ignored his training about not firing on the run, and when he pulled the trigger, that's when he stepped on the bottle. The shot flew wild; where he didn't know. Catching himself, he fired from one knee, placing a .38 slug deep in the perp's thigh, shattering the femur. He went down hard, losing his gun that clattered into the gutter.

On him in a heartbeat, Jason was clapping on the cuffs when he saw them. Two, shapely, high-heeled, black stockinged legs on the sidewalk; sticking out from behind the corner building. He froze for a fraction of a second while the scene sank in. Quick, short, unsure steps brought him to the prone figure. . . .

He no more had the answer now than he did then. He knelt where her head had been, touched the spot where the puddle of blood had flowed; it was that night all over again. The ugly gash in her neck where the slug had ripped straight through, severing the carotid artery, red and blue flashing lights danced off the wall, radio communications crackled in the sticky air. Her body still warm when he searched vainly for a pulse. The horror when he turned her over to see her face. All these things revolved around and assaulted his head. He needed a drink.

That first drink on the road to oblivion didn't come until after the Coroner's report which stated that if Carmen had received immediate attention she might have lived. He kicked himself for spending so much time on that perp. He got drunk that night.

If not for the blaring horn and the garbage mouth of the trucker assailing the driver in front of him he might not have snapped out of it. Reliving the past was not the answer; he had other fish to fry.

Something drew him in the direction of the docks. This always happened when he was on the scent of a missing person; much more so now since the accident. He didn't know why, it just happened. Sooner or later he'd always be drawn toward something or someone who could lead him to his quarry. This time it was the docks. The sensation was surreal.

Near the docks it occurred to him that if he were going to run away and hide this would be a likely spot. There'd be all kinds of produce around; and if you were a good sneak you'd eat.

Staying out of the weather would be another problem. If you were real careful you could probably find a warehouse to sneak into during the evening. You could curl up in a corner somewhere out of the way and maybe not get caught.

He didn't know if Tommy was that resourceful, or even if he came this way. But something was drawing him here and he had to check it out.

Nearing a local watering hole he thought it might be worth the effort to show Tommy's picture around. Maybe someone inside might have seen the boy in the area.

The bartender was far from helpful. "If he wandered in here it wasn't while I was working. Ahhhh, what the hell." He took the picture from Jason and held it up. "Anyone o' you yahoos seen this kid around?". Murmuring and shaking of heads were the only response. "Sorry chum," and he flipped the photo on the bar.

No one in the bar could tell him anything. But there was one big ugly brute at a corner table sent his *Esper* sense buzzing ever so slightly. A large man: probably in his forties, slope browed with a granite chin. His dimwitted expression led Jason to believe he only used it for a minimum of functions.

He finished his beer quickly, gave a grunt to the bartender and left in a big hurry.

This man could be the clue Jason sought. How, he didn't know; what connection he had to Tommy was a mystery. But he'd become accustomed to obeying his senses.

"Who was that big guy?" he asked the bartender.

He gave Jason that look he'd seen so many times in the past. He knew immediately what he was after.

In his Police Detective days he'd reach into his pocket, pull out his I.D. and badge and with a few idle threats, learn what he wanted to know.

Showing him his P.I. credentials would only get Jason a quick get lost. Instead, he reached for his wallet, took out a twenty, let him see it, tore it in half then stuck one half in the bartender's hand.

"I've got no time for haggling my friend. Tell me what I want to know and you'll get this half. Don't satisfy me and I walk out with this half and burn it."

"The dudes name is Sam."

"Got any idea where he lives?"

"Down on the waterfront."

"Strange place to live."

"He's got a shack down there. Ain't got no decent job or apartment, so he trades watchmen duties for a place to live."

"Not too bright I take it."

"Look pal. You got all you're gonna get from me. . . . Now fork over the other half of the twenty and get your fancy dressed butt outta here."

Jason rolled it around for a second. "I don't mind paying for information. But I expect to get my moneys worth. What you've told me isn't worth five bucks, let alone twenty. Sorry . . . pal."

Sliding his half of the bill in his pocket, Jason made for the door casually. A subtle motion from the bartender and two big ugly wharf rats got up and blocked the exit.

"Nobody leaves without paying their tab," said the bartender.

"I don't pay for what I don't get. And if you think these two monkeys can keep me from leaving, you got another thing coming."

The bigger of the two men stepped slowly into Jason's face.

"We don't like deadbeats around here," he said coolly while grabbing Jason's lapels with both hands. "Now I'm gonna have ta teach you a lesson."

Jason met the cold steel of the bouncer's gaze with the heated glare of his own. "Take your best shot bozo." Unimpressed, he tried to drag Jason towards the door and was perplexed when he could not move him.

"Oh, a tough guy. That'll make it all the more fun."

The troglodyte was struck dumb when Jason grasped his left wrist with his right hand; twisting it slowly around against all the force he could muster. Eventually ending up on his back on the floor with Jason's foot in his throat, his hand still locked on his wrist, twisting it around just enough to cause him discomfort.

The other Neanderthal felt it prudent to wrap a chair around Jason's head. Bad move.

When he swung, Jason thrust his free arm up to intercept the wooden bludgeon, shattering on his forearm. The dude's follow through brought him within reach of Jason's free hand, which he clamped around the idiot's throat. Purposefully slow, Jason raised him off the floor to arms length. His only recourse, to clamp his hands on Jason's wrist and hang on so as not to strangle.

"Now," he said to the bartender, "Do you tell me what I want to hear, or do you join your friends?"

DANGER flashed when the bartender ducked behind the bar; reaching for something.

Dropping the two jerks, who sat on the floor rubbing their necks, Jason was on the bartender before he could reappear.

He stood up with a sawed off double-barreled shotgun; pointing it at where Jason had been. To his consternation, he wasn't there. Before he could locate him: Jason yanked the shotgun from his grasp, grabbed the bartender's collar with his left hand, placed the business end of the weapon against the wide eyed man's nose and cocked the hammers ever so slowly till they locked into place with a deafening metallic click in the now deathly silent saloon.

"Now. Talk to me. Just make sure you tell me exactly what I want to hear. . . . Okay."

"Shoot. What do I care? . . . He lives on the wharf five blocks south o' here. He's a big dimwitted goof that don't think so fast.

Probably never went to school. Wouldn't hurt a fly, 'cept when he's been drinking heavy. Tore up the place once. Took ten guys ta hold him down. I pity you if he gets hold a you. He'll break your neck for you."

Jason mulled it around while he stared steely eyed into the sweating bartender's face. "Not a chance pal. Not a chance."

Lowering the shotgun while maintaining his grip, Jason broke it open, removed the shells then slid the weapon down to the end of the bar. Taking the remaining half of the twenty from his pocket, Jason stuffed it into the shocked bartender's mouth.

"Never. Never let it be said I don't pay my tab," he said while he shoved the stunned bartender toward the shelves behind the bar; eliciting a sharp clinking of the bottles there.

Backing toward the door, Jason juggled the shotgun shells in his one hand, dropping them in the lap of the brute still on the floor rubbing his neck. "Here. Try these," he said, clapping the man on the back. "These outta clear your throat for you."

Jason grinned then laughed sardonically while he headed for the door, then paused for one last insult. "It's been fun guys. Let's do it again some time, shall we."

Not staying for a reply, Jason ducked quickly out the door; heading south in search of this guy Sam, hoping he knew something useful.

Walking briskly, he mulled over what had just happened, wondering what he'd get into next. Halfway to his destination, *DANGER* flashed, jerking his head around to the alley on his right. Standing in ambush was the huge brute, Sam. He lunged for Jason's throat.

"Yer not gonna take Tommy!" he growled. "Yer not gonna take him."

Jason's reflexes coiled in preparation for hurling the Goliath to the far side of the alley. Barely in time he remembered his strength and got hold of himself. God forbid he should have a repeat of the incident with the gangster back in Philly.

When the huge man lunged at Jason He simply sidestepped him. Giving him a mild shove to the side.

Bracing himself against the wall the wild man whirled around, glaring savagely. While the brute prepared to lunge once more it struck Jason; he'd mentioned Tommy. Jason said nothing of the boy's name. Sam had the boy and Jason would have to find out if he was all right.

"Take it easy. I'm not here to hurt Tommy."

"You lie! Tommy said you would lie."

He lunged at Jason again. Again Jason sidestepped. Again with the same results. Again with the same insane glare in Sam's eyes.

"Now look," said Jason, his voice taking on it's eerie calm. "I'm not here to hurt anyone. I'm here to help Tommy. Now calm down fella. I'm a friend."

You could have brushed Jason over with a feather when the raging Goliath of a man stopped dead in his tracks, perceptively calmer. Like he'd been smacked between the eyes with a brick. This wasn't normal. He'd been led to believe nothing short of a regiment could stop Sam once he became enraged. He was too slow to be reasoned with logically. He just stood there like he'd been maced and chloroformed at the same time. No, this definitely didn't make sense.

Was he ill? Jason's enhanced ears heard a strong, regular heartbeat. The brute just stood there, almost catatonic, with no apparent physical irregularity. The only thing that made any sense was he'd developed some other power of which he was not aware.

A simple test would find out. Jason looked straight into Sam's eyes and concentrated. "Your left hand itches."

With little hesitation he scratched his left hand. Was it a coincidence? He made another suggestion. "Your right hand itches." Immediately he exchanged the scratching.

This was incredible. The accident had given him the power of suggestion. But he'd made several other suggestions to people in the recent past, forceful suggestions, but none with these results. Why only this man? Logically, it must be the power is only strong enough to work on the weak willed. Or, was it possible to catch a man off guard or in a semiconscious state, and implant suggestions in their minds? That would explain why the young mother in last nights accident calmed so quickly.

The answers would have to wait for another time because he had something else to try. Loathe to take advantage of Sam while he was so defenseless, he had to know; could he implant a suggestion in his mind mentally without saying it aloud?

He concentrated on the one thing he felt could be no coincidence. In this chilly weather no insects were to be found. If it worked, he'd implant the suggestion of a mosquito flying about Sam's head.

Unsure how to go about it, the experiment was somewhat of a mental strain. In the aftermath, he felt he should not be surprised, but to his awe, Sam began swatting at the non-existent insect.

Another suggestion dispatched the insect. Still another implanted one final suggestion, that of a friend, which he truly was.

"Friend," said Sam softly.

"Yes. Do you know where Tommy is?"

Nodding, he showed Jason the way. He told of how Tommy and some of the other boys in the area became his little friends and would come to visit.

Tommy would always bring him presents and just generally hang around.

Sam learned that Tommy's parents were divorced, and that his father didn't come around much.

Sam, in his own way, knew he was just taking the place of a father in Tommy's eyes. He welcomed it; trying to teach Tommy as best he could what he knew. Practical things: like tying knots, how to build boats and use tools, and to survive when times were tough.

Vivian had no knowledge of Sam; otherwise, this would have been the first place she'd have looked.

Sam looked forward to Tommy's visits. But he wouldn't let him hang around too long. He didn't want the boy to get in trouble with his mother.

Sam felt more like an uncle than anything else. That's why when Tommy came bursting into his shack Friday afternoon, half scared out of his wits, Sam took him in for protection.

"Why didn't you take the boy to the police or at least home?"

"I don't trust them. Alla time they arrest bad men but later they get let go 'cause the cops can't hold them. . . . 'Sides, I don't want no trouble with the Mob."

Jason hated to agree, but it was all too true. As an officer he'd seen it all. Build a case, collar the perp, see a shyster lawyer have 'em out before sunset. It wasn't the best system; but it's all they had.

"Tommy didn't wanna go home neither. He said his mom would only turn him over to his father to kill him."

That threw Jason for a loop. Why would Vivian be so frantic to find Tommy if she were going to turn him over to Rick to kill him? Was she mixed up in something so deep that it would force her to condemn her own son? He couldn't swallow that; but before he returned the boy to her he'd be sure of his safety.

He hoped it was just a misunderstanding; he'd know soon enough for they were at the door to Sam's shack.

Creature comforts inside were at a bare minimum. It was neat and clean, with one table, two chairs, and one bed. A sleeping bag spread on the floor next to the cot was where Sam slept each night. A pot bellied stove kept the place quite comfortable and doubled as a cook surface.

Tommy's face lit up at the return of Sam, then came awash with fear upon seeing the stranger. Backing toward the far wall his eyes darted about looking for an avenue of escape.

"It's okay," said Sam. "This is a friend of mine. He's a good man. Don't be afraid."

"Hi Tommy. My name is Jason. I'm a private investigator hired by your mother to bring you home."

"NO!!" screamed the boy in a fit of utter panic. "NO! I won't go home. They'll kill me for sure."

"Who would want to kill you?"

"My father!" said the boy, crying profusely. "H-He killed one man. Why shouldn't he kill me too?"

"Try to relax Tommy. I am your friend," said Jason, eerie calm.

"Only Sam's my friend," said the stubborn boy, plopping on the cot. His will was strong, but immature. Jason's suggestion power would take some time to convince the boy, if at all.

"Listen to the man," said Sam. "He's good."

Sam's gentle insistence coupled with Jason's calm demeanor reacted on the boy's hesitance; bringing him slowly around to their side. In time the boy began his tale.

Friday afternoon school let out early. With time on his hands before he should be home, Tommy decided to stop in at Sam's.

While skipping along the alley between two warehouses he spied a familiar looking car. Closer inspection showed it to be the limo his father usually rode around in. Knowing his father was near, not having seen him in several weeks, he paused to look for him.

Angry voices from the half open door to the warehouse drew him near. Curious, he crept cautiously inside; hiding in the shadows under a staircase. Nervous, he watched the drama unfold.

There were Rick and two other men. One, short, with a black mustache, wearing funny round glasses. The other, a tall, bald headed guy with a long ugly scar on his right cheek.

The three of them were yelling at and hitting a fourth man. Tommy never saw his face because his back was always to him.

Tommy saw Rick pull a gun from his coat and point it squarely at the unknown man. Then Rick said something about, "Here's the final kiss off brother," and shot the man several times.

They then stuffed the body into a steel drum and filled the remaining space with sand, then sealed the lid, putting it among the many drums stored there.

Rick said all the drums there were full of toxic waste; scheduled to be taken to a special dumpsite where they'd bury barrel and all. No one would notice one more.

"That was the easiest money I ever made from the Mob," said

Rick while the three laughed. "Imagine, fifty grand just to scrag a Councilman and make sure he's never found."

They left the warehouse and sped away. Tommy was so scared he ran straight to Sam for protection.

"Why didn't you tell the police?" said Jason.

"I thought if I ratted the Mob would send someone to kill me."

The boy's words had a ring of truth. The Mob doesn't like loose ends; they'd surely send someone to clean up the mess. Jason knew what he had to do. He used to have some friends on the force here. His only hope, would they still be willing to help after his disgrace?

He placed a call to the station from a booth on the pier. The time was late, after ten, with luck Capt. Bob Harris would still be on duty—fortunately, he was. Jason informed the Capt. he had a missing person for him and needed some answers. The Capt. met Jason's request with cold disinterest, but sent a unit to pick them up.

The unmarked car had them to the station in a half hour where they went straight up to Harris' department. He was with the Special Crimes Unit now.

"I thought I'd never have to see you again Jason," said the Capt., reluctantly extending his hand. "When did you blow into town?"

"I've been here a few hours."

"And still sober I see."

"That's uncalled for Bob!" Jason's anger rising.

"Is it? I want you in my office."

Jason knew the way but let him lead. The Capt. held the door; closing it after Jason entered.

"I can only offer you coffee," said the Capt.

"That's fine. Coffee's about the strongest thing I drink these days."

"You on the wagon?" he said as he poured two cups.

"No. Just . . . circumstances make drinking unenjoyable."

The Capt's anger spiked sharply on Jason's senses. "You were just about the best cop I had! You coulda gone a long way here."

"Don't you think I know that? But the Dept. abandoned me."

"Bullshit! We gave you every chance. Offered counseling and assistance. But you, you wallowed in your own self-pity. Good God man. You think you're the first cop ever shot an innocent bystander?"

It's not just that. Maybe . . . maybe you did offer me help. But it was too late. Internal Affairs roasted me over a spit. Carmen's brother turned his back on me. And after I was exonerated, it was business as usual. Here's your badge and gun Jason. Go back on the street. Just like nothing ever happened. But it did happen, and I couldn't forget . . . and you're to blame."

"Me? What've I got to do with it?"

"You lent me to Homicide! If not for that I wouldn't have been there that night . . . and Carmen might still be alive."

"Carmen was a hooker. Sooner or later they all die too soon."

"But it wouldn't have been at my hands"

Silence hung like the gloom at a funeral. Guilt crept in and sawed off the hard edges of the Capt's anger and disappointment. He knew Jason was somewhat right, but couldn't bring himself to admit it.

If not for Jason's *Esper* sense he might have left in a huff.

"Look. I can't change the past," said the Capt. "We were friends once. It hurt me to watch you fall . . . and it hurt even more watching you allow it. . . . You gonna be in town long?"

"I've done what I came to do."

"So now what? You going back to Philly?"

"Not yet. I've a few things to investigate."

Jason let him in on the whole story of Vivian's coming to see him, and of Tommy being missing. Telling him everything he could right up to his finding Tommy. Neglecting to tell him about his rather unique powers. Finishing with, "What do you have on Rick James?"

"Not much I'm afraid," said the Capt., his eyebrows raising.

"We've had our suspicions, but nothing we could make stick. We think he's connected with the Mob, but there's no hard evidence. Why do you ask?"

"Because," Jason said, checking Tommy who was asleep on the sofa outside, "this is Rick's son. He saw someone murdered by Rick in a warehouse last Friday. Near where your car picked us up. The boy can connect Rick to the Mob. He's probably one of their hit men. That's where he gets all his money."

"Did the boy see who was murdered?"

"No. He never saw his face. But let me ask you this. Are any of your Councilmen missing? One you've been investigating."

"Yes, there is. How did you know?"

"The boy overheard Rick tell the other two men he was with that the murdered man was a Councilman."

The Capt. leaned back in his chair. "If the boy's story is true, it's gonna clear up a few loose ends."

The Capt. allowed that the Councilman in question was suspected of being on the take. He'd been under surveillance for about six months. The man used his influence to get contracts for certain companies in the Metropolitan area. In return he was paid quite handsomely.

They believed these companies were tied in with organized crime; using them to hide their real operations. When the Councilman disappeared just before they were ready to pick him up, they checked and found all his records gone. All his bank accounts were emptied out that day, and they believed he skipped town.

Jason told the Capt. this was most likely done to make it appear he'd gotten wise and beat it before he could be picked up, when actually it was done to cover a murder. Time and manpower would be wasted looking for a man who no longer existed. Probably never realizing he was dead. They made sure he could never be caught and talk.

What bothered Jason was why pick that moment to off the

Councilman? Unless they were wise to the surveillance. Which means there must be a leak coming from inside the Dept.

"I agree with you," said the Capt. "But who?"

"I haven't a clue. For now I think you should hold the boy in protective custody as a material witness until we know more."

When informed of the whereabouts of the Councilman's body the Capt. said, "If possible, we'll try to retrieve it without too much fanfare. We don't want to alert the Mob we're on to them."

"I'll tell Vivian that Tommy's okay and he'll be held here for awhile for his protection."

"Agreed. Did the boy see the two other men?"

"Yes he did," said Jason, relating the descriptions.

"They don't ring a bell, but we'll have them checked out. They could be out of town help here for just this occasion. I'll get it on the wire."

"Let's hope they haven't left town yet."

After leaving the Capt., Jason went straight to Vivian's. The hour was late but he doubted she was getting much sleep lately.

"Jason?" said Vivian, drawn from worrying. "Come in. Come in. It's late. Is there something wrong?"

"Everything's fine," he said, stepping inside.

Closing the door, Vivian asked, "Do you have any idea where you're going to start searching for Tommy?"

"I've already found him."

Eyes like saucers, tears welling up, Vivian was astonished. "You've found him! Already? Well where is he? Why didn't you bring him with you?" Then fear set in. "He's not injured! Is he?"

She threw open the door and looked down the hallway in both directions, half expecting Tommy to be there.

Disappointed, she closed the door, angrily stalking toward Jason.

"If this is a joke it's not very funny."

"It's no joke. Tommy's safe. I have him in capable hands."

"When can I see him?"

"In the morning. First, I need some questions answered."

Her defenses came to the forefront. "What can I tell you I haven't already?"

"You knew Rick worked for the Mob, didn't you?" he said, half asking, half accusing.

"NO! NO! How could I?"

That was a lie.

"You also knew he was a hit man for them as well. Didn't you?" he accused strongly.

He caught the fear in her eyes—the apprehension—the frustration; even without his *Esper* sense this was evident. Among all this confusion he also detected, relief... relief that now she could stop hiding a big secret.

She sat slowly on the sofa, gathering her thoughts. Jason sat in the chair opposite, placing his hat on the coffee table.

In the beginning, I never really cared where Rick got his money . . ."

After they were married though, what and where seemed more important to her. After all, a wife should know everything possible about her spouse.

The first few times she asked, Rick just told her not to worry where it came from. When she began to insist more and more, Rick finally barked at her; it was none of her business and to just enjoy the ride. Not wanting to incur his wrath, Vivian just let it drop, never asking again.

By this time she was expecting the baby and had little need for upsets in her life. She had her suspicions but kept them to herself. She'd known Rick since they were teenagers. He'd been into gambling and the numbers racket even then.

Rick always showed her the best of times. Always taking her places, buying her things.

She was really busted up when he just up and left for a year, never telling her why. She thought he was gone for good.

During this time she met Jason, and they had their short relationship before Rick blew back into town.

Unknown by anyone save the Mob, at that time, during Rick's

absence he was off to St. Louis to make his first hit on someone the Mob wanted eliminated; then to lie low for a while. Surfacing again somewhere else to begin again. Rick traveled the west; performing Lord knows how many hits for the Mob before he returned to New York.

The light of truth about Rick's dealings came to the surface accidentally after Tommy was born.

Once she'd gotten her figure back, Rick started taking her out again.

The first place he showed her off was at the mansion of a business associate. They were having a large party that night. With scores of people in attendance.

Some she knew, some were strangers. Even so, it was good to be back out in the public again, enjoying life in the fast lane. She'd always been a real party animal that had no trouble having a good time.

She and Rick became separated during the course of the evening, but she was having so much fun she really didn't notice his absence.

After three hours of partying she had to excuse herself to go in search of the powder room.

The mansion was huge. Her first time there she thought she'd explore a little and got hopelessly lost among the corridors.

Hearing voices coming from one of the rooms, she thought she could ask directions. Being curious, she eavesdropped a little before knocking on the door.

To this day she wishes she hadn't. For in the room she heard a man's voice telling her husband he'd done a fine job on his last assignment. She also heard the man give him his next assignment. He was being sent to murder someone who was going to testify against their loan sharking operation.

Jason recalled the case. It was shortly after he'd gotten his Detectives Shield. A particularly grisly affair that was never solved.

Unnerved at what she'd just heard, she quickly found her way back to the party. The remainder of the evening she was more or less in shock. When Rick finally did return to her she told him she had to go home to check on the baby.

After that night she never felt quite the same about Rick. She begged off going out more and more; saying she needed to stay home with the baby. She spent less time in bed with him; using the babies crying as an excuse to sit up with him all night.

Finally, Rick couldn't take the neglect anymore—he moved out. Later, filing for divorce.

Vivian wanted the divorce more than Rick, but it was better if he asked for it instead of her. Because if she had he never would have given it to her. She just wanted Rick out of her life.

She told Jason that during this period Rick had gotten to her cousin Harry. Rick had paid off his gambling debts, for which Harry would slip him information. Just little tidbits at first; nothing too serious. Once he was in too deep to extricate himself, they started asking for top-secret info. Otherwise he'd tell Harry's superiors and ruin his career.

Jason's old roommate, Harry Reynolds, he was a Det. Sgt. Now, in debt to the Mob. There was the Capt's leak. He'd have to inform him of this in the morning when he took Vivian to see Tommy.

When asked why she never remarried, she told Jason that Rick had a nasty habit of discouraging would be suitors. If he couldn't have her he'd be sure no one else did.

No one ever knew what she'd heard that night. She never told anyone until now. The weight of what she knew had been pressing down on her all these years. Now, thankfully, it had been removed.

" . . . and every time I heard of a mysterious gangland murder I'd always wonder if Rick was involved."

"Why didn't you take what you knew to the Police?"

"What good would it do?"

"It would have saved a number of lives if Rick were off the streets."

"No it wouldn't," she glared. "They'd just get someone else to do it, and the same people would be dead anyway and so would I!

They'd never let me live for informing. And they'd probably shoot Rick after they made him kill me. That's how horrible they are."

The sad part . . . she was right. All the same people would be dead, along with Vivian, and they'd only have one dead gangster to show for it.

Listening to her tale, Jason had been formulating a plan that could wrap this all up without either Vivian or Tommy having to testify. A daring, almost insane plan that just might not work. He could be exposed for what he'd become. It required having witnesses around while he worked over a thug in the middle of their playhouse. There was little else he could do. Trouble was; he had to find one of Rick's accomplices in the murder to make it work.

The next morning Jason picked up Vivian and took her to Tommy. Appalled, when she learned that Tommy didn't come to her for fear she'd turn him over to Rick. Her only reasoning being Rick often told the boy that he and his mother would one day get married again.

The reunion was filled with tears, hugs and promises that things would be better; like so many others Jason had witnessed in the past.

Spying Jason, Capt. Harris called him into his office. "We got a line on those two guys Tommy saw with Rick. They're both from St. Louis. We showed him their pictures earlier and he confirmed it."

"That's great," Jason said, halfhearted. "But I've got some bad news for you."

"What?"

"It's Harry Reynolds. I think he's your leak."

"I find that hard to believe. He's had a fine record since he made Sgt."

"I think you'll find the Mob helped put him there by throwing him a few sacrificial lambs to make him look good in exchange for some rather large favors. Vivian's his cousin. She told me Rick got to him years ago. We've got to keep him out of the loop for Vivian and Tommy's safety."

"No problem. We can handle him in time. My main concern is getting Rick James."

"I think I can help you there. I've an idea how I can get someone else to finger Rick and all his associates. Leaving Vivian and Tommy in the clear."

"I can't allow that. You're a civilian. You tell me your plan and I'll discuss . . ."

"No can do Cap. What I've got in mind I don't think you'd approve of . . . officially."

"Now wait a minute. You're not a cop in this town anymore. You get your ass in trouble I won't be able to save you. . . . That's for the record. Unofficially, I'm only giving you a shot because we were friends once. If this goes sour we could both hang."

"And if I come out a hero you won't be able to give me any credit for the collar."

Jason wasn't ignorant of the Capt's precarious position, but as a private citizen he could get away with a lot of things their red tape wouldn't allow. If the Capt. were aware of the real plan he'd order a straight jacket and a rubber room for Jason.

The Purple Palace: a watering hole for most of the criminal element in this town, though nothing could be proved, was fifteen minutes away by cab. Jason would camp out there every night until who he needed to institute his plan came in. First: he needed to rent a tux; the bouncer would never let him into the Palace in his regular duds.

Rick always hung out here in the old days. No reason to think he'd change, or fail to extend to his buddies the hospitality of the place. Jason's only hope was they hadn't skipped town yet.

The Palace was full of glitz and glamour. All the well heeled congregated there. All dressed to the gills. Occasionally you'd see a celebrity or two in attendance with the regular crowd—but not tonight.

There were marble floors, marble steps even marble columns holding up the ceiling. Which was the only purple thing in the place, other than the drapes. Even the bar was solid marble.

Crystal chandeliers hung all around, giving the room a soft glow.

The band played all the contemporary music on the other side of the dance floor; which was sunken in two steps below the bar level. Dividing the dance floor from the main dining areas and the bar stood a highly polished mahogany rail supported by brass stiles.

Jason took a seat at the bar facing the door so he could watch whoever came or went.

What could have turned into an extended vigil consummated after but twenty minutes. In strolled Rick, bold as brass; close on his heels, his two compatriots.

This was more than Jason hoped for. Chances are he could round up the whole group tonight.

While they stood in the entry foyer, Jason listened in with his enhanced ears. Rick told them to have a couple of drinks while he went to the penthouse to talk to the boss. They went to a booth not fifteen feet from where Jason sat. Now, he had to get one of them alone.

Tuning in with his *Esper* sense, he needed to pinpoint which of them was the most impressionable; with the weaker will. The smaller one with the glasses checked out as a prime target. A guy who was only brave in a crowd. Alone he wasn't worth much. How to separate them? He knew his suggestion power might not work on a strong willed person, but maybe he could do some little thing to catch him off guard. He was so intent on his conversation he just might be able to plant a small suggestion.

Jason concentrated on making the man's foot itch. Within seconds he scratched his foot. Again he concentrated getting a similar reaction. Now for the crucial test. With a supreme effort he suggested, NOW IT'S ON FIRE!

With a violent start the man leaped out of his seat, stomping on his foot; yelling his foot was burning.

An attendant suggested he go into the men's lounge and remove his shoe to see what the problem was. He excused himself from his partner; hobbling off, saying he'd be back shortly.

The little man was right where Jason wanted him. He didn't hesitate in pouncing on the unsuspecting dupe. In the few minutes before his partner could return he'd initiate the seeds of doubt and confusion.

Jason slid into the booth where the other fellow had been.

"Who are you?"

"Who I am doesn't matter. But I know who you are . . . Benny."

"Big deal. You know my name. So What?"

"I just thought you'd like a little food for thought."

"What could you know that I'd wanna hear?"

While he talked, Jason began his suggestion ever so lightly and calmly. "Well, ya see Benny, it's like this. I work for the government. I'm investigating Rick James and I've been following him around for a few weeks."

"So?" said Benny, trying to sound aloof, though Jason knew otherwise.

"So, I know all about the guy you three bumped off last Friday. We had the Councilman under surveillance as well. We were all set to pick him up for questioning when you scragged him and stuffed him inta that barrel."

"I don't know what you're talking about," Benny said, looking around for his partner to return.

"Yes you do. And you know I'm right. Rick's got a lot of pull in the Mob. He's their best boy. You know that. He's not gonna take the fall for it. And neither will Monk; Rick needs him. So that leaves you Benny. Rick will pin it all on you and you'll take the fall; not him."

"What makes you so sure?" said Benny, beads of sweat popping on his brow.

"Take my word for it."

Benny's mind was racing. Jason could not be sure he was getting through to him.

"You're crazy!" he said so loudly it drew stares from nearby patrons.

It was time to pull out all the stops. He'd gone too far with this gamble to stop now.

Jason reached across the table and grabbed Benny's lapels with both hands. Standing up, he dragged Benny up with him. Then slapped him a few times to disorient him.

"You can't talk to me that way!" Jason said loudly, drawing a crowd of eyes.

Again he slapped him around, stopping short of knocking him unconscious. Then he concentrated on Benny in earnest while Security moved in. Silently suggesting that Benny would rot in a dank, dingy cell for the rest of his pitiful life for the murder of the Councilman. Rick would go free while he alone answered for all of Rick's evil.

He had time for one last suggestion before two of the bouncers could drag him off Benny, the biggest part of the gamble. If it didn't work He might be forced to reveal himself.

Physically, they couldn't detain Jason unless he let them. Essential, was that he stay here and detain Rick until the plan ran its course.

He let the two goons drag him out; assuming they'd take him upstairs to be questioned, but they headed for the door. This would not do, so. . . .

"Let go of me you goons!" he yelled. "Where ya taking me?"

"Out inta the street," one of them said. "We got rules against fighting in here."

"Oh, you don't like fighters. But you cater to murderers, gangsters and other sleazy types."

That stopped them in their tracks, each looking at the other in bewilderment. As expected, they needed to get further orders before they could deal with him now. One went off, presumably to make a phone call, while the other held on to Jason. If only he knew what he was holding.

The first goon came back two minutes later.

"The Boss wants the loudmouth upstairs till he can get to him."

Goody. Just where he wanted to go.

Jason got shoved into what obviously was a small waiting room to the bigger office just to the other side of the inner door. One goon watched over Jason while the other returned to the main floor.

Feigning disdain, Jason plopped onto the plush sofa and tuned into the inner room. Two men were conversing; one certainly the Boss, the other had to be Rick. Jason remembered the voice from downstairs.

The Boss was congratulating Rick on a job well done on the Councilman. Then told him he knew he'd been contacted by Mr. Big in Philadelphia; to come down and get rid of the lunatic who calls himself the Crime Czar.

Jason's surprise at the mention of the Crime Czar reflected forcefully on his face.

"What's yer trouble?" said the overseeing goon.

Jason replied with a repugnant sneer, then settled to listen.

"Look Rick," said the Boss, "we know you free-lance more or less, and you take the jobs you choose. We just want you to hold off on this one for a few months."

"How come?" said a restrained Rick.

The Boss clued Rick in on the deal made between the Syndicate and this upstart Crime Czar. The bet had to be allowed to run its course. The Syndicate just wanted to see how far this punk could get. There'd be plenty of time to kill him later . . . and he'd be paid quite well.

Jason shook his head at the unmitigated gall. This Crime Czar, whoever he was, certainly was sure of himself. Mindforce would have to stop in to the Commissioner's office with that little tidbit.

Jason had to act fast. What they were saying could ruin all his preparation. The Boss was telling Rick he had to speak to some jerk making a ruckus downstairs. Since Rick shouldn't be seen with him, he should use the back exit. Jason knew what he had to do and sprang to his feet.

"You can't hold me here! I know that no good Rick James is in there!" he shouted at the door. "What're you idiots trying to do, sneak him out the back door?"

Startled at the outburst, the guard tried to shut him up. When the goon attempted to grab him, Jason slapped him against the far wall.

Rapid footsteps came from beyond the office door. While the guard reached for his gun the door flung open. Jason whirled to face Rick's head poking out the door.

"What the hell's the trouble out here?"

Before the guard could speak Jason cut him off. "Plenty of trouble for you Rick."

The humiliated guard launched himself off the floor and strong-armed Jason into the office. Rick hadn't seen him in years, not since Jason's days in uniform. The mustache and slicked down hair didn't hurt either. Jason scanned Rick's emotions for any sign of recognition. He gazed at Jason vaguely but wasn't making the connection.

"Who the hell are you?" growled Rick, nudging Jason over to the front of the Boss' desk.

"Your downfall Rick."

"My downfall huh. You got a name pal?"

"You figure it out."

The guard took a light poke at his ribs. Jason never flinched nor wavered from Rick's glare. "You wanna end up with your ass against the wall again?"

"Oh, a wise guy," said Rick. "See if he's carrying any I.D."

Jason didn't make the frisk easy. "He's clean."

"You didn't get any greasy fingerprints on the tux, did you? I just had it cleaned."

"How bout a coupla bullet holes?"

"Enough!" said the Boss.

He and Rick put their heads together to decide what to do with Jason, who knew as soon as they did.

"All right. We don't know who you are," said Rick, "but you seem to know me. And since I can't take any chances, my man here is gonna take you for a tour of the countryside."

"Oh hell. And me without my camera. You don't suppose we could stop for it?"

Rick, the Boss and the goon exchanged quizzical glances.

"You're either the most cocksure man . . . or the biggest fool I've ever met," said Rick.

"I say he's a nut." chimed in the goon, trying to twist Jason's arm to no avail.

"You'll never stop us Rick. You get rid of me, which you can't, and another will take my place.

"What are you? A Fed?" said Rick,

The seeds were planted.

"You're so smart. You figure it out."

"I don't have to, smart boy," said Rick, sticking his nose in Jason's face.

"You've had your dance Rick. Now it's time to pay the piper."

"And just who's gonna make me? You? You're in no position to make threats you can't back up."

"No threat Rick. Face the facts. You can count the minutes you have left on one hand."

"This guys gotta be a Fed," said the Boss. "And if he is his back-up can't be too far away."

No problem. We take this one out the back and when his partner comes looking we off him too.

"You should get so lucky," said Jason.

All three men gazed blankly at each other trying to fathom this man's words. Certainly he must be bereft of his senses. Their emotions were all confused. Just what Jason wanted.

Rick opened his mouth to speak but never got a chance to vocalize anything because of the commotion erupting from the outer office.

Good ol' Benny. Jason's silent suggestion had worked after all. While he delayed Rick here, Benny went straight to Capt. Harris and spilled his guts. Capt. Harris had gotten a Judge to sign a warrant, and now stood poised to write the final chapter to this little drama.

At the sound of the commotion all heads turned to the door. Jason seized the opportunity to swipe the lamp from the desk. In the darkness he was quick and efficient. They never knew what hit them.

When the Capt. entered, Jason was turning on another lamp. Left hand on hip the Capt's right scratched his head at the sight of the three unconscious men.

"How'd you do it?"

"Doesn't really matter. But when they wake up, don't tell them who I am. They think I'm a Fed, and I'd like to keep it that way, okay?"

"Sure. All I want to know is how you got Benny to turn himself in and confess. He burst into my office babbling all he knew faster than we could get it on tape. We won't need the other witnesses testimony anymore."

"Precisely what I wanted. Now they can lead a normal life without looking over their shoulders all the time."

"But what about Benny?"

"Oh . . . I've just got the gift of persuasion," said Jason, placing a hand on the Capt's shoulder, then striding past him and out the door.

The Capt. stood rubbing his chin, shrugged, then knelt to cuff his prisoners.

The weather turned warm and sunny in New York; urging Jason to stay a few days longer to visit with some old friends.

Harry Reynolds, when confronted with what they knew, confessed all, adding to the list of charges on Rick. He turned in his badge and was taken into custody. Jason felt sorry for Harry, but law enforcement wasn't a two-way street.

Benny spilled so much about Rick's hit parade that the Judge ordered him held without bail, pending trial. He'd likely not see the light of day as a civilian ever again.

Jason paid one last call on Vivian before he set out for home. She still loved Rick in her own way. Jason was nearly certain the city would swallow her up again like it did before.

By now he'd gotten homesick. Foregoing the plane, he opted to use his own method. It was quicker.

Strange how fate works. If Tommy had been a little older, he'd have realized that Rick couldn't have seen him in hiding under the staircase; watching the murder unfold. If Rick had, he'd have torn the docks apart looking for the boy—and he wouldn't have stopped until he did.

All Tommy had to do was go home and keep his mouth shut, and no one would have been the wiser. Jason would never have been called in on the case, and Rick and his associates would still be on the streets; leaving the Crime Czar's connection with the Syndicate still a guarded secret.

As for his fee? Well, when he had Rick unconscious in the dark for those few seconds, Jason lifted Rick's wallet. Since he was the one who caused Tommy to run away, he could pay for it.

Now, all he could think about was getting home. There up ahead was the Delaware River and the lights of the city beyond. It sure felt good to be home again. The Crime Czar was going to wish Mindforce had stayed gone.

* * * *

CHAPTER SEVEN

Confrontation

The church tower struck ten as he flew over the late evening city. His flight home took him over the area of the city where the cream of society likes to graze. He paused to take in the crowd exiting the theater below. The opera, La Traviata, being performed there was just ending its opening performance. The high class were now strolling along in search of their autos.

If anyone were a prime target for a crime these people were it. What with their fat wallets, loaded with: cash, plastic money, their jewels and so forth.

The crowd, so engrossed with their egos, their noses so far up in the air, they never paid any attention to the beggar man filtering through their midst. Mindforce, as he'd chosen to call himself, was not so incautious and caught sight of him right away, and exactly what he was up to. This little beggar man was more than he appeared. If those snooty, stuck up people had any sense they'd reach for their belongings and clutch them tightly to their breasts.

Zeroing in with his binocular eyesight to the beggar man's nimble hands, Mindforce observed his actions while the man sifted through the crowd. He occasionally bumped someone, muttering apologies. While he did he lifted wallets from pockets quite deftly with those educated fingers of his. Not one person coming into contact with the beggar man had any inkling they'd just been robbed.

He lifted five wallets in all and now sought the safety of the shadows and dark alleyways to count his ill-gotten booty.

He'd seen enough. Time for Mindforce to take a hand in this game. Setting his bags on a nearby roof he made after the thief.

Flying stealth-like along the alley ahead of the pickpocket he landed softly and waited for him to pass by. When he did, Mindforce spoke.

"Good haul?" he said, stepping from the shadows into the light filtering in from the street.

"Not bad," the thin man said reflexively.

Startled, he whirled round to see who was his inquisitor while drawing from his belt a Smith & Wesson revolver.

Mindforce's *DANGER* sense screeched just before the pickpocket fired the gun.

Two shots sped for his chest. He'd not expected gunplay. Braced for the pain of impact he again felt the sting of hot lead on supple flesh.

Visibly shaken, the pickpocket turned to flee. When he rounded the corner of the back alley there was Mindforce leaning on the brick wall. Whirling to escape the other way, there the stranger stood again. With his speed, Mindforce could have toyed with the pickpocket like this all night, but he ended the game, grabbing him by the collar, lifting and turning him around so he could see the crooks face.

"Well, well, well. Lightfingers Leroy," he said, recognizing the slight, little black man he once arrested in New York. "I know your record Leroy. You never carried a piece before. Why're you packing now?"

"Y-You don't know what it's like out there in the s-streets with the Crime Czar takin' over everthin!"

"Enlighten me."

"He's tryin' ta be the big B-Boss o' all the rackets in the city."

"I'm well aware of that. Tell me something I don't know."

"His goons are ever'where. Tryin' ta intimidate all the small timers an' grifters in town. T-That's why I got the gun. F-For protection. I was tryin' ta get enough money an' blow this town. Honest!"

"Strange word coming from you." Still, his *Esper* sense corroborated all he heard. "Well, Leroy; you'll be getting plenty of protection. Plus room and board; courtesy of the taxpayers. Let's go!"

Returning to the crowd with Leroy, Mindforce informed the people there that if anyone was missing his wallet he could pick it up at Police Headquarters and file a complaint while they were there.

The precinct was abuzz when Mindforce walked in with Leroy in tow to make a citizens arrest. Distrust and confusion draped the air like a shroud. The desk Sgt. had been around a long time. He'd seen it all and didn't blink an eye when Mindforce handed Leroy over to him.

While Leroy was being booked Mindforce asked if the Commissioner was still in his office.

The hour was late but James "Jake" Parman was a dedicated man, if nothing else. This problem with the Crime Czar kept him in his office to all hours trying to solve this case.

"YOU!" said the Commissioner when he turned from staring out the window at the night. "What do you want?" he said, sitting at his desk.

"I've got some info you might find useful," he said, strolling over to the desk.

"Oh! I don't deal with vigilantes the likes of you."

Even though he knew the Commissioner was somewhat agitated he wasn't expecting an attack when he came in. He was just trying to be a good citizen; though now he wished he hadn't bothered. His blood began to simmer against any control.

"I'm no vigilant!" he said, leaning over, placing his knuckles on the desk. "All I'm doing is trying to be of help."

"How? By yanking the arms off every crook in town. Or maybe you'd like to cuff them to every railing in the city. Rescue had to use the Jaws of Life to get that guy loose."

"You got me wrong," he said through clenched teeth; his blood reaching the boil while he stood erect. "Everyone makes mistakes."

"Not like yours." Pointing an accusing finger.

"And just how do you figure that?"

"That strength of yours can be deadly if uncontrolled. You might even kill someone."

"All right! . . . All right," he said, trying to calm himself. "I admit . . . I made an error in judgment. But so does everyone else occasionally. My reflexes overruled my head. But I can overcome that—in time."

"Oh! Is that so? And what happens in the meantime if you can't? With all those powers, how the hell am I or any of my men supposed to arrest you?"

"Don't worry. I'd turn myself in."

"So you say now. But you vigilantes are all alike. You break the law then you run and hide."

"I told you, I'm no vigilante!" he shot back, pacing the room. "And what about you and your men?"

"What about 'em?"

"Haven't you or they ever made a mistake with that hunk o' iron you carry on your hips?" he said loudly.

"Make your point mister."

He hit a sore spot.

"How many innocents have been shot by someone on the force either by accident, or on purpose?" he said. "And how much of it was swept under the carpet? Forever hidden! . . . Huh?"

"You're nuts!"

"Am I? That debacle in North Philly last week was just as much your men's fault as mine! Maybe more so because I didn't start it!"

"My men had nothing to do with starting that gun battle!" the Commissioner shot back, not really believing it.

Now he got it with both barrels.

"Don't lie to me. I overheard your men when they reported to you on the radio."

"You didn't hear nothin'!" he said, raising his voice—placing clenched fists on his desk—leaning toward the costumed man.

They were yelling so loudly at each other and were so animated it brought a horde of officers storming into the room; guns drawn, ready for action.

"What the hell do you want?" demanded the Commissioner.

"We thought you were in trouble," said the Sgt.

"Well I'm not. Now get the hell out."

"Will you be all right?"

"Go on. Get out," he insisted, shoving them out the door; then closed it firmly behind them.

In a way, Mindforce was glad for the interruption. He was on the verge of one huge frustration attack. Without those few seconds of distraction. . . . Well, he hated to think of it.

Jake was being secretive as he returned his attention. He walked back to his desk, pensive.

He took a deep breath. "Now. Like I said. You heard nothing."

"Oh? Let me refresh your memory," Mindforce bit off. "Your men stated there was only one gunshot heard from inside the building. Instead of holding their ground and waiting for the SWAT team to arrive they went in guns blazing; lobbing teargas, shooting up the place. They weren't prepared for the opposition they faced and were beaten back.

"When I got there they were in a standoff. I'd have stayed out but for the chatter about tossing in some Semtex to rout the gunmen from the site."

"That's not true!" The Commissioner stood erect; beads of sweat forming on his brow.

"Yes it is! I wouldn't have been there otherwise."

"No!" he repeated firmly. Pounding his fist upon the desk.

"It is and you know it. No one died that day because I was there. My God man! Can't you see the carnage there would have been had I not intervened? How many lives might have been needlessly lost. On both sides."

"That's bullshit."

"It's the truth. You know it. And so do I."

"You're nuts."

"I've been told that before. But it still doesn't alter the facts."

"You made the Dept. look foolish."

"Were they?"

Sitting slowly back in his chair, Jake wrestled with his thoughts. Long seconds passed while he struggled with the truth.

"You're . . . right. You're absolutely right. I've been going over the preliminary reports from Internal Affairs all day." Mindforce's head lolled back. "It states, basically, everything you just said; leaving me to suggest discipline. But, if you knew all this, why didn't you tell it to the press when they tried to interview you afterwards?"

"Because I'm not wired that way. I don't care to be Judge, Jury and Executioner. But the people of the city have a right to be informed. That's your job, not mine. So I'll leave it up to you to tell them."

"I guess I shouldn't expect more than that. You know, that skirmish could have been the 'MOVE' incident all over again."

He got that right.

"Now, what was that information you had for me when you came in?"

"It's about the Crime Czar. This whole damn gang war is over a bet he made with the Syndicate big shots. He's gambled that he can take over the city rackets and throw out Mr. Big."

"That's it. A friggin bet?"

"That's it in a nutshell. I don't know how much time he's got, but they're not going to let him try for long."

"What can he hope to gain?"

"It's safe to assume if he can pull it off he probably thinks he'll get to keep everything and take Mr. Big's place in the Syndicate."

"And if he fails?"

"The Syndicate boys will come down and take everything he owns. Starting with his life."

"And that's what this is all about."

"You got it. But there's a joker in the deck."

"How's that?"

"The Syndicate is planning a double cross should the Czar manage to pull it off."

"Why?" he asked; though he knew the answer he felt better with confirmation.

"If the Czar loses they gain all his wealth. They also learn basically where all their weak spots are and can fix them."

"And if he wins?"

"Then it's World War III. The Syndicate doesn't like upstarts and loose cannons; they're too unpredictable. If he can take over like he plans he might get delusions that he could challenge the big boys. So the plan is to dump the Czar no matter what he's able to pull off. Win or lose, the man is a walking target. Only he don't know it yet."

"You realize what this means, don't you?"

"What else? If the Syndicate doesn't take him out on the first try we're gonna need a lot of body bags! At least until then, we know that we won't have any outside muscle to deal with."

"And If I allowed the Syndicate to take him out I'd be a party to murder."

"Exactly."

They must know who he is. Otherwise they wouldn't have accepted such a crazy proposal."

"That would be logical."

"You didn't happen to discover who he is, did you?"

"That'd make our job a hell of a lot easier, but no; I didn't."

"Too bad. Say. You never told me how you knew all this in the first place."

"That's gonna have to remain my secret for now, Commissioner. Trust me when I tell you that I did find out by accident while working on something else unrelated. Other than that I can't tell you any more."

"I'd like to trust you somehow. Do you have any sort of plan for dealing with this?"

"One. . . . But if it doesn't work I haven't a clue what to do."

Mindforce felt the skepticism. The Commissioner only half trusted this stranger. It would have to do.

"All right. I'm going against the grain with what I'm about to say. My necks out a mile letting a civilian get involved in police business but I'll do anything to stop the upcoming blood bath. You do what you can from your end and I'll gear up the Dept. for what it has to do. Just keep me informed on anything you find out."

"Will do. And thanks for the support."

"Just make sure that support is justified."

For better or worse it looked like he was in the super-hero business, for now. His head had been clear for some time, and that trip to New York had dispelled a few ghosts . . . though the guilt was still there.

Not totally entrenched in his convictions, his thoughts returned to a young police rookie with stars in his eyes. The young man who'd dedicated himself to those who couldn't help themselves. He had a chance to make amends to that young rookie for falling from grace. Once this caper was over he could decide if Mindforce should continue or just disappear into fantasy.

"Do those arches on your chest mean something?"

"Yes. The first letter of my working name, Mindforce."

"Mindforce. At least now I know what to call you."

Expecting the costumed man to leave by the door, Jake went to open it. Jason, however, wasn't prepared to run the gauntlet of the crowd and media gathering outside. When the Commissioner had turned around, Mindforce had opened the window and was gone, leaving the cool night air to fill the void.

Jake looked to see him fly away but was too late. Questions spawned themselves wanting to know why he allowed the aid of this costumed man. Only time would tell.

Would history regard him as a great law enforcer, or just one more fool led down the garden path?

The Crime Czar had to be stopped before all Hell broke loose.

Easy to say. God only knew how he was going to accomplish it. At least, for now, he had the Commissioner on his side.

As Jason Parks, he never cared much for Jake Parman. Maybe Mindforce could.

* * * *

CHAPTER EIGHT

In Search of the Crime Czar

Soaring through the night sky he thought about how easily he'd found Tommy James with nothing to go on. Why couldn't he do the same to find the Crime Czar? Hell, it was worth the try. If it worked he wouldn't need a plan to flush him out.

Cruising over the city in ever widening circles for over an hour brought nary a tingle. Nor did he feel drawn to any particular area of the city. It didn't make sense. He'd found hundreds of missing people in the past.

True, runaways always did seem to be harder to find than the kidnapped or lost, but runaways never sat still either. He'd tracked one runaway all the way to California; though he did get lucky a couple of steps along the way.

Could there be some connection between the type of missing person he was after and his ability to find them?

Landing atop one of the support towers of the Ben Franklyn Bridge he paused to ponder.

Removing his hood the cool breeze was relief upon his flesh. Leaning against the safety railing he looked out over the river and the electric lit city inhaling the crisp night air.

What was so different about the types of missing people he'd tracked down in his career; other than the obvious?

The accident did a lot to enhance all of his physical abilities and given him several new mental ones. It hadn't, however, done much to improve his memory or detective skills.

Detective skills? Yes. . . . Of course! His fingers snapped repetitively when it occurred to him. As he recalled, the kidnap victims and those that were simply lost, he always seemed to just . . . feel where they went. Call it a hunch or whatever. When he was close he just zeroed in on them. Even a few runaways were found this way, but not many. Most of them he had to rely on his detective skills learned over the years.

But? What was the difference between the runaway and all the rest?

A runaway leaves of his own choice; that's a fact. The others have no choice. In fact, they're really looking to be found—even praying.

"Of course! That's it! It must be!"

The runaway, more often than not, doesn't want to be found. They want to hide from detection. All the others are actually hoping to be found, even praying. That had to be the explanation. Nothing else fit.

They must be giving off some kind of signal or aura that his *Esper* sense is attuned to. Once triggered by the need to find them it alerts the tracking mechanism. Otherwise the hundreds of people giving off the same aura'd constantly tug him in all directions. It could only be some sort of directional signal that keeps him on course.

Obviously, this was why the Crime Czar's trail remained cold. It was all so simple now; he just doesn't want to be found.

It was time for the alternate plan—as soon as he thought of it.

The clock tower chimed in the distance; 1 AM. The night was just beginning for the low life that prowled the seedy areas of the city. Plenty of time to comb the streets for talkative cockroaches before calling it a night.

He flew over the area, looking for someone who could be intimidated easily; a virtual brook of information waiting to babble. It might not be much, but at least he knew he could not be lied to or sent on some wild goose chase.

There below. Coming out of that filthy gin joint. Well whata-ya-know. This he had to check out.

The fella in question exited the front of the joint, stood in the doorway and lit a smoke. He peered nonchalantly along the street in both directions like he wasn't sure which way was best to go. He opted left and swaggered off north, up the street; whistling a happy tune while he went. Not a care in the world. That'd change real soon.

"I thought I had you locked up nice and tight in the slammer."

Alarmed, the butt dropped from his gaping mouth. Eyes darting, head twisting he spun around and stammered. "Wh-who s-said that?"

"Some mouthpiece get you out on bail already? I didn't think they worked so fast for small time."

"Where you at?!" he shouted, eyes glared open wide while he contorted himself around looking for the mystery speaker.

"Up here, Leroy."

Leroy stepped back. Looking up over the glare of the street lamp he saw the crouched shadowy caped figure in the gloom.

"Aw Shoot! Why don' cha leave me alone?"

"What are you doing out of jail so soon?" said the masked stranger while he glided down in front of Leroy.

"Weren't no shyster or bondsman got me out. The heat had no case, so they hadda let me go."

"Whata-ya-mean, no case? I caught you with five stolen wallets on your person."

"So ya did. So ya did," came out wrapped in a nasty snicker. "Don't blame the law now. It weren't their fault. They did all they could ta keep me. No. Blame the owners o' them wallets I lifted."

Mindforce grabbed the back of his neck; rubbing the knot forming there. "You wanna run that by me again." He had a feeling he wasn't going to like what he was about to hear.

"Suurrre. Seems them snooty, Society types don't wanna get involved. Not one o' them wanted ta spend the time in court. . . . An' their egos was so fat they didn't want no publicity. They didn't want their friends ta find out they had their pockets picked right under their blue noses."

"You GOT to be kidding!"

"Nope. They got their goods back, so they didn't want to press no charges. The blue boys had no case. So, here I am."

"But, what about the gun?"

"It's mine—all registered—legal and proper. Ain't my fault the cops didn't look ta see if it was fired."

"Well I'll be. . . . The pompous, lazy, no good—"

"Well. Be seein' ya. It's been nice chattin' wit' ya," said Leroy as he turned to walk away while Mindforce cursed under his breath.

"Whoa! Hold on there," he said, grabbing Leroy by the collar, waltzing him back into the gloom of the alley. "You're not getting off that easily."

"Leggo o' me! Ya got no right ta hold me!" shouted Leroy, squirming, trying to pull free.

"Don't count your chickens buster! There's the little fact I never told the police about the two shots you fired at me." He shook Leroy extra firmly, making his large brimmed hat slip down over his face. "That's attempted murder! What say we go down to headquarters again and fill out a complaint. I'm sure we can get you five to ten. Hmmm?"

"Your word against mine."

"Oh, I don't know. . . . It won't be hard to prove this gun was fired tonight. And I'm quite sure I can find those two slugs you shot at me. . . . Well, how about it? Want to take your chances?"

Mindforce watched with glee while Leroy agonized over the pros and cons of his dilemma. Leroy's heart rate doubled during the few seconds of troubled deliberation; coming to the only decision left him.

"Al-All right. Ya got me over a barrel. Whata-ya-want from me?"

"Information," he said as he released his grip.

"I don't know nothin' 'bout nobody," was his clipped reply while he straightened his hat and collar.

"I think you do, but since you're unwilling to talk to me." Mindforce reached for a scrap piece of two-by-four lying in the alley. He grasped it about mid way and showed it to a trembling Leroy. "Pretend, if you're able, and I think you are, that this is your arm." Agonizingly slow, with ever increasing pressure, Mindforce increased his grip on the lumber. In the echo chamber of an alley the fibers of wood popped, grated and snapped while Leroy winced at each sound. Soon, the halves released and fell away; the double "thunks" bouncing off the walls. In his hand were the crushed pulp fibers, which he let, drift down from his open palm. "Care to change your story?"

"You wouldn't."

"Wanna bet?"

Leroy's lips retracted between his teeth then returned abruptly. "Let's not be hasty here. Maybe I might know somethin'."

"That's more like it," he said as he smoothed Leroy's lapels. "Now. Tell me what you know about the Crime Czar or any of his men."

"Aw no! I can't help you there man," was his uneasy reply as he raised his hands in protest.

The Liar! Mindforce's *Esper* sense nagged something fierce.

"Don't lie to me Leroy. I get unpleasant when people lie to me," he said through clenched teeth, gripping Leroy by the lapels again. "You must know who some of the Crime Czar's men are. You were packing heat to protect yourself from them."

"You're asking too much man!" he protested, yanking his lapels free.

"I'll be the judge of that," he said, grasping Leroy's arm firmly. "Now. What do you know?"

Visions of splintered bone slapped Leroy smack in the face. "Rumors, man! All I know is rumors," he squeaked out as he tugged on his arm.

"So, lay it on me."

Leroy looked around cautiously in both directions as if someone might hear, then dropped his head and spoke in a whisper. "It's . . . Alfie . . . Alfie Tulio! H-He's sposed ta be the Czar's second in command."

"Alfie Tulio. I've heard of him. Big time gambler and small time hood."

"Yeah. Yeah. Y-You got it."

"And if Tulio's involved," he said, letting go of Leroy, "then his buddy, Freddy Lester, can't be far behind."

Outwardly, Leroy was all cool and collected; inwardly he was a sack of jiggling entrails. His emotional level rose through the roof while his heart raced like a trip hammer. Mindforce was afraid he was going to have a stroke, or at least a nervous breakdown.

"C-Can I go now? I can't tell you nothin' else."

"All right, but don't leave town. I may need you again, and it'll piss me off if I have to take the time to find you."

Leroy ran like a scalded dog while Mindforce paused to take in what he'd just learned. Leroy believed what he said was true. If it was, Mindforce was one step closer to finding the Crime Czar and short-circuiting his reign of terror.

It was doubtful he could have made the attempted murder rap stick. The evidence was skimpy at best, and there were no witnesses. A rookie lawyer could have gotten it thrown out of court. Leroy just didn't have the guts to call the bluff. If he had, the two-by-four trick wouldn't have worked either.

Standing there, he got the feeling of waves of uneasiness. People were halting then walking back the way they came or crossing the street to avoid him. There was nothing to fear, but people being what they are. . . . It was late and he was ready to go home for some sack time. He left the locals to their private little fears and flew off into the night.

He arose bright and early. Though he'd turned in after two he was awake by six. Ever since the accident he'd needed only three to four hours sleep each night. The exception being the night he'd pulled those muscles lifting that trailer load of steel; he'd slept a full seven. Otherwise there was no change in the pattern.

Sleep had usually been beneficial; it shut out the stress of living—except when the nightmares invaded. Now there were more hours of consciousness to bear. Only the current crisis kept it suppressed.

Nothing unnatural was occurring in the city this morning. Fear of the Crime Czar kept all the small time off the streets. He'd have to check with the Commissioner about that; sure he'd want to know what Mindforce heard from Leroy about Tulio and Lester.

The morning paper made Jason wish he hadn't bought it. Among the usual depressing stories was one about him, or more to the point, his alter ego. There'd been a fire in a hotel two days earlier that took three lives; one of them a firefighter, and a major gang fight. The reporter asked if this strange costumed freak was pretending to be a hero, where the hell was he? Jason fumed as he strode the last few blocks to his office. No matter what you do it's never enough! The ungrateful. . . .

Checking into the office at 9 AM, opting for the stairs instead of the elevator; the walk up the three flights gave him time to cool down. With him, to be typed and filed, was a tape he'd dictated in New York on the Tommy James case. As usual, Sheila was there before him.

"Good morning, Jason," she bubbled. "How was New York?"

"Just as I remember it; all filthy and scum ridden."

There were pleasant and beautiful spots to be taken in but being ex NYPD all you ever faced was the decadent side of the city. It's no wonder you become jaded.

"I trust everything went well?" she asked.

"Quite well indeed." In more ways than he could let on. He handed her his dictation. Then he saw it or more to the point, didn't see it. "Where's the typewriter"

"That old thing. I put it in the closet after I brought in my laptop and printer. We've got to bring this office into this century." He nodded. This was her responsibility and he was more than glad to let her handle it any way she wanted.

"Any interesting calls while I was gone?"

"Just one. A Mr. Greenleaf called Saturday morning. Said his daughter hadn't been home in three days."

"Has he filed a missing persons report with the police?"

"Yes."

"And?"

The police took all the pertinent information and told him they'd check it out."

"I see. Which means; that there's no reason to believe there was any foul play, so they'll put it in the pile with the rest of the reports and get around to it when things are slower."

"The father did say she just didn't come home from work one night. She'd done this before but had always called home first.

"Ohhh-kay. Well, it could be she just forgot this time. Did he leave her name, age and description?"

"She's 23—First name, Charlotte—five feet seven—blonde— 125 pounds."

"Does he know where she works?"

"No. Only that she works nights from ten to six."

"Okay," he said as he started for his office. "There may not be much to this but call Mr. Greenleaf and tell him if he doesn't hear from her in a couple-a-days, I'll be glad to take his case."

He paused at his door. "Did Mr. Greenleaf say why he came to me?"

"Yes he did. He said he'd read about your rescue of me in the paper."

"But that hero guy really saved you."

"True. But your name was printed as the one brought me home."

His double identity was becoming confusing.

Sitting at his desk he thought of this Greenleaf case. Women of that age were known to just up and leave on a whim. She could have met some guy and decided to spend the weekend with him somewhere. It was odd that her father had no idea where she worked. Fellow employees can usually give you some kind of lead. Anyway, he had a description for the morgue. If there was no Jane Doe there fitting her description there was a better than even chance she was still alive.

Reaching into his desk for a smoke, all he found was a note:

I STRAIGHTENED UP YOUR DESK WHILE YOU
WERE AWAY. YOUR CIGARETTES ARE FILED UN-
DER TRASH!

                                              SHEILA

He stared at the note and grimaced; then went to the doorway to speak to the witch.

"You're determined to stop me from smoking, aren't you?"

"Around me and the office. It's taken a week and several air fresheners to get rid of the smell in here. And you're not going to foul it up again. And before I'm finished I'm going to clean the smoke stains off everything as well."

Thoroughly put in his place, he knew she meant every word she said. First the booze, and now his smokes. He was beginning to believe he was functioning under the delusion that he was running this office.

"It's a small vise."

"So you say. But it's one that'll turn your lungs to hamburger if you persist. It's hard enough to breathe out there with all the pollution."

The look on her face told volumes. He wasn't about to win this argument. No way, no how.

"Okay. Okay. I'll behave myself. But it'll be your fault if I turn to food for satisfaction and get fat and dumpy in the process," he said turning to return to his office. "Then you'll be sorry," he said over his shoulder.

"No problem. I've got a killer diet you can go on."

He swore she snickered when he stopped dead in his tracks. He was about to say some smart-ass remark but caught himself; mouth open. Best he retreat, lick his wounds and live to fight another day.

Poring over the backlog of mail that piled up while he was away he tossed out all the advertisements for a bunch of stuff he'd never need. There were a couple of bills and a reminder from the state that it was time to renew the registration on his Mustang. Great! Now that he thought of it, he'd likely be flying more than walking in the future. He'd be paying the state for the use of a dust collector. Maybe he should lease and take the whole thing off his taxes as a business deduction. But then . . . he'd miss that old 'stang.

Nearing ten o'clock, it was time to check in with the Commissioner. Grabbing his hat and coat he told Sheila he'd be gone for a while and would check in later. From there he went to the roof, changed quickly and launched himself into the air.

Arriving at the Commissioner's office he was immediately ushered inside. Jake had left orders that if Mindforce were to show up to let him in immediately.

"Come in Mindforce. Come in." His interest in seeing him was genuine. Have a seat. Have you found out anything we can use yet?"

"Not much," he said, sitting on the corner of the desk. "Last night I brought in a pickpocket, Lightfingers Leroy. You had to release him."

"Yes, I heard," dripped with disgust as he sat behind his desk. "Not one! Not one of those society jerks would press charges. They got all their stuff back and clammed up with indifference. No amount of talking could convince them to sign a complaint. Tomorrow those self same people will be bitching that the force isn't doing enough to clean up the city."

He threw up his hands in disgust. "What's the matter with these people? Can't they see that their indifference only condones crime. . . . Well, enough of this. What was it you had about Leroy?"

"He took a couple of shots at me when I apprehended him last night."

"You want him picked up, say the word."

"No. Don't bother. I didn't mention it because he couldn't hurt me, and I thought the felony charge would keep him locked up."

"It should have."

"Doesn't matter. It's better for us he's not locked up."

"How so?"

"I ran into him coming out of a bar up town. He wasn't very cooperative, but he gave me a couple of names to work with. Do the names, Alfie Tulio and Freddy Lester mean anything to you?"

"I've heard of them," he said, perking up. Couple small timers. As I remember, we picked them up a coupla times in the last nine months. Never could pin anything serious on them. Had to release them due to lack of evidence. Judge threw out our case."

"Well they've hit the big time, Commissioner."

"They working with the Crime Czar?"

"Tulio's worked his way up to second in command."

"Are you sure of that?" said the Commissioner, leaning forward.

"I've only got the word of our friend, Leroy, but if it's true, we may be able to get Alfie to lead us to his boss."

"Can you be sure Leroy wasn't just blowing smoke?"

"I can't tell you how I know, but trust me, Leroy believed everything he told me." For now, it seemed best that no one knew about his *Esper* senses. The less anyone knew about his abilities the better.

"So, what have you got in mind?"

"First, I'll need the mug shots of Tulio and Lester."

"No sooner said than done," he said, reaching for the intercom. "Frank. Bring me the mug shots of Alfie Tulio and Freddy Lester. . . . That'll take a few minutes. Go on."

What I want to do is scour the local hangouts. If Tulio or Lester shows, I'll have a surprise for them. I also want to pay a visit to Mr. Big. I want him to know he'll not be getting any help from New York, or anyone else. I want him to know he's alone in this."

"Rattle his cage."

"Something like that."

"That'll certainly make his day," laughed the Commissioner, leaning back in his chair. "But speaking of Mr. Big; we've noticed a sharp decline in the number of hookers he has on the streets."

34-MILL

"Isn't that a little out of character for him? I'm sure it's not their safety he's concerned about."

"Actually, the grapevine says the Czar's men are pulling them off the streets and holding them somewhere. We've no proof because no one's ever reported a missing hooker before."

Somewhere in the back of Mindforce's mind a buzzer went off, softly. He passed it off as nothing particularly important.

"If what I have in mind works, Commissioner," he said, clenching a fist, "you'll have enough on Mr. Big to put him away for a long time."

"God, I hope so. We know that he's running the rackets here in Philly. We've just never been able to dig up enough evidence to make it stick, nor have we come up with anyone willing to testify."

"They'd come down with terminal lockjaw if they did."

A knock at the door drew their attention. The Sgt. came in with the mug shots. Taking a quick look, Mindforce shoved them in his belt.

"By the way, Commissioner," said the Sgt. "the boys from the media are here to see you as you requested."

Thanking them for the pictures, Mindforce got up to leave, halted by the Commissioner's hand on his arm.

"Stay around awhile, Mindforce. I called these boys in for a press conference. What I have to say concerns you and I want you to hear it first hand."

Evidently, the press was not expecting to see Mindforce here. While the TV and radio people set up the print media flocked around him. After several "no comments" the electronic boys signaled they were ready.

"Gentlemen and ladies of the press. I've called you here to make a brief statement about the shootout two weeks ago in the north end of the city, between factions of the underworld and the Police Dept."

An audible murmur buzzed from the crowd.

"Please now, no questions until I'm finished. After a thorough investigation by our department, our conclusion is that the shootout . . . could have been prevented, and need not have taken place—"

The murmurs were agitated now. Mindforce was hard pressed to shut out all the accumulated emotion in the crowd.

". . . the blame for the incident rests solely and only with my own department. Mindforce here, I am glad to say, has been completely exonerated of any and all wrongdoing in the affair."

You could have knocked Mindforce down with a whisper. His head snapped around to face the Commissioner when he finished.

"It is the belief of this department that if not for the timely intervention of Mindforce, the loss of life and property, on both sides, would have been considerable, and is hereby commended for his heroic action. Those within the department, deemed accountable, will be disciplined. And . . . after such discipline has been handed down a complete account will be turned over to the media."

"What about the man that Mindforce, as he calls himself, busted up in the alley!" came and adamant voice from the crowd.

"That has been declared self-defense by this department and we will stand by that decision," the Commissioner said curtly.

"There's been a question of excessive force in that incident," came a female voice.

"The man in question was out on bail for having beaten up several other people; including a police officer. He was resisting arrest and was injured while being subdued."

So, if the man had not resisted he would not have been injured. And that it was his own fault that he did indeed receive those injuries," came the voice.

"Precisely."

"And you're sticking to that story?"

"Exactly."

"Sounds like a cover-up to me," came another voice.

"Now you tell me," interjected the Commissioner, "just exactly what you would do if you were in the middle of all that gunfire and some 300 pound goon was trying to snap your neck? My guess is that you wouldn't just stand there and let him kill you. You'd use whatever means you could to get free . . . if you could."

"But no one has his strength," suggested another.

"That's irrelevant. What if it were a normal man with a billy club or gun. It's all the same."

That remark got mixed reviews; some nodded mildly in agreement, others scoffed. Some just went on frantically taking notes; indifferent.

"Whata-ya got to say about it, Mindforce," came a gruff voice.

"It wasn't my intention to hurt anyone. I only wanted to stop the battle before it escalated out of control. Which I believe you'll find, I did."

"How come you're wearing that mask if you're here to do so much good?"

"To keep you people from hounding me 24 hours a day. I work for a living too, y-know."

That brought more laughs than groans from the crowd, and the conference soon broke up.

While the electronic media gathered their gear, one reporter asked. "Does the Mayor know about your decision Commissioner?"

"He's got a copy of the report. If you want to know how he feels about it you'll have to ask him."

"One last question, Commissioner. After the incident you said you were against vigilantes—"

"I still am. But I see no vigilantes here." Whereby he closed the door in the reporter's face.

"Thanks for the vote of confidence, but I don't think you endeared yourself to them with your statements today."

"Ahhh. I like to throw them a bone once in a while and watch them fight over it like a pack of hungry dogs. By tonight they'll have the Mayor and myself at each other's throats. No matter what I do in this town I'm never going to please them all. Besides, everything I said was in the report from Internal Affairs. It was just our discussion last night that convinced me the decision was correct.

I was opposed to their decision . . . and you. But I'm also smart enough to see when I'm wrong." He was quite sincere.

"Truthfully, Commissioner, I'd rather work with the Dept. than have to butt heads with it."

"My feelings as well. I'll probably get my head handed to me for this, but until they relieve me from this job, I'll run it my way. . . . Now. Do me a favor."

Sure. Name it."

"Call me Jake. Commissioner is too formal if we're going to work side-by-side."

"Okay. Jake it is."

"May I ask what you have planned for Mr. Big?"

"I think, for now, I'll just say that I'm going to make him answer for his crimes."

"Don't get yourself into anything I can't get you out of. I'm an officer of the law first. You bend the law so severely it breaks I'll have to come down on you. I'll have no choice."

"I know, Jake. But you can't make an omelet without cracking a few eggs. Now. If you don't mind, I think I'll leave out the window. I'd like to avoid any of those reporters who might be lingering around."

They shook hands on this fledgling partnership.

Flying into the sky, the first thing on his list was to pay a visit to the new Commerce Building where Mr. Big was reported to own a suite of offices. What he had to tell Mr. Big wouldn't make his day . . . and Mindforce couldn't wait to louse it up for him.

* * * *

CHAPTER NINE

Mr. Big

Rumor had it the new Commerce Building had been built with the help of a large chunk of Syndicate money. That's how the additional floors, with the penthouse, got added to the plans. They wanted a modern base of operations with which to run their bogus businesses and harbor wanted felons. Nothing could be proved though. They'd covered their tracks too well. The D.A. couldn't prove just cause; the law couldn't even get a search warrant for the place.

Several hundred legitimate businesses rented space there to mask the true character of the building owners.

A tall building; the first of the new skyscrapers allowed in the city. Mindforce was only interested in the top three floors. Specifically, the penthouse, where Mr. Big kept his private offices and living quarters.

It was inaccessible to the general public via the normal route. he could surely muscle his way through the gauntlet but that would make a lot of noise. Attaining the office unannounced and unobserved was his objective. Fortunately, he had the means, but before that he had some preparations to make.

The penthouse had a large, open balcony, which was unguarded, unlike the lower offices. The balcony was considered inaccessible; but that was before he came along.

Floating above the building from a distance, Mindforce focused his binocular vision on the balcony. As expected, no one was in sight. Neither were there any surveillance cameras. After all, this was Mr. Big's private home; certainly he didn't want any snoops watching him.

Flying in noiselessly, landing softly, he hoped the glass patio doors were unlocked. Luck was with him. As long as there were no other alarms he'd have the element of surprise.

This time of day Mr. Big should be in his private office below. There'd be no reason to set the alarms. Of course, there was no accounting for paranoia.

Reaching out with all his senses there appeared to be no electronics present; no invisible laser beams.

The balcony doors entered into the living room. Very large, very elegant, it sported the finest that money could buy from furniture to entertainment equipment. He sure knew how to spend the Syndicates loot.

Tiptoeing inside, he reconnoitered the place. The kitchen and dining room were to one side through open doorways. Down the hall was, he assumed, the bed and bathrooms. To the right was a landing, one step up, with an elegant door. This should be the way to Mr. Big's office.

Lacking x-ray vision to tell him what or who was waiting beyond the door he resorted to the next best thing. Sitting in a chair he employed another of the powers discovered when he'd rescued Sheila. There was some queasiness when the invisible, ghost like wraith left his body. It was still eerie to turn and see his body sitting there in its coma like state.

He didn't have much time, so he'd better get on with it.

He passed through the door as easily as smoke through a screen, into a large adorned foyer. Obviously a waiting place for all visitors before they were admitted to the apartment.

An elevator stood to the far side and what he'd hoped to find; a stairwell to the lower level.

As expected, there were no guards the entire route to the offices below. This was Mr. Big's private entrance to his inner offices; accessible only from the penthouse. No one got on the elevator without proper clearance.

There he was, alone. Good.

Having all he needed, it was through the ceiling, into the living quarters and back into his body; all in a matter of seconds.

Once merged, he retraced his steps, pausing before the door to Mr. Big's office. Less than a minute since he'd left. He entered quickly and quietly.

"I hear some of your prostitutes are missing," cut through the silence with the desired effect.

Startled at the break in the silence he nearly swallowed the cigar clamped in his teeth.

"How the hell did you get in here?!"

Doesn't matter. I'm here and that's all that should concern you."

"Get out or I'll have you thrown out!" he said, reaching for his phone.

Behind him in a heartbeat, Mindforce had his arm around the fat man's neck, raising him on his tiptoes.

"Calling your goon squad won't stop me. You know who I am and you know what I can do . . . don't you?"

"Get your grubby paws off me!" he gurgled out.

"I could snap your neck like a twig," he bit off, tightening his grip on Mr. Big's fat neck. "But I got something I want you to hear. For your ears only. . . . Get me?"

He was sharp. The futility of his struggles sunk in quickly. He nodded.

Released unceremoniously, he flopped on his fat ass, like a shot down rhino into his chair while Mindforce strode around to the front of the vast desk.

"All right! You got two minutes to say your piece!" growled Mr. Big, massaging his neck. "Then haul your ass out of here!"

"What I've got to say, LARD ASS, is going to take more than two minutes," he said while placing clenched fists on the desk, leaning toward the fat man. "You won't like it, which makes my heart go all a flutter, but you'll be glad you heard it."

"That's your opinion," he rasped with an offhand gesture.

"It's a fact. And here it is, shorty. You're missing several prostitutes from—"

"Wait a minute! Wait just a fucking minute! I've got nothing to do with prostitutes! Or any kind of corruption for that matter!"

His *Esper* sense lit up like a Christmas tree.

"BULL! You're the guidance behind just about every crooked operation in the city."

"You got no proof of that. Now. Finish your piece and beat it."

"All right. Straight out. The Crime Czar is kidnapping your prostitutes and holding them till they come over to his way of thinking."

Mention of the Crime Czar got a definite rise in Mr. Big's emotional state. Outwardly, he was the poster boy for cool. Inwardly, Mindforce knew, he was a roiling inferno, a volcano on the brink of eruption.

He'd struck a raw nerve, and now, quite happily, he was going to rub salt in it.

"I also know that the Crime Czar is trying to take over all your operations in town and throw you out on you fat ass."

Standing erect he added, "And then, I suppose, he'll move into your office here, live in your penthouse, drink all your booze and screw all your women."

That straw had the expected effect. The enraged fat man stood as tall as his diminutive frame would allow. Then with his balled fist, slammed the top of his mahogany desk with such force it rattled everything on it. After which he leaned his scarlet face as close to his adversary as possible.

"That son-of-a-bitch will never, *ever,* take over here while I'm alive! I'm too powerful! My organization is too big! I'll see the Fucking Bastard in Hell before I'll let him take over!"

Animated, he whirled his arms, hurling epithets. So vocal now that if not for the sound proofed walls to prevent listening in, Mindforce was sure he would have been besieged by the muscle on duty outside. As if he cared.

"Now. Now. Now. Is that any way for an honest business man to talk?" he said while crossing his arms before him.

"ALL RIGHT! All right. Let's cut the bull," he said, cutting short his ire. He'd allowed himself to be baited. That hadn't happened in years. Many others had tried, even the cops, to no avail. He knew the extent of the cop's bluffs. But this costumed geek . . . he didn't have a clue and it unnerved him. He rationalized it to all the stress of the previous weeks.

Sitting back in his chair, more reserved, he was ready to spar with the demon.

"Suppose. . . . Just suppose, I do admit that I run things here?" he said, lighting a fresh cigar; blowing smoke rings at his adversary. "Suppose I admit to being the big *Boss* of all the rackets in this town? What can you do? Really? It's your word against mine. Right?"

The man was good. No wonder he's got the job.

"True."

"I got the aid of a nationwide syndicate to help me get rid of that two-bit punk."

"*WRONG!* Fatso."

"I don't have to stand for this," he griped, rising to his feet again.

"I'm doin' it, tubby. . . . Now, si'down. I'm going to tell you something you don't know," he said, pointing a sharp finger at the rotund man. "You see, shorty, it's like this. The Crime Czar made a bet with your bosses."

"What kinda bet?"

"Simply this. . . . He bet your so called friends he could throw you out on your fat ass and take over the whole operation."

"Baloney."

"'fraid not. And the kicker is; you won't get any help from your boys in the Syndicate until the Crime Czar proves his point. One way or the other, you're all alone in this fight."

"You're full of it," he hissed through clenched teeth. "They won't do that to me," he said, thumping the desk lightly.

"Oh, but they have. They have. . . . I also know about the hit man, Rick James, you tried to hire to rub out the Crime Czar. Only he didn't show up."

"Don't mean nothin'. The bum got himself arrested before he could get here."

"Uh uh, fat boy. Wrong, wrong, wrong. Your pals in New York wouldn't let him come down here. They want to see what you're made of—if you still got it. They want to know if you can hold your own; just how good you really are. The fact that James got himself locked up had nothing to do with it."

"Ahhh, you're just blowing smoke."

"Am I? . . . Tell you what. . . . Call your friends for help after I've left and see what they tell you. I'll guarantee you all their men are busy."

"Still don't prove nothin'." His sweat evident.

"Oh wise up man! You've been thrown to the wolves by your so-called friends. You may come out on top after it's all over, but what about the next time someone wants to muscle you out. Will they be there to help?"

"Why shouldn't they?"

"Why should they? Think about it."

"Ahh, bull. Where do you get your information? From some old lady on the street. D-you actually expect me to buy all this crap?"

"It came straight from the horses mouth, tubby."

"Oh sure. Now I guess you expect me to believe they just up and took you into their confidence."

"I didn't say that."

"How do you know then?"

"I got my sources."

"You got nothin'."

"Simple to prove."

"Yeah? How?"

"Call your friends and find out."

"My friends are loyal to me." Trying to convince himself.

"That's your biggest mistake right there. . . . But then, it's your neck. Isn't it?"

"Whata-ya mean by that?"

"You're not as smart as I gave you credit."

"Smart enough to keep the law in this town runnin' in circles tryin' to find the bad guys."

"You're a puppet. When the boys in New York pull the strings you jump."

"Your two minutes were up a long time ago," he bit off. "Now. get out of here."

"I'm going. . . . Make the call."

That said, he made his way to Big's private exit, turning at the door for a final comment.

"You're a man in the middle. And neither side gives a rat's ass for your chances. I'd hate to be in your shoes right now. But if I was . . . I'd be covering my ass right quick."

Ducking out, Mindforce paused long enough to catch sight of Mr. Big hurriedly reaching for the phone.

As predicted, the Syndicate boys gave some lame excuse for not being able to help him crush the Crime Czar. He was told he'd just have to hold out on his own till they could get to him. Unless he'd like to step aside and let someone else do it for him. He nearly broke the phone in two, he slammed it down so hard.

Calling his muscle from the outer office he laid it out for them. He wanted the Crime Czar found and brought to him . . . alive! He wanted the pleasure of killing the Mother Fucker himself.

Step one was in motion. Step two involved Alfie Tulio. If he fell for the scheme, things would come to a head quite quickly. The Czar's whole house of cards would come crashing down around his ankles.

* * * *

CHAPTER TEN

One of Our Hookers is Missing

Late afternoon shadows crawled lazily up the sides of the edifices when Mindforce finished his patrol. Time to check in with Sheila at the office. But first, he'd fly by Jake's office to bring him up to speed.

Jake was busy on the phone when he let himself in the window. Catching sight of Mindforce, he motioned for him to take a seat. He opted to stand.

"That was the Mayor," he said when he hung up.

"Good news?"

"Well, that depends on how you look at it." A touch of disdain framed his words.

"How's that?"

"Those reporters we had at the press conference went straight to his office after they left here."

"From the look on your face I'd say it didn't go well."

"That's not the half of it. First, he wasn't pleased with being stormed in his office without a prepared statement at the ready. Second, he wasn't very pleased that I'd changed my position on you without consulting him so we could reach some sort of accord."

"And?"

"I told him he should read the reports I send to his office instead of simply filing them; then he'd know."

"And did he?"

"That was what the call was all about."

"And the verdict?"

" 'After thorough consideration and learned advisement, he

will be taking a position in the periphery until conditions warrant his further participation.'"

"In other words, he's going to sit on the fence until he sees which way popular sentiment blows. If you're caught with your pants down he doesn't want his underwear flapping in the breeze next to yours."

"Exactly. Those chicken-livered politicians are all alike," he said, leaning back in his chair, clasping his hands behind his head.

"And if you come up smelling like a rose, it'll all be his idea."

"You got that right. And I'll be roasted alone if it goes down badly. Now. What have you got for me?"

"First off. If you hear any loud noises coming from atop the Commerce Building, it's just Mr. Big blowing his stack."

"Then you did pay him a visit," he said, leaning forward.

"Oh yes."

"No witnesses, I hope."

"No. We were alone. I made sure of that. He can't prove anything. Just his word against mine."

"Good. Did you learn anything?"

"Plenty. He admitted to me, he does, in fact, run all the rackets in the city."

"No kidding?"

"Yeah. He obviously feels no one will believe anything I might say if it ever got to court."

"I wish we could prove all that."

"Would a tape recording help?"

"You didn't?"

"Did." From behind his back, hooked to his belt, he produced a miniature tape recorder. He played for Jake the most incriminating parts; deleting most of the references to Rick James, which could compromise his secret as Jason Parks. By the time the tape was finished the Commissioner was nearly salivating.

"You know this isn't admissible in court."

"True. But a voice print match from some of his other interviews should give the D.A. some leverage.

"It's worth a try."

"Besides," said Mindforce, with Mr. Big searching for the Crime Czar it'll help us flush him out. He's so incensed with capturing the Czar and so outraged at his friends for their complicity, he's bound to make some mistake somewhere. And then we nail him."

"It could blow up in our faces."

"That's the chance we gotta take. The body count will be a lot worse if we go completely by the book."

Jake nodded, and since there was nothing more to be said, they each began what they had to do.

It was quitting time for the masses. Looking down at the congested, narrow streets, he was glad he could fly. It'd take him a half hour or better to drive the few short blocks to his office this time of night. Flying took only a few seconds.

There must be over a million people down there; going in every direction out of the city toward home on every conveyance possible from a city that seemed to constantly be under urban renewal.

Most every street is cluttered with debris from demolition and construction. Remodeling and new construction abounded. A city, grown filthy and rotted with age, engaged itself in a giant facelift. Attempting to raise itself Phoenix-like from the ashes of obsolescence to take its place in a shining new future.

Dirty politics would always be evident. Unchanging and unaffected by time and man to tarnish that future.

Crime, on the other hand, would constantly evolve; always developing new ways to spread its corruption. Always modernizing; never standing pat. Growing faster than laws can be enacted to contain it.

And which is the more evil of the two?

Arriving at his office, Sheila was about to call it a day.

"Oh, Jason. You're back."

"Anything I should know?"

"Yes," she said, reaching for a slip of paper on her desk. "I called Mr. Greenleaf. When I told him you'd be willing to take his case he rushed right over to give me his daughter's picture."

"Hmmmm. Pretty. Did Mr. Greenleaf know any of her friends? Someone I might get a lead from."

"Not anyone he knew personally."

"That's going to make it tougher to track her down."

"He did say she frequented a bar over on 18th street."

"Not much to go on. Still, it's something. Maybe I can check out the bar on my way home."

"You're not going to be doing any drinking are you?"

She'd struck a raw nerve again. He was about to tell her to get the fuck out but caught himself. He tossed his hat and coat on the chair.

"Oh yee of little faith," he bit off.

"Oh yee of little will power."

"What's that supposed to mean?"

"I think you know. . . . Have you called AA yet?"

Why was she doing this to him? His anger crowding his ability to read her, he bit his lip. "NO!" he said, brushing past her to his office, Sheila hot on his heels. "What's the matter? Don't you trust me? There are no hidden bottles here. . . . But then, I suppose you've checked."

"Yes."

She came across remorseful. Like what she was doing was distasteful. He ignored the sense.

"Well, for your information, I haven't had a drink since before I left for New York!"

He couldn't tell her it was useless to drink anymore. That it no longer had any affect.

"If that's true, I'm very pleased to hear it."

"If? It is, thank you very much. And right now it's been very difficult to cope with reality. So if you don't mind, I don't need this."

"Well, that's what AA is for; to help you cope."

"I don't have time—"

"Then promise you'll do it soon."

She was sincere and he found it hard to maintain his anger. He took a long slow breath.

"All right. I promise."

She said nothing. Just nodded and walked for the door.

"Sheila."

She paused at the door without turning. "Yes Jason?"

"Thanks for the concern."

He'd remembered looking around the office when he'd come in. Sheila had folded up her laptop. The answering machine was switched on. Her purse on the desk instead of her usual place under it.

"Going home early tonight."

"What makes you think so," she said when he approached her desk.

"Hey. I'm a detective. Remember?"

The tension broken, she smiled that wry grin of hers. Putting her hands on her hips she gave him that cold look of indignation that he'd sadly learned to respect . . . and fear.

"Oh kay. That's one I owe you. Anyway, Mother called me this afternoon and asked me to help her with a dinner party Daddy's giving tonight. I have to stop at my apartment, pick up my dress and scoot over to the house."

"Well, have a good time, and give my regards to your family."

His *DANGER* sense tingled ever so slightly. It unnerved him when he could sense no apparent danger until he saw the coy look on Sheila's face.

"Jason. Mother says I can bring a friend if I like. Why don't you come with me?"

Was she trying to make amends?

"No. I don't think so."

"Why not?" Now she was dejected. "You've met my family. It's not like everyone there would be strangers."

"What about your father. As I recall, he was dead set against your leaving home and getting a job. And since I'm the one that gave you that job, he might not take to kindly to me."

"He also owes you for saving my life . . . and his wallet. Besides, Mother can handle him. So, how about it?"

There was time to check out the bar on 18th street before the party. Since he didn't figure on finding Tulio in any of the spots he wanted to check before 10 PM. . . . Heck. Why not?

"Okay. I'm in. 7:30 okay?"

"Sure."

"I gotta leave by 9:30."

"Okay." She was relieved. "See you there. You know where the place is. And scrape your face before you stop by."

Chicky's Bar was no dive by any definition . . . just a few steps above . . . barely. The night was young, the bar only half full right now. Mostly local laborers catching a few beers before going home.

Jason sat at the bar; ordering a drink out of habit, then canceled it in favor of a ginger ale. When the bartender returned he showed him the picture of Charlotte Greenleaf.

"I understand she hangs out here a lot."

The bartender gave it a quick scan, handing it back without recognition. "Sorry. Can't place her. She looks familiar, but, I can't place her."

"Would anyone else here know her?"

"Marge might. She's the night barmaid; knows just about everyone."

"Can I see her?"

"She don't come in till eight. Come back after that and she should be here."

Jason thanked the man, finished his drink, leaving a decent tip, and headed for the street.

Reaching the sidewalk, something told him he was on the right track. His gut feeling was there was more to this than met the eye. But it was only a feeling; something he was beginning to trust again. He'd be back later to see if his guts were right.

7:35 PM. He was pressing the doorbell to the entrance of the palatial estate owned by Sheila's father.

The butler who greeted him, challenged him for an invitation he did not have. He was about to explain he'd only been invited a few hours ago when Sheila came to his rescue. She called from across the foyer.

"Jason. I'm glad to see you could make it."

While she glided across the expanse of polished marble floor he took the opportunity to drink in her evening attire.

It was made of a white, satiny material, fitting ever so snugly to every rise and fall of her figure. It was floor length and strapless. Backless to a discrete point just above the cleavage as he soon discovered. Nearly topless as well as it was cut so low it made bending over extremely hazardous. To be certain, one good sneeze would leave nothing to the imagination.

"It's all right, Henry,' she said, taking my arm and leading Jason inside. "This is my boss and I invited him."

"Yes'm," he said stoically.

"Nice dress you got there," Jason murmured in her ear while they walked arm in arm across the entry hall.

"Isn't it great. Daddy doesn't like it. That's why I wore it."

"How do you keep it from falling down around your ankles?" he whispered from the corner of his mouth.

"Double faced taped. How else?"

"Hope it's not hot in here."

"Just right."

"Gonna be a bitch peeling it off later."

"Not your worry," she said tugging at his arm, smiling broadly as they entered the sitting room. "You're late," she chastised.

"Only five minutes."

The first to greet him was Sheila's mother.

"Welcome Mr. Parks," said Rita, warmly. "It's so good of you to come."

"My pleasure. And please, call me Jason," he said, taking her hand.

"Very well. And you must call me Rita. I have to thank you again for returning our little daughter to us safe and sound."

"Well, she's no little girl anymore as I'm sure you know. To be honest, I think it was Ray and Lyle who were in the greatest danger." Sheila gaped, giving him a light rap on the arm. "And, for what it's worth, she's becoming a fine girl Friday for me."

"Yes . . . well. . . . That's enough of that," said Sheila, tugging at his arm. "Let's go see what Daddy's up to."

"That wasn't nice," she said, piqued.

"What?"

"Lying to Mother. Fine girl Friday. All we seem to do is fight."

"I was just being gracious."

"Uh huh."

Anthony Alonzo DiAngelo. Born of immigrant parentage. A self made man. Owner of his own Real Estate/Accounting and Insurance firm. One of the ten wealthiest men in the state. A man of power and influence who has the ear of many of the top politicians in the northeastern part of the country.

He likes to occasionally gamble in Atlantic City or Vegas, usually breaking even.

He was having a quiet chat with a half dozen men in his den. Jason recognized only one of them, the former Governor of Pennsylvania.

Mr. DiAngelo, seeing Sheila and Jason, strode toward them.

Sheila's attire drew a scornful gaze. She silently reveled in his disdain, looking him square in the eye as one heavyweight would to the other in the ring.

Turning his attention to Jason with a grin, he stuck out his hand. "Jason, Jason! It's good to see you again," he said, wringing Jason's hand profusely. "Sheila told me you were coming. I'm glad you could make it."

"Likewise," he said while managing to get his hand back intact.

"Gentlemen," he announced. "I want you to meet the man who returned our little girl to us, unharmed"

"Keep the Ray and Lyle crack," she said through clenched teeth.

With the Governor were three current members of City Council and Mr. DiAngelo's two younger sons, Allen and Albert.

"I must apologize for my oldest son, Alonzo," said Mr. DiAngelo. "He was supposed to be here tonight, but he called and begged off at the last minute."

With the usual pleasantries exchanged the original conversation resumed.

"Now Anthony," said one of the Councilmen. "Won't you reconsider our offer?"

"For the last time, gentlemen. I'm not interested in running for Mayor. You guys need an airhead. Someone you can manipulate. I'm insulted that you would even consider me."

"Let's get away from this," said Sheila, tugging lightly on Jason's arm. "This kind of talk grosses me out."

Excusing them, Jason and Sheila left the group to their discussion.

Dinner announced; they all filed into the large grand dining hall.

The seven-course meal was pleasant and uneventful. Quiet but for the usual chit chat. It was after dessert, over the coffee, that the conversation intensified.

"It must be fascinating being a detective," said Sheila's youngest brother, Albert.

"How So?"

"Well. The thrill. The excitement. The shooting of criminals," he said while leaning over the table. Hate and anger emanated from Albert.

Jason knew of Sheila's brother's protectiveness, but this was much, much more.

"I perform a necessary service for the people. Many times what I have to do is dull and routine. Any thrill I get is secondary to my purpose. As for shooting criminals, as you put it, I haven't shot at anyone since I was on the NYPD."

"But, you carry a gun, don't you?"

"I'm licensed to carry one, yes."

"Some big 9mm, I presume."

Some of the guests fidgeted while Sheila's anger hit a fast simmer.

"I don't think—"

"It's all right," Jason said to Sheila. "He's asked an honest question."

Her father sat quietly while Rita bit her lip. All seemed interested in the answer he was about to give.

"I carried a 9mm when I was on the force in New York, but I gave it up for the .45 I have now."

"Not much muzzle velocity in them. Why the change?"

"9mms have a nasty habit of going straight through the target and walls and hitting things behind them."

"But they're better at shooting things at a distance, aren't they?"

"Look, Albert, I'm not going to be shooting at anyone from two blocks away. Anything I shoot at will be within twenty feet. The .45 will do."

Jason reached for his still untouched wine glass but was intercepted by the gentle touch of Sheila's hand on his.

"I suppose you have it on you right now."

"Oh Albert! Why don't you give it a rest?!" interjected Sheila, jumping to her feet. "If you had any guts—"

"Now now now," said Jason, taking Sheila's arm, motioning for her to sit down. "Let's not get testy here," he added, turning to Albert. "It's all right.

"In answer to your question, Albert. No! I'm not carrying it right now. . . .   Unless you feel I need it to protect me from the servants."

That sliced through the heavy air. Sheila gave a smug look to her thoroughly put in his place brother. Then her father ended it by saying "Enough is enough."

Announcing that it was time for him to depart, Rita asked Jason if he couldn't stay a little longer. Apologizing, he added he was on call twenty-four, seven, and had several leads to check out on a pending case.

Driving back to the city he reflected on what Sheila had said of her brothers.

Allen and Albert were all but useless. They had the finest education money could buy but had no ambition what so ever. They were a couple of playboys living off their father's money.

Allen liked fast women and fast cars. Keeping to himself a lot, he chose his associates carefully. When it pleased him he'd show up at the office for a few hours to make it look good but actually did very little work to earn his pay.

Albert liked life in the fast lane but was unwilling to pay for it. He looked for women who would pay his freight. He'd disappear for days while some woman indulged him. When the ride ended he'd turn up at home again.

Alonzo Jr., "Lonny" to Sheila was the only one with any drive. He'd started at the bottom of his fathers firm, working his way up to Vice President. He was on the fast track to the top. It almost seemed like he couldn't attain anything fast enough to suit him. Sheila didn't know where he got the money to buy his one third of the business; sound investments she was told.

As she put it. "Daddy wasn't about to give anything away. If the boys wanted the family business they'd have to buy it from him." Of course, Allen and Albert didn't believe this. They were in for a rude awakening one day.

Alonzo Jr. had his own apartment somewhere in the city. She didn't know where, and didn't care much. He was a private person, never letting anyone know too much about him, and everyone respected his wishes.

There was one thing that Albert had been right about. Jason did enjoy the thrills that were involved in his new life now.

It was a few minutes to ten when he got back to his office. Before Mindforce took off to find Tulio, he'd pay a return visit to Chicky's. Marge should be there now. He hoped she'd be able to shed some light on this case.

Chicky's wasn't far. Rather than fly over and have to change twice, and since he wouldn't need the car, he opted to walk.

The mugger that accosted him in the alley wished he hadn't he was sure.

Flashing a formidable looking blade in Jason's face he demanded his wallet or he'd turn Jason's face into dog chow.

To be sure, when he returned from his trip to lullaby land, the unfortunate mugger will be wondering how he got hung up by the collar from the fire escape. Jason would have loved to have seen his face but there were more pressing matters at the moment.

Striding into Chicky's, scanning the room, no Charlotte was in sight. Sitting at the bar he ordered another ginger ale and asked for Marge. Walking to the front of the bar the bartender said a few words to the woman serving a drink and pointed to Jason.

The woman that ambled toward him looked about 45, 5'10", about 165-170 pounds. A lovely woman of ample proportions, with pendulous breasts that, though they were securely harnessed in her bra, swayed rhythmically as though of a mind of their own while she sashayed along the bar. Showing a hefty expanse of cleavage, she was in good athletic shape. One who's ·not about to take any crap from anyone.

"You wanna see me?" she said, pushing my order in front of me.

"You Marge?"

"Depends."

"On what?"

"On what you got on your mind."

Suspicion jumped out of her every pore.

"I'm looking for this girl," he said while handing her the picture. "I've been told she frequents this bar. Do you know her?"

Her eyes showed recognition but her mouth didn't.

"Nope. Can't help ya Ace. Never seen her before."

His *Esper* sense did hand springs when she handed the photo back. She was hiding something. Was she protecting the girl or was she the one who made her disappear?

"I think you have," said Jason, searching for a reaction. "Your eyes betray you."

"You're loco. I don't know what you're talking about."

She started to walk away when Jason had her by the wrist.

"Hey! Leggo Ace!"

"Look. You can either speak to me or the police down town."

"Ain't *you* the heat!"

"Uh uh. Private."

Releasing her wrist Jason reached in his pocket for his ID, tossing it in front of her. When she picked it up he felt the steel like grip of powerful fingers on his upper right arm.

"Ya want I should throw this bum out for ya, Marge?" rasped the voice connected to those fingers.

One very large dude held Jason's arm. Broad shoulders, thick arms and chest, narrow hips and waist compared to the rest of him. All brawn with very little thought process. If he got a half dozen brain cells to hold hands he might get out a cogent thought.

Jason's *DANGER* sense had given him a mild tingle just before this troglodyte grabbed his arm. Being so intent on getting Marge to come clean he ignored the signal, otherwise this brute would never have come close to laying a finger on him.

"You can either, remove that hand, or I'll break it off and shove it where the sun don't shine."

"Inyer dreams, Fel-la!" he said, squeezing harder.

Jason's left hand whirled around, grabbing the ape's wrist, twisting his arm up behind his back. His free hand grabbed the brute's collar, raising him off the floor.

He wriggled and groaned for several seconds, when Marge intervened.

"That's enough! Let 'im go! Let 'im go!"

Jason let him go less than gently, shoving him away brusquely.

"It's all right, Geoff," she said, standing between Jason and the seething dude, her hands firmly on his chest. "I can handle this ya big stiff. Now, get lost."

The bruiser, unable to scrounge up a decent come back, gave

in reluctantly to her demands. Slowly backing off into a corner of the room. Never once taking his eyes off Jason.

"He's the bouncer here. He's got a short fuse on his temper. Thinks I need protection all the time."

"Someone oughta put a short leash on him before he gets hurt."

"You want the job? You're the only one's ever been able to handle him."

"No thanks. I got other troubles right now."

"What's a PI want with Charly?"

"Charly?"

"That's what we all call her."

"She disappeared a few days ago. Never came home from work one night. Her father hired me to find her. This place is the only lead I have."

He sensed she knew something he didn't.

"Let's go over to the booth," she said, motioning behind him. "It'll be more private."

Sitting in the booth, Marge leaned over the table. Brazenly pushing her ample cleavage forward. He wasn't interested. Her words came out in a hushed tone as if she cared if someone heard.

"I thought you was a cop in here to arrest Charly."

"What would the police want with her?"

"What I'm gonna tell you can't get back to her father," she said succinctly. "Charly don't want him to know about her work. Deal?"

What she did for a living was no concern of his. If she didn't want her old man to know what she was doing, that was her prerogative. What did he have to lose? "Deal."

"Well, her and three or four of her friends always come in here at night before they go out to work."

"So?"

"So! Don't ya get it?"

"Get what?"

"They was all *HOOKERS*, ya dumb stiff!" she let out in a harsh whisper.

The light strobed in Jason's head so bright you would have

thought that others could notice it. That pretty, baby faced little girl, was a hooker. Her picture, so innocent looking. No wonder he didn't come to that conclusion himself. She did not have the stereotypical look of a lady of the evening.

"She was a prostitute?"

"Ain't that what I said? Boy. For a gumshoe, you're awful dumb."

"I'm a little slow on the uptake sometimes. So where is she tonight?"

"That's just it. No one knows and no one's talkin'. She ain't been around in over a week, and neither have the other girls. Even their pimp ain't shown his ugly kisser in here."

Jason had a bad feeling about this. Only Mindforce was supposed to know about it. So he couldn't relate it to Marge.

"Pretty strange behavior. Wouldn't you say?"

"Well, the cops is always on a purge now and then. She's been picked up now and then for soliciting . . . but her pimp always got her out the next day."

"That would explain all the other times she didn't come home from work."

"Yeah. She once told me she lived with her father and he didn't know she was hookin'. But she always called with some excuse so's her old man wouldn't get too nosy."

"Well she didn't call this time. In fact, she hasn't been home since last week. That's why her father looked me up."

Marge nodded. "I just thought she and the other girls was lyin' low for awhile, till the heat was off."

"Well, if you learn anything else that might be helpful, give me a call." He handed her his card and got up to leave.

The hairless gorilla, trained as a bouncer, was waiting at the door. When Jason attempted to remove himself from the premises the brute stopped him with a hand on his chest. The jerk hadn't learned his lesson.

"I ain't finished with you yet," he growled.

"You talking to me?"

"No one makes a fool o' me," he snorted.

"You're doing all right by yourself. You don't need my help."

"All right wise mouth! That smart remark is going to cause you some teeth."

This poor man's Atlas was pushing it; Jason felt his anger rising.

"Take your best shot, Bozo. . . . But let me warn you. I got chunks o' guys like you in my shit! Now. You can either remove your grubby paw . . . or you're gonna have to learn to tie your shoes without it. . . . You can tie your shoes, can't you?"

Jason glared straight into the Cro-Magnon's eyes, detecting the conflict roiling within, his anger seething, but. There was doubt. Doubt in his ability to carry out his threat. Maybe he wasn't all muscle and no brains after all. Otherwise, he'd never have even thought about it.

Slowly—hesitatingly—reluctantly, he removed his hand from Jason's path.

"Good night one and all," he said, tipping his hat. Striding out into the night he listened while he walked away.

"You're lucky he didn't clean your clock for ya," said Marge, casually.

Obviously, Charlotte being a hooker was marked for kidnapping by the Crime Czar; along with all the other hookers.

Two separate cases. Now ironically intertwined.

Mindforce, in search of a flock of hookers being imprisoned by the Crime Czar, and Jason Parks, hired to find a missing woman who happens to be a prostitute. Solving one case would solve them both.

Now. Where would someone hide about a thousand ladies of the evening?

* * * *

CHAPTER ELEVEN

Next Comes Alfie Tulio

Where someone would keep a thousand women undetected was a mystery. They'd need a good-sized hall for their purpose Jason concluded while walking back to his office. Like as not, they'd need a small army to contain them; unless they were in a place that made it futile to try escaping. That seemed the more likely.

It was a sure bet they'd want those women alive. To kill them would mean an awful lot of bodies to dispose of, and if the Crime Czar was able to take over the rackets here, he'd need these women to add ready cash to his coffers. This gave Jason hope that Charlotte was still among the living.

With all these ladies off the streets, Mr. Big must be losing a lot of money every day. He'd have to get out his calculator when he got back to the office.

Someone had been kind enough to release the mugger he'd left hanging from the fire escape in the alley. He hoped it was a suspicious officer.

Digging his calculator from his desk, Jason started crunching numbers.

Figuring girls must average $400 a night to satisfy their pimps. That each girl could only work three weeks per month—the percentage the pimps kept—the girls cut—then Mr. Big's tribute multiplied by roughly one thousand ladies working, he stood to lose . . . *SIX MILLION DOLLARS* each month the girls were off the streets!

HOLY COW! Was this ever big business. Even with the figures

being conservative, he believed, it was no wonder the Crime Czar was grabbing all the hookers from the streets. Surely, this couldn't be helping Mr. Big's emotional state either. This definitely wasn't penny ante here.

The Crime Czar's chances of reaching retirement age were slim at best if Mr. Big caught up with him.

At any rate, it was time for phase two of his plan to smoke out the Crime Czar.

A fast change—a short walk up to the roof—then a leap into the sky.

There were two places on his list where Tulio was likely to show. A supper club down on the river or a nightclub down town that was suspected of having an illegal gambling room.

Knowing Tulio's habits from his yellow sheet he opted to stake out the gambling room. A two-bit gambler like him couldn't stay away from the action for too long. If it were illegal, the allure would be that much greater.

Landing on the roof of a building across from the club, Quincy's Nite spot, he set out to dispatch his ghost to check out the joint. It still amazed him how this ghost could have all his sensory powers. He just couldn't grasp anything or make his voice heard.

There was nothing illegal about the dining hall on neither the second floor, nor the dance floor on the first level; nothing behind the stage as well. That left only the basement to check out. Another swift drop through the floor coming up, or down as it were.

Nothing. Nothing looked out of the ordinary—anywhere. Shit! He should have known it wasn't going to be easy.

There were only the usual things you'd expect from a musty old basement: the furnace room, a well stocked wine cellar, plenty of storage, a modest utility room with a few tools; but nothing that could be construed as a gambling establishment. Could the rumors be wrong? Was the place really legit? Or was it a smoke screen to keep the cops busy sniffing around the wrong hole while the real gambling den went unnoticed elsewhere. Possibly, but he doubted it.

He was about to chuck the whole thing; chalking it up to a wild goose chase, when something on the floor caught his eye. He moved in closer.

Intangible in this state he couldn't pick it up. His enhanced vision only worked in his physical form but his levitation power brought it to eye level; a white poker chip.

It still meant nothing but it gave him the incentive to keep looking.

A quick poke of his ghostly head through the walls proved fruitless. All he found was dirt, a couple of small sewer tunnels and the neighboring businesses basement, which was similar to the one, he was in.

Something was going on around here and he was determined to find it. Returning to the wine room where he found the chip, he gave it a closer look.

Standing in the gloom, he reached out with all his senses. To his ears came the unmistakable sounds of gambling: dice clicking, slot machines being pulled, roulette wheels, cards being shuffled, a number of voices calling out bets; and it came from all places, below his feet.

He'd believed he was as deep as he could go. Now he knew there must be a sub basement. But where was the entrance? No matter. He just descended through the sixteen inches of steel reinforced concrete like a good ghost should.

The complexity was incredible. If he found anything he expected a crap table or two—a couple of poker tables—your odd slot machine, not this. This was far above what he would have imagined.

The room was easily fifty feet by seventy-five. Fully carpeted in a French Argyle pattern. A huge mirrored marble and mahogany bar stretched the entire width at the far end of the room. A room sporting every form of gambling available. If you were brought in unconscious and placed on the floor, when you awoke you'd swear you were in Vegas or Atlantic City.

This set up was too vast—too elaborate. Not some private,

penny-ante little parlor. This couldn't slip beneath the scrutiny of
Mr. Big and his organization. It had to be owned and operated by
him.

What brass Tulio must have. To work for the Crime Czar yet
show up, big as life, in the Syndicate's own game room. And there
he was. Tossing his money away at the blackjack table. Across the
table stood someone losing heavily; someone the D.A. will be
interested to hear about.

This shed new light on things. How could an insignificant,
small time pickpocket, like Leroy, Know about Tulio working for
the Crime Czar, yet Mr. Big Didn't? His operatives must have
their ear to the same grapevine.

Could he have missed something when he questioned Leroy?
Does he have a bigger part in the scheme of things than meets the
eye? Could his fear of Mindforce and his apprehension have masked
the fact that he wasn't telling the complete truth?

He'd look up Leroy later to get the answers to those and other
questions.

Scanning the room for other means of entrance or escape it
became apparent why he could not find any door to this place.
Not ten feet from where he'd slipped through the floor, in one
corner, stood a free-standing hydraulic piston. The whole storage
closet above could be lowered to this level. Anyone knowing the
proper password would be brought to the closet then lowered to
the casino. Ingenious, but he couldn't see this place not having
some other means of egress.

He spied a door next to the bar marked *"Private"*. This could
be what he was looking for.

Inside was an office some twenty-five feet square. Plush, leather
furniture sat arranged around the perimeter: sofas, chairs, lamps
and the like. In the middle stood a regulation walnut pool table
with mother-of-pearl inlay. A large ornate desk stood to the far
side with a private bar behind; lined with mirrors floor to ceiling
along the whole wall making the room seem twice it's true
dimension.

No one was in at the moment. He didn't see anything that looked like an exit anywhere, but that didn't mean there wasn't one.

He was about to slip through the walls when the bar behind the desk slid to one side with barely a whisper of noise.

Wonder of wonders. Who should step through the opening in the wall but ol' tubby himself. The short little lard bucket popped through the opening; followed by a couple of his goon squad.

That clinched it; this little establishment was the property of the Syndicate. This was Mr. Big's private entrance; doubling as an emergency exit should the casino be found and raided.

Checking the corridor behind the bar he discovered the mirrors were two-way. Anyone standing here could check out the room to make sure it was safe to enter. Only the trusted few were privy to this entrance.

Beyond the corridor lay a series of old abandoned subway tunnels, long forgotten by the City Engineers and kept that way by Syndicate moles in the system. Mindforce was certain one of the tunnels had to lead back to the Commerce Building so that the little fat man could commute without fear of connection to the casino. Real shrewd.

Without warning, waves of dizziness crashed over him like breakers on the beach. He'd foolishly allowed himself to forget he could be away from his body for only fifteen minutes.

His vision blurred rapidly; disorientation rapidly twisting his senses. He had to find his body immediately, but where was it?

UP! All he could think of was up! He was forty feet underground. His body sat somewhere up there on top of a building. He had to return to it. *NOW!!*

A speeding truck flashed through his ghostly figure when he emerged through the middle of the street. Extremely disoriented he acted convulsively, flinging his arms before his face for protection.

WHERE? Where was his body? . . . Up—still up—on the roof. What roof? There—over there! Yes—over there.

His vision, blurring—swirling–dimming; he could barely see. He was . . . dying!

No! No! He mustn't think that. Must . . . must go on! DAMMIT! Try harder. Try . . . HARDER!

There! There. Against . . . air-conditioning . . . unit. His body! Must reach it! Can't.. see. Can't SEE! Going to . . . going to . . . DIE!

NO! NO! Must go on. Can't . . . stop now. So Close! So clossssee. . . .

With one final supreme effort, Mindforce flung his ghostly wraith toward his unmoving, trance induced, mortal form. Upon touching there transpires a symbiotic union of body and soul. Could this merging of two entities be too late?

For several seconds there is no movement. Then a twitch; a minuscule twitch of a finger.

The feet and legs jump convulsively. The eyelids, concealed behind the mask, flutter, then snap wide open, uncomprehending. The head rolls around. The mind: grasping, fighting for understanding.

His stomach was the first thing he became aware of; it felt like it was full of rusty razor blades and coarse gravel. His brain felt like the skull was lined with broken glass and was abuzz with the drone of a million angry hornets.

This was a new experience in agony when he tried to convince his body to sit up. If not for the cradle he formed with his hands he felt his head would fall into his twitching lap.

"Oooooh! My aching head," he mumbled when he found his voice. "Feels like someone used it for a wrecking ball."

Within five minutes the pain and queasiness abated; his recuperative powers in high gear.

Standing on rubbery legs, he leaned on the air-conditioning unit. Pushing back his hood he sucked in the dusty air.

He'd stayed from the body too long, almost fatally. Why hadn't his *DANGER* sense warned him? Or, was that initial queasiness it? He didn't know.

The effect of time and distance from his body nearly was his undoing. He'd been lucky, very lucky. He never wanted to be that close to death ever again.

"Christ! Why am I bothering. . . . Shit!" He knew why. His conscience, now that it's clear, won't let him do anything else.

Only out of it a few minutes, he felt it safe to assume that Tulio was still in the casino.

After what he'd seen below, it became apparent he'd need to formulate a new plan of attack. He'd expected to find a small back room, not the elaborate set up built there. Expecting only a small grouping: he was going to barge in, chase out everyone except Tulio, push him around, toss a few threats, then tell him exactly what he wanted his boss to know; to be sure, that plan had to be scrapped.

With this new data, this would be a golden opportunity to nail Mr. Big. If he were to rush in after Tulio now they'd know he was on to their operation. There'd be nothing but an empty sub basement there by the time he got the cops to move in and they'd be back to square one.

No. This required stealth. A well thought out, organized plan. No one man or small group could hope to accomplish what had to be done. He'd have to be satisfied with waiting for Tulio to come to him.

Since it was unlikely that Tulio would be using the secret exit, he'd have to come out the front door. After all, he was putting on the image of a respectable citizen. Why should he sneak around?

2 AM: He'd wished he'd brought along some coffee or something. The evening had dragged on slowly. Without the presence of a partner to while away the time, he settled in for a boring evening. Finally, his quarry had had enough and exited to the street.

Alone, he climbed into a waiting cab.

He could, in all likelihood, lead Mindforce to the Crime Czar if he waited long enough, but that could take days. No. He had to make Tulio want to go there right away. With nothing to charge him with that anyone would be willing to testify to it would be no good in arresting him now. He'd have to be pushed into that fatal mistake where he would incriminate himself. It was doubtful knowing who he was would be of any advantage. They knew all about Mr. Big and it hadn't helped one bit.

The cabby must have been in total shock when he realized his fare had disappeared from the back of his cab and he hadn't made any stops.

Following the cab for several blocks until they were a safe distance from Quincy's, at top speed, he swooped down. Opening the door to the cab he extracted Tulio from the back seat and soared off with him.

They were several hundred feet in the air and still climbing before Tulio comprehended what had happened.

"HEY! Put me down," he bellowed. "You can't do this to me! I got my rights y-know!"

The flurry of foul language that followed could have curdled milk.

Climbing steadily to an altitude around two thousand feet, Mindforce refused to acknowledge any of Tulio's raving.

He held Tulio at arms length by the collar of his overcoat. He could easily have used his levitation power but he wanted the scum to feel the helplessness of dangling in mid air.

When Tulio pulled his courage, a .357 Smith and Wesson, from inside his coat, Mindforce flinched ever so slightly when it was pointed directly at his heart.

"Oh, gimme a break," said Mindforce. "Don't tell me. This is where you go into your, 'Do as I say or I'll fill you full of lead', routine. Look around you pal. Even if you could kill me, which you can't, it's almost a half-mile to the street. Granted. The fall won't kill you. But that sudden stop; that's the bitch! You'd look like a puddle of strawberry jam wearing a tux. The ambulance boys'd hafta pick you up with a sponge."

"Nah, nah, nah. It's a fucking trick of some kind. You're just tryin' to scare me."

"A trick is it? Maybe you'd like I should let go o' you and we'll see."

Mindforce lowered his arm as if in preparation to release him when Tulio blurted out.

"Okay. I believe you. But no matter what you do to me I ain't gonna tell you nothing!"

"That's where you got it wrong, tough guy. I don't want anything from you."

"So, What do—"

"Shut your yap and listen, asshole. I've got some information for your boss. I just brought you up here so we could talk, privately. Now. Put that popgun of yours away before you hurt yourself."

The wheels spun rapidly in Tulio's head while he weighed his options. Since he had none, he released the hammer on his weapon and jammed it back in its holster.

"It's your play amigo. But you got it wrong. I ain't got no boss. I run my own affairs."

"Just what you'd like everyone to believe. I'll bet Mr. Big would be tickled pink if I were to give you to him. How do you think he'd feel if he knew you were the Crime Czar's right hand and you've been spying on his operation?"

The Czar's mention got a spike in Tulio's emotions. He was extremely tense now and Mindforce was sure he had the right man.

"Crime Czar? You're crazy."

"All right. Let's cut the crap! My fingers are getting tired," Mindforce said, giving Tulio a gentle shake. "I'd hate to lose my grip. But then, Freddy Lester wouldn't care. He'd just move into your spot next to the Crime Czar."

"He'd never put Lester in my place," he spit out, then immediately shut up; knowing he said too much.

"Thought you said you had nothing to do with the Crime Czar."

"So, you got me. So What? You got no proof."

"I couldn't care less. Your petty problems are your own. Now. Listen and listen good. I and the Commissioner know all about the bet with the Syndicate. Furthermore, so does Mr. Big because

I told him so. You better warn your boss that Biggy knows he can't get any help from his cronies in New York and he's quite put out about the whole thing. He's mobilizing everyone who's loyal to him that he can just to smoke out the Czar. . . . Crime Czar? Only a self righteous nut case gives himself that name."

Tension and astonishment welled up inside Tulio, spilling over its levy in a torrent. He'd been under the misconception that their little escapade would remain a deep dark secret.

"I told him he was out of his mind."

"So why throw in with him?"

"'Cause he just might pull it off."

Tulio's initial disorientation was clearing now; his true self coming through.

"All right. All right. You want some truth."

"That would be refreshing.'

"The asshole knows nothing of the Mob. Yeah. Maybe he can pull it off. But he'll never keep it."

"And you feel you're the logical successor."

"Why not? The Mob knows nothing about me here. I can redeem myself by offing him for them later."

He really believed all the garbage he was spilling.

"And what if I tell him all this?"

"You gotta find 'im first. And even if you did, I've got him convinced of my loyalty."

The man had some grand delusions, and Mindforce was about to let the gas out of this airbag.

"I don't give a shit. But keep this in mind . . . if I found you out, so can they. Only, they're not going to be nice like me."

Now for the big bluff.

"You tell your boss I know he's working within a specified time frame, and the two minute warning is fast approaching. He doesn't have an unlimited supply of cash and he can't rely on the loyalty of half the army he's recruited. All I've got to do is throw a monkey wrench into the works. Delaying his schedule long enough will bring the vast army of a nationwide syndicate here to collect what's due them. Now. You got that straight, or shall I repeat it for you in words of one syllable?"

"Don't bother. I heard you. Now leggo of me," he said, shrugging his shoulders.

"Don't tempt me," he said just before Tulio remembered he was still two thousand feet above the street. "If I didn't know I'd have to find Lester and go through this all over again, I'd be glad to let go of you."

Tulio looked down between his dangling feet, swallowing hard; quiet the few seconds it took to reach the sidewalk. Mindforce dropped him and was gone in an eye blink.

If the Czar was the megalomaniac Mindforce envisioned, his scheme should goad him into chucking his well thought out plan, thus forcing him to accelerate his timetable. If he were reckless, he'd have to make some fatal mistake, and Mindforce would nail him to the wall.

What he couldn't tell Alfie was he wasn't about to wait for the Syndicate to step in. The carnage would be devastating while they tore the city apart looking for him; though some of them probably deserved it. Innocent people always got hurt no matter how careful the Syndicate boys were. That wasn't going to happen here.

Now. He had to get Jake out of bed. Like it or not, he had to be informed of what he'd discovered below Quincy's.

* * * *

CHAPTER TWELVE

Several Birds; One Stone

2:45 AM: Mindforce stood at the front door of the Commissioner, leaning on the bell. It was a quaint, unobtrusive little place in the suburbs.

He knew approximately where Jake lived since the Commissioner and his wife moved in six years ago. The media had made a big deal of it; though they weren't allowed to be specific. Prominent people drew attention with little provocation.

He'd found the street and the block, but the concrete jockey on the front lawn with the name PARMAN on the hanging plate that clinched it.

Now. If he'd just answer the door.

He hated waking Jake at this late hour, and he'd likely be all bent out of shape about it, but this couldn't wait for regular office hours. Plans had to be made quickly if they were to be successful.

Another push on the bell and from the other side of the door came odious grumbling.

"All Right. All right. I'm coming. Hold your water."

The curtain by the window lights next to the door, receded. A sleepy eye sprang open followed by the door at the sight of the costume.

"Mindforce," Jake said with a yawn. "What are you doing here at this Godforsaken hour? Don't you ever go home to bed?"

"Sorry to disturb you, Jake. What I have to say can't wait."

"What is it?" said Jake, hustling him inside, scanning the area out of habit.

"How well do you know the DA?"

"Leonard Taylor? Why, I've known Lenny for over twenty years. Why?"

"Can he be trusted?"

"Look! Lenny became the Asst. DA about the same time I made Detective Lieut. When he became DA I moved up to Captain. It was largely through his influence that I got appointed Commissioner. I'd trust the man with my life."

"You may have to."

Jake's eyes narrowed. "What's this all about?"

"I just want to be sure which side he's going to be on when it hits the fan."

"Then before you tell me anything, let me call him up and get him over here. He only lives a couple miles away. If what you say is worthwhile you can bet he'll act on it accordingly."

A hurried call—a few choice words—some moans of protest from the other end, then a petulant okay.

Twenty minutes later a very rumpled, very sleepy DA was leaning on the doorbell.

"This better be good!" he protested, striding in the door held by the Commissioner. "I hope you got some coffee on."

"Coming up."

Once settled, Mindforce related his discovery tonight.

"Are you familiar with Quincy's Nite Spot down on Broad?"

"Yes," returned the DA. "Rumor has it there's illegal gambling going on there, but the rumors haven't panned out."

"Well, it's there all right. I found it earlier this evening."

Over the next several minutes Mindforce went into elaborate detail about what was contained under the sub-floor—the secret elevator—the room size—all the games to be played there, and the secret exit to the abandoned subway tunnels.

"Then it's a full scale casino, not some penny-ante gaming den," said Jake.

"You got it."

"And it's got to be under the control of the Syndicate," added the DA

"Operated by Mr. Big himself."

"You saw him there?" perked up the DA

"In the fat little flesh."

"You got any proof of this?"

"No. I'm afraid not. That's going to be up to your office."

Lenny took a deep breath and slowly exhaled. "This isn't going to be easy. And it's going to take some time."

"We've got some time. You heard the tape I made in Mr. Big's office?"

"Yes."

"Okay. I got 'im riled up, plus I found Alfie Tulio tonight. He's the Crime Czar's right hand. With what I put in his ear I hope to goad the Crime Czar into speeding up his timetable and coming into the open. Hopefully, they'll be so involved with each other they won't notice us undermining their foundation."

"You're setting the city up for a blood bath," said the DA

"There's no other way. We've got to play them off against one another. Planned properly, their operatives will uncover and we'll have them out of business before they know what hit them. Long before any innocent blood will be shed."

Jake rubbed the back of his neck. Lenny tapped his fingers on the coffee table. Both men agreed in principle. They knew some chances had to be taken if they were going to get a wedge between the different factions. If only there were another way.

"What do you suggest?" said the Commissioner.

"We've got to prove that Mr. Big actually owns Quincy's. I think if the DA's office checks further we'll find it's all part of Mr. Big's corporation.

"Next, we need to get any maps or blueprints of the old abandoned subway system. We'll need men we can trust to sneak down there to make sure we get access to all possible escape routes so we can bottle them up. Plus make sure there are no new tunnels added by the Syndicate."

"As far as the street entrance goes," said the Commissioner, "when the time comes I'll have enough men in the basement to cover the elevator should anyone try to leave that way."

"We'll need warrants to get in there," said the DA. "After we make our search and determine there could be criminal action involved, it shouldn't be hard to get a judge to sign them."

"We can't use Judge Bradley."

"Why not?" said the DA cocking his head to one side.

"I hate to say this, but he was gambling quite heavily in the casino while I was there."

"Are you sure it was him," said Jake with a measure of doubt.

"Quite sure. He's been in the news often enough. I couldn't mistake him."

"You know, Jake," said Lenny. "The pieces are all finally fitting into place."

"How so?" said Jake.

It's like this. I've got a private file on Judge Bradley at home. On my own I've been investigating him; putting together notes on the Judge's actions in hopes of proving malfeasance."

"You got much on him?" said Mindforce.

"Bits and pieces that on the surface, could be just coincidental. For the past couple of years, several suspected Syndicate members who have come before Judge Bradley, have been getting off Scott free. And those that were convicted, received light sentences or parole."

"A real bastion of law and order," said the Commissioner. "Why didn't you tell me. I could have put a few detectives on it."

"I was about to once I had enough evidence. If it went sour I didn't want to take you down with me. With what I have I could turn it over to Judge Mercer for consideration. I just wish we could catch the Judge in there when we raid the place."

"Maybe we can," said Mindforce.

"You got an idea?" said the DA.

"Maybe. Most people are creatures of habit. Why should the Judge be any different."

"I think I know what you have in mind and I like it," said Jake.

"Good. Last night was Tuesday. I assume the Judge isn't on call that night, so it would be safe to say he gambles there every Tuesday, more or less. Once we're ready we set the raid for a Tuesday night."

"It won't be easy to have the Judge shadowed. He's too smart," said the DA. "I'll see if I can get his phone tapped just in case he crosses us up."

"Then we can trust Judge Mercer?" says Mindforce.

"I've known him since Law School," said the DA. "We shouldn't have a problem."

"Fine. We'll need him to know ahead of time, but we don't want him to sign the warrants until about thirty minutes before we move in. That should prevent any leaks."

"We've got to keep this as tight a secret as possible. Everybody works on a need to know basis. One slip and they can have the place empty in an hour."

"Since this has to do with *Organized Crime* we're going to have to inform the FBI," said the Commissioner. "They'll want to be in on this."

Mindforce agreed. "It might be better to have some unknown faces on surveillance if they're so inclined."

"Well, so much for Mr. Big," said the DA.

"There's been something I've been wondering," said Mindforce to the DA. "What the heck is Mr. Big's real name?"

"Francis, Aloysius, Bigsby," said the DA.

"No wonder he changed his handle to Mr. Big."

"What about the Crime Czar?" said Jake.

"We know he's taken over most every bookie joint in the city and the people running them. And for certain he's picked up all the prostitutes working the streets."

"To what end?" said the DA.

"It's only chump change to the Syndicate on the whole, but locally, Biggy stands to lose about a million and a half every week."

A short clipped whistle issued forth from the DA. "Those are staggering figures over a years time. You sure they're accurate."

There's a small margin of error, I'm sure, but near as I can tell, they are."

"Whata-ya think of that, Jake?"

"Well, Lenny. None of the districts have arrested a hooker in the past ten days; which isn't much in itself. And there hasn't been anyone seen soliciting anywhere in the city. And that's not all. The weekly reports show that the incident of rapes is up 400 percent; wife beatings and child molestation's have nearly tripled in the last week."

"Now, Jake. You're not going to sit there and suggest these increases are due to these hookers having been taken off the streets, are you?" said the DA.

"It sure looks that way," said the Commissioner, throwing up his hands.

"Mindforce?" said the DA.

"Well. I, for one, find it hard to believe that rapes and so forth would increase in direct proportion to the decrease in the availability of prostitutes . . . but figures don't lie. It's a coincidence I can't buy either."

"I'd sure hate to have it get out that having hookers on the street actually helps reduce the incidence of other, more violent crimes." said the Commissioner.

"Don't even think it." said the DA.

"Let's face it," said the Commissioner. "Like it or not; the girls do serve a useful purpose."

"That's still no defense in a court of law," said the DA, waving an accusing finger.

"Yet," said Mindforce.

"Don't worry," said the Commissioner. "If they ever show up on the streets again, and until the law changes, my men will continue to arrest them for soliciting."

"Do you think they're still alive?" said the DA.

"I would think so," Mindforce said. "The Crime Czar may be insane, but he's not stupid. He knows the longer he holds those girls the more pressure he applies to Mr. Big. The way I see it, he's after a bloodless coup. He's out to discredit Mr. Big, to shame him before his peers. When and if he takes over he'll have someone to gloat to."

"And with all those girls he'll be able to line his pockets quickly," said the Commissioner.

"If this blows up in our faces he may decide to kill them all," said the DA.

"I doubt that. It'd be easier to pull out and abandon them where they are. Depending on how they're restrained they could be left to starve to death. Which is why I have to find them before we can wreck his plans.

"Which leads me to the other hitch in his whole scheme."

"I know. Either way, he loses," said the DA.

"With the city caught in the middle. That little nugget I neglected to tell Mr. Big or Tulio. If Biggy knew of the time limit as well he'd just stall until the Syndicate collected their prize. We'd never be able to sneak behind his back to nail him. And if the Czar new of the double-cross he'd go into hiding and we'd never find him."

Having found the casino, we've got Mr. Big dead to rights," said the DA. "It doesn't matter what he does."

"We don't have him behind bars yet."

"This Crime Czar must be someone we'd certainly recognize without the mask," said the Commissioner.

"Or he could be someone who's never run afoul of the law," Mindforce added. "No face or fingerprints makes a person hard to spot. He could be right under our noses and we'd never know it. Free to pursue his private life, laughing at us while we searched for him."

"Like you, for instance," said the DA, turning an accusing eye in the direction of Mindforce.

His *Esper* sense had caught Lenny's suspicious instinct. The insinuation was intolerable but he had to agree with his reasoning. He'd scanned the DA's emotions all during the conversation. Skeptical of him all the time, his words came across with honesty.

"Say what's on your mind, Lenny," Mindforce said flatly.

"What do we really know about you? You come outta nowhere at the same time as the Crime Czar."

"If not for the Crime Czar I'd never have shown myself, ever."

"That's what I mean. For all we know, *YOU* yourself could be the Crime Czar!"

"You're outta line here, Lenny," said the Commissioner. "He's no more the Crime Czar than you are."

"How can you be sure? How does he know all he's told us? And is it the truth? This could all be an elaborate hoax to confuse us!"

Typical. Mindforce was on his feet, headed for the door when the Commissioner caught his arm.

"Now listen to me," he said. "This man saved the departments collective ass a few weeks ago in that north Philly shootout. If he were trying to take over the city, he'da let us blow ourselves up."

The DA was more animated now. Stalking around the room and Mindforce, sizing him up.

"Don't you see?" pointing an accusing finger. "That's exactly what you'd expect the Crime Czar to do. To help the police break up Mr. Big's organization."

"I knew I never should have gotten involved." Mindforce kicked himself mentally. His fingers balled up into fists.

Jake laid his hand gently on Mindforce's forearm.

"Don't be an *ASS*, Lenny. If you were the Crime Czar, would you throw away an extremely expensive, already established casino in a perfect hiding place? Have some sense man."

Mindforce was about to stalk off and forget the whole thing. He didn't want to be a hero in the first place. Who needs this shit? Then he felt the DA's emotional pattern change. Whether it was the Commissioner's words or his respect for the man's judgment, he was questioning his own position.

"Besides. Just by luck, one of my men was planted in one of the bookie joints where the Crime Czar showed. According to the description, the Crime Czar is a full head shorter and hasn't got nearly those shoulders."

"Well why didn't you say so in the first place?"

"Because you can be such a knot head at times," said the Commissioner, placing a hand on Lenny's shoulder.

The DA turned to Mindforce. "It's the nature of the job, I guess. To be a little suspicious of everyone."

"You can take it or leave it," said Mindforce. "I don't give a shit. I'll go it alone if I have to. My only interest is in seeing the Crime Czar stopped. I've no time for your petty problems."

"Now don't go off half cocked," said the Commissioner. "You've accomplished a lot. Don't blow it now."

Jake was right. He'd let his ambivalence toward the DA and the law here, get in the way. There was only one course to take and he needed the respect of the law or he'd just be an outlaw himself.

"So, what do we do about the Prostitutes?" said the DA.

"Leave them to me," said Mindforce. "I'll find them. And when I do you'll have a thousand counts of kidnapping to slap on the Crime Czar."

"If you can, get one of his men to roll over and finger him as the brains behind it."

"Well, we all know what we have to do," said the Commissioner. "But first, I'd like to get a couple more hours sleep before I have to go to work."

"You and me both," added the DA with a yawn.

"I've got one more thing I have to do before the nights over for me," said Mindforce. "But first I need a favor, Jake."

"Anything. What is it?"

"I need the address of Lightfingers Leroy."

"No sooner said than done. Let me call downtown."

While the Commissioner made the call the DA made his exit. Grabbing Mindforce's hand before he left, he again made his apologies.

The DA was a hard man. Cynical, he was dedicated to this job with its consternation and disappointments. Law was placed above friends and professional courtesies. Mindforce doubted he could become accustomed to him.

"Here's the address Leroy gave us after you brought him in. What do you want with him?"

"This little weasel knows more than he let's on, and I'm gonna find out just how much."

"You're not going to do something rash, are you? The Mayor and the press would love to have a reason to crucify you."

"I can't be concerned with that right now. This punk has got to fear me more than the Mob; otherwise he's not gonna talk. All I'm gonna do is point out that it'd be safer talking to me than having to run from the Mob."

"The ends may justify the means, and you know I can't authorize that," said the Commissioner, placing a hand on Mindforce's shoulder. "Be careful, son. We need you more than you know."

He took the slip of paper and tucked it into his belt.

He'd missed something when he last questioned Leroy. Or maybe he just didn't ask the right questions. He'd relied on his *Esper* sense to tell if Leroy were lying; discarding his detective skills. If Leroy hadn't lied, he held something back. He'd not make that mistake again.

One way or another, Leroy was going to tell what he knew. Bet on it!

* * * *

CHAPTER THIRTEEN

No Honor Among Thieves

While Mindforce was busy getting the Commissioner out of bed, Alfie Tulio was driving to a rendezvous with the Crime Czar.

After his release he flagged down another cab, returned to his apartment uptown and made a few hurried calls. After which he took the freight elevator to the parking garage and sped away in his car.

He took a circuitous route. Down dark, narrow, one-way streets and alleys. Checking again and again his rearview mirror for supposed followers. He had no way of knowing there was no cause for all this caution.

Certain he wasn't being followed, Alfie made his way to the headquarters the Crime Czar had made for himself. *Manayunk*, a suburb northwest of the city.

It was a quiet little place whose elevation rose sharply from the Schuylkill River. A town carved practically out of the stone cliffs there. The streets appeared to run almost vertically. San Francisco had nothing on this town, except for the cable cars.

With the closing of the Armory, most of the shipyards packing up and moving south, and the TV manufacturers leaving the country altogether; much of the labor force that lived there packed up and moved as well.

Vacant buildings abounded. One such was an old, empty rooming house that Alfie pulled to the rear of. At least it appeared empty.

The second floor of the musty old house was quite clean and

well kept. Meagerly outfitted, it was only a place to meet in secret and make plans. No other functions were desired.

The Crime Czar planned this little coup d'etat for well over a year. He knew he'd need a base from which to work unnoticed. Systematically, he bought this building and the ones around it through dummy corporations.

The rooming house was but four blocks from the river. A four foot storm drain ran adjacent, not six feet from the basement, draining into the river. He chose the house for that reason. It was a simple matter to cut into the drain and have it ready as an escape tunnel should the need arise.

Waiting impatiently was the Crime Czar with Freddy Lester who busied himself with a bug crawling up the wall. They'd been there for nearly forty-five minutes.

"Al! Al! We got trouble!" said Alfie upon entering the room.

"How many times've I told you not to call me that?" bit off the Crime Czar.

"What difference does it make? We're alone here."

"That's not the point. It leads to bad habits."

"Oh for crying out loud. Since you put your plan into action, me and Freddy ain't been allowed to come around to your apartment anymore. We ain't even allowed to associate with you in public."

"You know why I instituted that policy."

"Yeah. So you won't get implicated with scum like us."

"You're missing the point here," he hissed. "I wear the mask to conceal from one and all exactly who I am. From the beginning you've both known it was imperative I keep my identity a secret.

"I'm running a legitimate business right under Mr. Big's nose, in his own building where I can keep an eye on him. You two have past records in St. Louis. If you're seen with me all the time some smart ass just might put two and two together. Then over a years plans will be in the dumper.

"This whole plan depends on secrecy. While openly attacking Mr. Big's sources of cash, keeping his people busy, my lawyers are secretly undermining all of his holdings. Then we take him over. Legally!"

The Crime Czar took on a Napoleonic strut behind his desk while he replayed his plans of conquest to his underlings. Alfie stood seething under the skin.

"You don't gotta remind me! But it's all for nothing. They're on to us!"

"What the hell are you talking about?"

Freddy Lester, who stood idly, snapped to full attention with this revelation.

"They're on to us, I said." He wiped his sweaty palms on his jacket.

"WHO?!" demanded the Crime Czar, his eyes flaming.

"The cops. And Mr. Big too."

"How do you know this? Who told you?"

"That dude, Mindforce, put 'em wise to us."

"MINDFORCE? How the hell did he find out?"

"I don't know," shouted Alfie, throwing his hands up while he paced the floor. "I don't know. But he's going to queer this whole deal for us!"

"And he told you this?"

"Yeah," he said, still wiping his sweaty palms.

"Just why the hell were you doing talking to him?"

"I wasn't talking to him! He was talking to me! Besides. I didn't have no choice. He had me stuck a half mile up in the air!"

"Stuck? A half mile up in the air! How, for Christ's sake?"

"Well, the dude's pretty strong. And he flies y-know. I was hangin' out at the casino, like you wanted. Tryin' to get some info—"

"So he snagged you there?"

"No! No! It was after I left!" Would the damn sweat ever come off his palms? "I got in a cab and was riding for about ten minutes, when he grabbed me outta the back seat and flew me into the air."

"Out of a moving cab? I'm supposed to believe that!"

"Yeah. Yeah. Exactly. He held me out at arms length. Told me he'd drop me to the street and squash me like a bug if I didn't listen to him."

"To what?" His patience wearing extremely thin.

"He told me all about our operation. About how we're snagging all the hookers offa the streets. How he told Mr. Big and the cops all about it. And about the bet you made with the Syndicate boys."

"The BET! How the HELL could he know about the bet?" he roared, nearly having a fit.

"How the hell should I know?" screeched Alfie. "But he knows all about it. About the time limit, the limited funds you got and the fact that you can't trust halfa the goons we conned into working for us! He says he's gonna throw a monkey wrench into the works, delay our plans and wait for the time limit to run out. Then he'll watch the Syndicate boys come busting in here and take care of alla us."

"Is . . . that . . . so?" said the now suddenly calm, Crime Czar.

"Yeah. And that ain't all. In the mean time, he says Mr. Big's got his whole outfit working overtime trying to track you down."

"You know what, Alfie?"

"What, Boss?'

"I think I smell a rat."

"A rat? Whata you mean?" Alfie's guts churned. He was certain he didn't want to hear the answer.

Toying with nothing in particular on the desk while he gathered his thoughts, the Crime Czar spoke softly.

"There's no way that anyone could have found out about the bet." His voice rose in intensity with every word. The only way they could know . . . is if somebody told them."

"You can't mean me?"

"I can—and I do! You've lost partners before, back in St. Louis."

"You don't know nothin'."

"Oh, but I do. You only left St. Louis because you ratted on your friends to get immunity."

"You're full of it!"

"Not hardly. You were so fearful for your life you left town."

"What liar told you that?!"

"Why, your buddy over there, Freddy."

Freddy had been doing what Freddy did best. He sat and kept his mouth shut while the others argued. Only when everything was decided did he take sides.

"Why you back stabbing little weasel!" said Alfie through clenched teeth before he strode toward Freddy; fists ready.

"Let him alone!" ordered the Crime Czar.

Alfie stopped short, seething. Glaring cruelly into Freddy's ashen face. After long seconds he returned his attention to the Crime Czar. Freddy trembled inwardly.

"All right. So what? That happened years ago!"

"If I'd known ahead of time I'd never have included you."

"Yeah. And who woulda recruited all the thugs you needed?"

"True. But what says I need you . . . now?"

Realization slapped Alfie across the face—hard. He could count the remaining seconds of his life on one hand unless he took action.

"You won't pull it off without me."

"Don't flatter yourself. Admit it. You sold us out!"

"No way Al. Honest. There's no profit in it."

"Then how'd they find out?!" erupted the Crime Czar, pounding a gloved fist on the table. His eyes glowering hotly behind the mask.

"I don't know, I told you! All I know is it wasn't me! And if I did, why in Hell would I come here and tell you all this?"

"To cover the fact you're the one sold us out."

"Oh get real," said Alfie, the color draining from his face down his neck.

"What'd you do? Try to make yourself a better deal than I made you?"

"That's crazy. And so are you if you think that!" shot back Alfie, losing the last of what good sense he owned.

"Crazy am I!" raged the Crime Czar, nearly throwing a tantrum. "Maybe I am for keeping you around."

Alfie flinched when he caught the incensed, maniacal glare in the Crime Czar's eyes; instantly knowing he'd said too much.

"No Al! Wait! I didn't mean that!"

"I told you not to call me that!" roared the Crime Czar, his eyes flashing with insane rage. "I've had enough of your filthy lies!"

All the Crime Czar could see was the intricate web he'd woven over the last year suddenly fraying and unraveling at his feet. His great dream of conquest and power denied him by the traitorous Judas in front of him. Here's when the last remnants of his brittle sanity crumbled like the Philistines temple before the mighty arms of Samson.

Bereft of all restraint, the Crime Czar's hand flashed for his gun in the desk drawer.

"You're a DEAD MAN Tulio!"

Simultaneously, Alfie's own hand leaped inside his coat for his .357.

"NO AL! DON'T DO IT!"

BLAM! BLAM! BLAM!

In the last seconds of his life, he stood transfixed. Three .45 caliber, copper jacketed, hollow point slugs ripped their way through his torso. Two irreparably shredded his lungs. The third ground his left ventricle into so much hamburger, all before erupting on the far wall of his rib cage.

Body fluids draining rapidly into his lungs and chest cavity, oozing quickly from the entry points, he turned slowly on stuttering legs that were rapidly turning to jelly, to face his executioner.

The smoking, Sig-Sauer, still in Freddy's trembling hand. Freddy, who had stood silently by, watching the drama unfold, had been its terminator.

Bloody spittle dribbled from the corners of his trembling lips, running quickly down his chin and neck; collecting in a growing crimson stain along the top of his starched, powder blue collar. His arms dropped, hanging limply at his sides. His weapon slipped from his feeble grasp, clattering at his feet on the wooden floor, useless. Gaping hollow eyes, full of surprise and fear, burned into Freddy's gaze, asking the impossible to mouth question. . . . Why?

There was a last, gurgling, strangling noise from his blood-engorged throat. The last sounds he would make on this planet while he teetered there for that briefest of seconds.

Freddy had had his gun out for several seconds before the fatal gunshots. Up until he pulled the trigger, he had no idea who was going to be the target. Come what may, he'd made his choice.

Alfie was dead before he hit the floor.

Fortunately for Freddy, if also fatal to Alfie, he hadn't the opportunity to reveal that Mindforce knew of Freddy as well.

Truly. There can be no honor among thieves. Not when the lust for money and power can erase the bond of loyalty to a friend.

Would Freddy be alive now had Alfie told his boss that Mindforce knew of Freddy's involvement? Would Alfie not be dead? Would they be lying in their own fluids on the floor? Or, would they have both turned on the Crime Czar and slain him? A moot point now.

Finally finding his voice, Freddy asked apprehensively, "Whata we do now?"

"Take his filthy carcass out through the emergency tunnel." His words bitter. "At the end of the tunnel you'll find my boat. Weight him down and dump him in the river where he won't be found."

"All right. But what are we going to do about Mr. Big and the cops?"

"Since they all know my plans and the wager I had with the Syndicate, all bets are off. Mr. Big and anyone with him are gonna keep Alfie company at the bottom of the river. They're all dead! They just don't know it yet."

Freddy knelt next to the body, retrieved the .357 and stuffed it in his belt, with nary a glimmer of remorse for an old friend.

"What about Mindforce? No bullets are gonna stop him."

"Don't worry about him. I've got a carload of dynamite in a

warehouse down the street. When I set it off with him in it no way he comes out alive."

"How you gonna get 'im to show up?"

"He wants me so bad we'll let him know where to find me. Only we've got to be subtle about it. If he smells a rat, the whole things gonna blow up in our faces. Ha ha ha ha ha ha ha ha ha ha!"

The crime Czar's maniacal laughter trailed off while they took Alfie's body to its watery grave.

If Freddy had any regrets about pulling the trigger he kept them to himself. Probably the smartest thing he'd done today.

4:30 AM. His quarry should be at home at this hour. If he still lived at the address Mindforce was given. A rundown, rotting tenement on the north end of the city; a real slumlord's delight. Eight floors—no elevator. The fire escape barely met the code. Rotting staircases with dangerously loose or nonexistent railings. Litter was everywhere, with the usual assortment of rats. Those of both the two and four-legged kind; a real firetrap.

For their few meager dollars a week, a person gets: four walls, a window, a floor and a ceiling over his head; nothing else. You want a bed and furniture, go buy it?

A common john was at the end of the hall on each floor.

How the powers that be could allow such a structure to house human beings was beyond him. For the right amount of money, however, some officials could be persuaded to go blind. The tenants weren't about to complain if the price was right and no questions were asked.

He entered through the front door. Of modest dimensions, the entry hall was filled to capacity with the derelicts of society; sleeping anywhere they could find space. The foul stench of the pickled liver society assaulted his senses; each holding on to their drained liquor bottles. The view sickened him along with the memory of his own downfall. Had he really looked like them those few short weeks ago?

Not wishing to run the gauntlet of boozed up, passed out bodies, he simply floated over them up the stairwell.

He came to a landing in front of 6C.

One good kick and the door was open. Leroy, who was asleep on a cot under the window, instinctively plunged his hand under his pillow for his weapon. Faster than Leroy's sleepy brain could pull the trigger Mindforce gestured and the .45 flew from Leroy's hand to his.

Leroy scrambled for the window and the supposed safety of the fire escape beyond. Mindforce had him by the belt before he scarcely had his shoulders out. Flinging him back on the cot, Leroy cowered with his hands across his face.

"Don't kill me man! Don't kill me! Please?"

"No chance. . . . That is, if you cooperate like a good little boy."

Realizing who his assailant was and that he was in no immediate danger, his attitude changed to one more brusque.

"What'sa matter wit chu man? Comin' in here an' disturbin' a honest man's sleep."

"Honest? That'll be the day. You're as phony as a three dollar bill."

He removed the clip from the pistol, ejected the last shell from the chamber then tossed the empty gun into Leroy's lap.

"You should be more careful with your toys. Someone might get the impression that you're unfriendly."

"At least I ain't gettin' ripped up inna papers."

"You can't believe all you read at the checkout counter."

"Now. The press don't lie. Do dey?"

"They gotta sell fish wrap somehow."

He was beginning to piss Mindforce off. If he didn't need whatever Leroy knew, He'd just as soon wring his scrawny chicken neck.

"So, whata ya want me for now?"

"Answers."

"I tol' ya before. I don' know nothin' 'bout nobody!"

"You know a hell of a lot more than you should! And you're going to tell me all about it!"

"Oh yeah. Like what?"

"Like how you knew Tulio worked for the Crime Czar and both Mr. Big and the police don't."

Even in the gloom he could see Leroy's face turn ashen.

"I don' know what you're talkin' about."

"That's a DAMN lie! What are you mixed up in that you'd be afraid someone would kill you?"

NOTHIN'! Nothin' at all!" he said fidgeting across the cot. By now they were making enough commotion to awaken the entire floor, above and below. True to their nature, not one of the cowardly types that infested the stinking rat hole ever bothered to investigate. They turned their backs, pulling their heads back into their stinking little burrows. As long as they were left alone they didn't care.

"Look pal! We can do this the easy way or—"

"I AIN'T talking!"

" . . . the hard way. Okay. It's your choice. Get out on the fire escape. NOW!"

"What! . . . No," he said, throwing his hands up in protest.

"You wanna go under your own power or shall I help you?"

He grabbed the shoulder of Leroy's T-shirt and pushed him firmly toward the window.

"You can't do this!"

"I'm doing it anyway," he said, pushing harder.

"You ain't no cop."

"A pity for you I'm not. A cop couldn't get away with this."

"I know the Captain."

"So, if you survive you can sign a complaint."

The substandard ironwork swayed, and groaned its displeasure when they stood upon it. Mindforce was sure the whole thing was headed for the alley if anyone else should try to step out on it.

"I've got a lawyer. There's laws against this."

"Sue me."

Leroy's foggy breath came in rapid spurts while he stood shivering in the cold. The ironwork shivered in tune.

"So? Ya got me out here. Now what?"

"Tell me what I want to know."

"An' if I don't?"

Mindforce grabbed Leroy, turned him upside down by the ankle, climbed up on the rickety iron railing and held him out at arms length over the alley.

"If you don't, I watch you do a mean swan dive to the bricks."

"No! You can't do this!" shouted Leroy, arms flailing about.

"Don't thrash about so much, Leroy. We're six floors up. If I lose my grip your head's gonna look like a squashed cantaloupe after you hit the street. Either that or you're gonna bring down all this rotting iron. With the same result I might add."

Only a small part of him hated doing this. Most of him couldn't care less. If he didn't make him fear for his life now he wouldn't be able to make him overcome his fear of whoever might want to do him in later.

"Put me down or I'll never tell you nothin'!"

"Tell me now," he said, shaking Leroy's ankle, "or I let go."

Discretion being the better part of valor, Leroy decided to save his ass and talk.

"Okay. Okay, man! Whata-ya want to know?"

"That's more like it. . . . How come you know Tulio works for the Crime Czar?"

"I-I know someone who works for him," he screeched out.

"Who?"

"F-Freddy. Freddy L-Lester."

"How do you know Lester?"

"Me . . . me an' him grew up together . . . in St. Louis. We got into some trouble w-with the law there. . . . and we decided to split up."

"So, what are you two doing here?"

"W-We split up, like I said. I g-got away b-but Freddy, he got caught an' did time. We just ran into each other by accident last year."

What's his connection to the Crime Czar?"

"I don' know nothin' about that!"

The liar. He was hiding something. He'd come clean or Mindforce just might let him bounce.

"You're a damn lousy liar, Leroy! You wouldn't want me to lose my grip. Would you?" He shook Leroy's ankle again.

"NO! NO! Don't drop me!" he squealed. I'll talk! I'll talk!"

"Good boy. Continue."

'F-Freddy tol' me he had this gig, see, that was gonna make Tulio an' him rich. They an' this Crime Czar dude was g-gonna take over the rackets an' he asks me if I wanna piece of the action. Honest!"

"How big a piece?"

"I dunno. Honest. I didn't want no part of it. That's too big a scam for my blood. C'mon, let me go!"

"Did he tell you who the Crime Czar is?"

Leroy's tension level shot through the roof. He knew and Mindforce was going to know. Now.

"NO! NO! I can't! They'll kill me if I do!"

"I will if you don't! Now. My arm's getting weary, along with my patience. Talk!"

"Okay, okay!" he said, nearly strangling with fear. "B-But Freddy never tol' me w-who he was!"

"I've had enough of this crap! Say you're prayers sucker."

Mindforce began to uncurl his fingers, one at a time.

"NO! NO! PLEEEASE!" he gasped out, sobbing. "He didn't tell me the man's name. Honest! All I know is the guy is the son of some big shot downtown!"

"Politician, lawyer, businessman; what?"

"I-I dunno. Alls I know is the dudes got money. Lot's of it."

He wasn't lying, and what he said made sense. Mindforce was sure everything to date had to be a smoke screen. The real threat would be through the back door. The man was insidious, and criminally insane for sure.

"Does the Crime Czar know about you?"

"No, no," choked Leroy. "If he knew Freddy'd been letting me in on his plans, he'd probably kill us both. I thought you was them when you come bustin' in the door."

"Why'd Freddy tell you this?"

He n-never could keep a secret," he blubbered. "He hadda tell someone an' I guess he figured I'd keep my mouth shut. W-We was pals y-know."

To Leroy's relief, Mindforce returned him to the relative safety of the fire escape. Whimpering, he cowered in one corner of the railing.

"One last question."

"Ain't chu got enough from me, man!" he shot back.

"Just one more. Then you can go crawl back under your rock. Where they keeping the hookers stashed?"

"Try the catacombs," he sobbed. "Tha's all I know."

"All right. I'm through with you for now, but don't leave town. You keep your ears open. You hear anything I should know, contact me through the Police Commissioner's office. Remember, Leroy; you can't lie to me. If you do I'll know it. Got it?"

Leroy nodded feebly; left to his own fears. Mindforce would never have dropped him, but Leroy didn't have the nerve to call his bluff. Even now he had a bad taste in his mouth, but what other choice had he? Leroy would never have spilled his guts any other way and he'd be nowhere now.

6 AM saw the first faint glow of morning on the horizon. He wanted at least a couple hours sleep before beginning his search for those hookers.

They'd keep a little while longer; they were safe for now. He'd need a logical plan. The catacombs covered a large area; he'd need all his senses at their best if he were to be successful.

Alfie's body, tied at the ankles to an old engine block, went over the edge of the boat. Sinking swiftly in the icy, early Spring waters, of the Schuylkill River.

The Crime Czar looks on scornfully while Freddy tosses Alfie's .357 into the dark waters after its murdered owner.

"Let that be a lesson to you," says the Crime Czar. "You even get a glimmer of trying to betray me and you'll be joining him."

"I'd never turn on y—"

"Is that what you told Alfie, too?"

Freddy was stumped. He'd not really thought about it. When he pulled the trigger, he wasn't even sure he'd done it till he saw the smoking gun in his hand.

The Crime Czar would only trust him so far. He'd have to stay on his toes from now on.

"Don't bother. Your silence tells me all I need to know."

"Whata we do if someone asks about Alfie?"

"Don't worry. Your secret's safe with me. Just tell anyone who asks that Mr. Big's men got him. Got it?"

Freddy offered a meek nod.

"Now get us out of here. The sun's coming up; I don't want to be spotted by some early morning rower out for some exercise."

While Freddy fired up the engine, the Crime Czar opened his fly to piss over the gunwale where Alfie was dropped.

"That to you, and anyone else who gets in my way from now on."

In the cool, damp morning air, Freddy's throat was suddenly very dry.

* * * *

CHAPTER FOURTEEN

The Catacombs

Jason got his usual three hours sleep and was in the middle of his morning shower, when it struck him. The Crime Czar's next move might be to hijack the Syndicates shipments of illegal drugs into the city. Another means of causing chaos among Mr. Big's troops and cash to the Czar's coffers. They might already have begun for all he knew.

Proving it was another story. No one in the business of selling a controlled substance was about to call the police if he'd been robbed. They had their own means of justice.

Truth is; he couldn't be sure he wanted to stop them if they try. Let ol' Biggy suffer some more. It'll just make him more careless.

Aw. He knew that wasn't the right attitude either. The Crime Czar'd only sell the stuff himself and the junk would still be on the street.

No. These drugs had to be cut off at the source; and the bastards that sell the slop put behind bars.

Still, if he did hear of anything going down, he could let the hijacking take place, then rip off the hijackers. Thus pissing off two birds with one hijack. He'd have to touch base with Jake on this when he saw him later.

Checking in at the office was his first priority. After which he'd begin his search for a thousand hookers held hostage somewhere in the city.

He arrived at the office around ten o'clock. Strangely but not surprising, Sheila was not in yet. The dinner party at her parent's house must have gone on into the wee hours.

He collected the mail piled on the mat below the slot in the door. The phone bill, ads for a half dozen things he'll never need, and a letter from a young man he met last week.

Tommy James wrote to thank Jason for saving him from the Mob and seeing to it that he and his mother wouldn't have to testify.

The letter went on to say that he and Vivian were planning to move out of New York City to some place Rick and his friends could never find them.

Tommy had little to worry about his father. With what the Feds had on him it was unlikely he'd ever bother Tommy or his Mother.

The Mob, on the other hand, was a different matter. There was doubtful any place one could go on this planet they couldn't find you if they really wanted. Though, with the trail Jason left, they'd believe it was a Federal man who'd caused all the trouble, not a ten-year-old boy.

Jason was finishing the letter when his harried secretary burst through the entry door. She couldn't see Jason at his desk and went straight to her station. He quickly went to the doorway.

"You're late. Rough night?"

"Dammit Jason! You startled me," she said, flinching. "I didn't know you were in."

"How was the party?"

"Oh, all right, I guess. I had it out with Albert again after you left. He had no call to talk to you that way."

"My hide's tough."

"He's such a snob. His only enjoyment in life is to look down on everyone. He and Allen are like two peas in a pod. If it weren't for Daddy's money—"

"So, how's your Mother?"

"Oh fine. Really. We sat and had a long talk. That's why I'm so late. We must have talked to well after four."

"She seemed disappointed when I left early."

"She was. But I explained you were working on a missing persons case and had to follow up a hot lead. That seemed to satisfy her."

"And you father?"

"Daddy. Oh, he tried to talk me into coming home, but I told him I had to live my life; not his."

"There are some definite advantages to living at home."

"Only money!" She paused for a moment, then went on. "Y-know, Mother was right."

"How so?"

"She was the one suggested I get a job and learn to take care of myself. I've never felt so good since I've been out on my own. Mother told me I'd feel this way, and she was right. So, did you learn anything last night?"

"More than I expected. It turns out Miss Charlotte Greenleaf is a hooker."

"Get out."

"It's true. I also found out that several of the hookers in the city have been disappearing from the streets."

"Have you found out why?"

"Only that they're not doing it of their own free will," was all he could safely tell her. "Someone's pulling them off the streets and it's not the police."

"Do you think they got Charlotte?"

"Seems so. She obviously didn't come home because she couldn't."

"What about her father?"

He caught her drift.

"I'll find and bring her home if I can. It'll be up to her to tell her father where she's been and why. It's not my place."

"She sounded like such a nice girl when I spoke to her father. Why do you think she got mixed up in prostitution?"

He couldn't think of a good reason why anyone would risk life and health for that business then nor two hours later when he prepared to enter the catacombs.

There was no telling what action he might run into down there. So he was going in as Mindforce. Surely there'd be guards and if there were trouble it wouldn't do for Jason to be seen doing things no ordinary man could.

He'd been shot at a few times now. Though he came away unharmed, it still hurt like hell. He shuddered at going into a den of crooks with Lord knows what weapons, facing a hail of hot lead if things go badly. He had a screwy idea that might not work. His experiment called for a secluded area.

In the short time he'd had these powers he'd discovered most of them by accident. Now, he was about to see if he could make one happen on purpose.

Approaching the area he'd chosen for his experiment he felt the area where the slugs had once bounced off his chest. The memories were still quite vivid. Though sore and somewhat bruised, he was okay. Something needed to be done about that.

He entered an abandoned building in the suburb of Chester, which once held an old machine shop. The walls were thick and heavy, encrusted with decades of oil, dust and metal shavings, as were the floors. The humid air, laden with dust, was permeated with petroleum and solvent odors. The gloom meant nothing to his enhanced vision. He knew how a cat must feel while it negotiates the dark night. Anything he did or any sound he made wouldn't be noticed by anyone.

He was hoping there might be an old vise left behind still attached to a bench. After a short search he found his objective in a corner. A large, sturdy old vise. Must have weighed two hundred fifty pounds. Little wonder why some looter never took it.

From behind his back, tucked in his belt, he pulled his .45 automatic, then clamped the butt between the jaws of the vise.

He believed it might be possible to use his levitation power to create a field around himself that just might be strong enough to repel bullets or other objects hurled his way. In his new vocation one couldn't watch all sides at once.

He could, in all likelihood, learn to withstand a gunshot or two, but suppose some joker comes at him with a Tommy gun or a portable rocket launcher, or something of that order. That was more pain than he wished to deal with.

He imagined the bewildered look on someone's face if he handed him his gun and asked them to shoot him. He might look strange to people in this costume now but a stunt like that and they'd be convinced he was straightjacket material. That's why the vise.

Centering the gun in the vise he hooked up a cord he'd found to the trigger. From there he threaded the cord around to a spot where he might stand before the muzzle and discharge the gun by remote control.

Now, how to set up the field? He'd have to practice that several times before he firing the gun.

Visualizing a barrier around himself appeared to be the likely way to go. Taking a deep breath he tried to employ the concept. Trouble was, after a several seconds of concentrating he didn't feel any different nor could he see any field around him. Was it there or was he wasting his time?

The answer came when he lowered his gaze to his feet. On the floor the puddle of oily water he stood in had receded to about two inches from his feet and remained there. Releasing his concentration the tide slowly rolled in to shore.

Again he concentrated; again the water receded. Several times he practiced this until the field engaged with a mere reflex.

Confident, he stood before the gun. His only doubt, the muzzle velocity of a .45 caliber slug was a hell of a lot more than a puddle of water. Would the field be strong enough to withstand the impact? There was but one way to find out.

Cocking the gun, he made sure the safety was off. He stood about fifteen feet in front of the muzzle. Picking up the remote cord he took a deep breath and swallowed hard, concentrating.

"Well. Here goes nothing."

The pistol roared while the muzzle flash threw deep shadows against the near wall. Flinching slightly, Mindforce stiffened in his stance. Tensed muscles anticipating the stinging impact, but there was no need; the slug never reached his chest. It slowed to within two inches of his chest, stopped completely, then fell harmlessly to the concrete floor. Elated at his success he tugged on the remote cord repeatedly, emptying the clip, all with the same result.

Never again would he worry about bullets stinging his flesh as long as he set up the field before going into battle.

A brief stop at the Commissioner's Office to let him know what he scared out of Leroy, before going to the Catacombs.

The FBI alerted, they deployed agents to help with surveillance. There were only a handful of officers that Mindforce knew personally that he could trust, and they were working with the Feds.

When asked, the agents knew of no drug deals going down but would keep him posted.

The DA's office geared up for the research work they needed. Stealth was the key. They didn't want to alert any mole that might be in the loop. The DA had a lunch date with Judge Mercer and would keep them posted.

The *Catacombs* are a network of unused tunnels beneath the city's surface, out to the suburbs. Once they were the pathways for the old subway/surface cars used by the old transit authority.

With the passing of time and the addition of all the new superhighways, their use rapidly decreased. Stopping altogether when the present Transit Authority bought out the old. According to them, the old lines weren't bringing in enough money to warrant their operation. Surface buses were far less costly to operate for what little ridership existed.

Ten years ago the tunnels were permanently sealed, except for a few locked access doors. After a young child had wandered in and gotten lost the tunnels were condemned as dangerous and unsafe. His corpse was found six months later.

The meandering tunnels were dubbed so from one of the searchers that volunteered to go in there. They've long since been forgotten by the general public. Few in the city's service or the transit authority for that matter, remember their existence.

Apparently, someone has. For, if Leroy was right, those tunnels make a perfect hiding place for all those women. Once in there, no one without a map could hope to find their way out.

You couldn't make enough noise down there through all that concrete and stone to attract anyone's attention.

With plenty of room and little in the way of escape routes, few men would be needed to keep the girls in check. Only a fool would risk sneaking off and becoming hopelessly lost.

Walking down a little used auxiliary subway tunnel, Mindforce spotted one of the sealed entrances to the Catacombs. It was entirely filled with concrete blocks; a barred and padlocked steel door to one side.

The door showed no appearance of ever having been opened since its installation. The perfect place to sneak in unobserved.

He attempted to dispatch his ghost to pop through the wall to reconnoiter, but to his consternation, try as he might, it would not appear. No amount of concentration would make it come forth.

Could the near fatal brush with oblivion last night have provoked some subconscious defense mechanism to refuse to allow the separation of body and soul? Frustrated, he still had other powers at his command. There'd be time enough later to sort it all out.

Standing in the gloom he directed his enhanced hearing to the chamber beyond the block wall.

Sounds of dripping water and rodents scurrying about their daily existence revealed themselves, but nary a human heartbeat anywhere.

No one in the interior would be alerted to his twisting off the encrusted padlock or removing the iron cross bar. Rusted hinges balked at his insistence, nevertheless, giving way to his increased strength; protesting with a screech like a cat with a trod on tail.

The foul, acrid stench of brackish water and rotting flesh of numerous dead rats and their excrement, assailed his senses first.

The filth and accumulation of years of debris, that managed to find itself here, lay piled a foot high in the doorway and several feet around.

Never was he more grateful for his power of flight. At least he wouldn't have to go mucking around through this slop and ooze to get to the other side.

Drifting above the slimy mess he pulled the door shut behind him. Several feet down the tunnel he landed in a dry area.

Since leaving the Commissioner's office he'd been reaching out with his *Esper* power in hopes of latching onto Charlotte's aura to no avail. Receiving zilch, he wasn't drawn to any special place.

Could she be dead? He hoped that wasn't the reason he couldn't tune in to her.

Searching the many miles of multiple tunnels by normal methods could take weeks. He wasn't normal. Determined; he was going to find those women—today!

At this point, his only recourse was to fly along the tunnels, reaching out ahead with his enhanced hearing and night vision. Wherever they were he should sense them long before they were aware of him.

Roughly fifty miles of tunnel branched off in all directions. With his speed he discarded most of it within an hour.

Zeroing in on the last sections of the tunnel he became more cautious with every bend of the tunnel. It wouldn't do to pop around some corner smack into the face of a hood on guard. Lord only knew what chaos would result. One nervous Nellie could start a shooting spree that'd leave several people dead or wounded.

Every fruitless mile increased his apprehension. Was Leroy wrong? He'd checked what he felt were the most likely places and come up empty.

He assumed they'd be using some outlying area. Possibly where the old depots were. These had large storage areas for tools and supplies used by work crews assigned to them. Power lines and lavatory needs were easily accessed.

All that was left were the downtown areas.

His *Esper* sense proved Leroy was telling the truth, but that doesn't mean he was right. He wouldn't know until he'd checked every foot of the place, and that was rapidly running out.

Despair ran high now. He was believing he was on a fool's errand when the faint sounds of human heartbeats and muffled murmuring triggered his enhanced hearing.

They were here! Added adrenaline set his heart pumping rapidly, forcing him to pause to restrain himself and think of a plan of attack. This required stealth not flamboyance.

He needed to locate every guard to find out exactly how many were on duty. Each had to be neutralized without alerting the others. Before that the women had to be located to see that no harm could come to them. He was determined there would be no casualties. This would not be another Carmen.

Again he attempted to dispatch his ghost but it was still down for the count. Oh well. That wasn't the only trick up his sleeve.

He'd been able to sneak through the underbrush in Southeast Asia beneath the noses of trained jungle fighters searching for POWs and MIAs. These guys were a walk in the park.

The ceilings of the tunnel were over fifteen feet high and quite gloomy. If he hugged them closely he could float over their heads without being spotted.

The lights they'd set up were a hundred yards down the tunnel. Listening, he did not hear the sound of a generator. They must be hooked into the main grid somehow.

Floating aloft, he passed over two men on watch at this end of the tunnel. One lied through his teeth about a female conquest he'd had over the weekend. They didn't realize they'd just been boarded.

Ahead, two men stood guard about fifty yards away on the other side of the old station platform.

On the platform sat four at a rigged up table playing cards. Three shot craps at the far end of the station.

Across the tunnel from the platform stood an iron fence from the floor to within two feet of the ceiling. Eight feet behind the fence an open door led behind a stone wall to what must be a tool and supply room. Tuning in he heard many women in idle chatter. They were here all right. If all of them were here this job could be done in record time.

While studying the fenced area one more guard came from inside the gate, taking a position in front of the fence. Twelve guards in all. Four had Uzis, the rest carried semiautomatic handguns. No other weapons were in sight.

The plan required getting into the room that held the women. He had to know if all of them were here and if they were okay. The guard on duty made it more difficult.

A diversion was called for, one that wouldn't arouse the guard's suspicions. Dousing the lights would do it.

Tracing the wiring from the lights led him to the fuse box. It was over forty feet away. Effectively out of his levitation range. To do what he had in mind required getting closer. With a little luck, as long as no one looked up, he was home free.

Once in range of the box he reached out with his levitating power. He'd open the box and loosen the main fuses enough to make them arc. The accompanying heat would soon cause them to burn out. The hitch in the plan being, one of the guards might see the door open.

This required a certain amount of finesse on his part. To open the door slowly without slamming it back on the brick wall.

The first attempt caused the door of the box to wiggle only slightly. A little more force and it popped off its stops. The click of the door unlatching with the subsequent squeak of rusted hinges was audible only to Mindforce. The nearest guards made so much noise at their crap game they had no idea they were in deep shit.

Once the lights winked out he quickly closed the fuse box.

Then swiftly sailed over the fence, careful not to cause a draft in his wake.

Entering the makeshift dormitory he listened while the guards were shouting at one another, wanting to know what happened.

One yelled. "It's gotta be the fuse box. Hold your damn water while I check it out."

While some played their flashlights around the tunnel the guard at the fence never left his post. Never aware of the swift, silent presence of Mindforce.

His only concern was, when the lights came back on, the women spotting him might make such a commotion it would alert the guards. He had a minute at best.

Taking a position on the high ceiling he checked out the place. The girls, essentially blind in the darkness, unlike himself, froze in place.

The large room, some seventy-five feet by a hundred, twenty, studded with concrete support columns held up massive steel beams, which supported the infrastructure above. Obviously an underground storage depot long ago; an easy access to parts and tools. It had the look of a locker room for the old Transit Authority employees. The filing cabinets along the far wall suggested it was used for records storage as well.

Cramped was an understatement with all these women packed in there. Many had cots. Most didn't. Even without his enhanced sense of smell he would have known these women hadn't bathed in some time. The conditions, as bad as concentration camps, could serve no purpose 'cept to break the girls will. The Crime Czar must really hate women . . . the prick!

The alcove, to the right of the doorway at the end of the row of lockers, must lead to the lavatory. Of course, the sign above the entrance helped.

Flying to the alcove he grabbed the nearest girl, covered her mouth and carried her into the lavatory.

Struggling and kicking like a wildcat she clawed at his hand in an effort to free her mouth.

"Stop struggling," Mindforce whispered in her ear. "I'm not here to hurt you. I've come to rescue all of you."

Muttering muffled epithets, she tried to bite his hand. Mindforce didn't catch it all but he got the idea.

"Now look!" he said while she struggled harder. "This is Mindforce."

His name brought about a calming effect. Reaching over her head she slowly felt his hood then down to his collar and cape.

Relaxing his grip on her mouth, he stood ready to clamp his hand back on should he sense her wanting to scream. She turned to face him in the gloom.

"I brought you in here because the lights will be on again soon and I don't want to start a commotion that'll attract the guards."

"Is that really you, Mindforce?"

"In the flesh."

"This better not be some cheap trick."

"It's no trick," he said when the lights snapped on.

"It really is you!" He caught the skepticism in her voice. "Look. I want to trust you but I gotta have some proof you're really who you say you are."

A smart cookie, but if the roles were reversed, he'd say the same.

"Watch," he said while levitating off the floor, turning to stand on the ceiling. "Satisfied?"

"You're the real McCoy all right," she sighed. "How'd you get past the guards?"

"Wasn't hard. These guys think nobody knows they're here. I killed the lights and floated past them. Now. What's your name, hon?"

"Vicky."

"Okay, Vicky. Here's what I need you to do. Someone's apt to miss you shortly. Go out and bring back a half dozen girls you can trust. We've plans to make."

Within five minutes Vicky returned with her friends. Taking precautions, Mindforce was nowhere in sight.

"Mindforce? It's Vicky," she whispered. Where are you?"

"Up here. On the ceiling, sweetheart," he said while returning to the floor. "I just wanted to make sure it was you."

"Thank God! I thought I was going whacko for a second."

The girls milled around, wanting to touch him. Each wanting to make certain for herself that he was real and not a ghost while Vicky introduced them.

"This is Diane . . . Ruth . . . Violet . . . Mary . . . Phyliss and Joanne." Each girl nodding when her name was spoken.

"Okay ladies, here's how it is. But first, one of you stand by the door and warn me if anyone wants to come in."

Diane, being closest, took a position by the door.

"What I need to know is, are all the girls that were kidnapped, here?"

"We're all here," said Violet. "All 986 of us. Boy are we here. Throw in a quart of oil and we can go as a can of sardines."

Someone still had a sense of humor. Even if it did lean toward the sarcastic.

"Right. O . . . kay. Is there a Charlotte Greenleaf among you? I believe you know her as, Charly."

"Yeah. She's here," said Joanne. "What's your interest in her?"

"A detective friend of mine was hired by her father to find her after she went missing."

"That's right," said Mary. "Her old man don't know she was hookin' to pay her tuition."

"*Tuition?*"

"What's so strange about that?" said Mary. "It's the only way she could raise the money the State College wants. She told her father she got a scholarship is all."

"Hey. I'm not here to judge. I just want to know if she's all right."

"She was fine when they brought her in," said Ruth. "but she sorta freaked out on us."

"Look! She's got this thing about being underground, y-know," said Phyliss. "She and I have been friends for some time. Anyways, after awhile she couldn't stand being down here and started freakin' out; screaming and banging on the cage. She sleeps most o' the time now 'cause they keep her drugged."

"I see. What about meals?"

"They don't keep her doped up all the time," said Phyliss. She wakes up on her own and they leave her be till she freaks out again."

That's why he couldn't tune in on her with his *Esper* sense. Being drugged and unconscious she had little brain activity for him to tune in to.

"Is she all right now?"

"She's fine. Just sleeping."

"Okay. Now, how often do they change the guards?"

"Every three days," said Mary. "These guys just came in this morning with the new food supply."

"I didn't see any means of communication when I scouted this place earlier. Cell phones won't work down here, so I assume these guys are cut off from the rest of the world till one of them goes up to the surface to a phone or the next crew comes in."

"That's about it," said Joanne.

"Then it's probably safe to bet no one will check on these guys till Friday."

"So! How do we get out of here?" said Ruth.

"Tell me. Is there anyone out there among you who's liable to spill the beans on what we're doing?"

"Well. There's Marcie and Carol," said Vicky. "They've been doing special favors for the guys to get more privileges. If you know what I mean."

"I'm sure he's been around," said Mary. "And don't forget Gerry. She's been sucking up to the guy at the fence since he came in this morning."

"Good. When we're ready you'll have to find some way to get them in here without attracting too much attention. Much as I hate to do it, we're going to have to tie them up and gag them. Now. What else can you tell me?"

"Well, at meal time they put everything inside the fence," said Phyliss. Then they lock it before we're allowed to collect the food."

"Yeah! And that fence is electrified at night when they want to catch some shuteye," said Mary. "Just in case one of us is stupid enough to try to find her way out of here."

"They brought us in blindfolded, a few at a time," said Vicky. "We don't even know where we are."

"By my reckoning, we're about five blocks from City Hall."

"No shit!" said Ruth. "Right under the cop's noses. I tolja them pigs couldn't find the armhole in their shirts."

"Oh stuff it will ya!" said Phyliss."

"Look. Mindforce," said Vicky. "I don't know what you have in mind but we're all agreed we want to be a part of it."

"Could be dangerous. Someone could get killed."

"We don't care!" said Vicky while the others nodded. "We just want to get our mitts on those bastards for keepin' us in this toilet and treating us like shit!"

To attempt to dissuade them would be fruitless. They saw an opportunity to get even and weren't about to be denied. With some reluctance, Mindforce agreed to scrap his original plan, bowing to their wishes. To be sure he would have had a full-scale riot on his hands if he hadn't.

"All right. You're in. . . . Tell me. Have there been many fights among the girls?"

"Have they ever," said Ruth. After all this time down here it doesn't take much to set some of them off."

"What do the guards do about it?"

"Usually nothing," said Vicky. "They just let the girls fight until they wear themselves out."

"But these guys just came in this morning," said Joanne. "It's the first time for most of them down here. No one wants the job, really."

"So it's safe to say if some of you started a fight a few of them might come in to check it out."

"And when they come in we jump them. Right," said Ruth.

"Right. Now. Go out and collect Marcie, Carol and Gerry. Then I want you girls to inform everyone they're about to be rescued . . . and keep it down, for God's sake."

Twenty-five minutes later everyone was informed and the preparations made.

Pressing himself against the ceiling, the girls went into their act.

When the screams and sounds of battle drifted out into the tunnel, Mindforce heard the guard at the fence call out to one of the others. "Hey! Sounds like a catfight in there! Whata ya wanna do?"

"Let 'em fight. They'll soon stop."

"Sounds like they're killing each other."

"Don't worry about it."

They weren't getting the desired response, which was Vicky's cue to go into her prearranged routine. She ran out to the fence screaming hysterically, yanking on the fence.

"HELP! Ruth and Violet found some knives! MY GOD! They're slicing up anyone trying to get near them!"

"What the Hell?!" said the confused guard.

"DAMMIT! Get in here! I think Diane and Mary are already dead!"

That had the desired effect.

"Joe! Frank! Eddie! Go with Buddy and see what's going on!" said the leader. "I'll juice the fence once you're inside."

The boys were confronted with a circle of women trying to get at Ruth and Violet. Pushing the girls aside, they made their way in. Diane and Mary lay deathly still on the concrete floor. Covered with blood made from left over ketchup, it was convincing just long enough.

Mindforce dropped from the ceiling behind the two men with the Uzis. The other two were aware of him for only a second before he sent them to la la land along with their partners.

While motioning for the girls to keep up the racket, Mindforce picked up an Uzi in each hand after tossing the handguns to Diane and Ruth. They then opened up on a stack of mattress piled up in the corner.

All Hell broke loose before the stunned guards when several of the girls ran out to the fenced off area. Screaming uncontrollably, they screeched that the guards had lost it and were killing everyone.

Enhanced hearing told Mindforce the leader ordered someone named Phil to go call for help and the rest of them to follow him inside.

"What the hell's the matter with them?! They lost their fucking minds?"

Cutting off the electric fence, they charged in.

The first three who entered were taken out almost as one before they were even aware of their danger. By this time the girls were in such a frenzy they disarmed and clobbered the next two on their own.

The last two, seeing what they were up against, lost their courage in a heartbeat. Turning tail, they took the time to squeeze off a few shots. Thanks to Mindforce's force field the slugs fell harmlessly to the floor.

The girls shoved one of them toward Mindforce who quickly disarmed him then handed the hood to the girls crowding behind him. They gleefully beat his brains out.

The last one panicked. In desperation he grabbed Vicky about the throat from behind. Holding his automatic weapon at her head, all fell silent.

"I'm takin' this broad an' gettin' outta here! You follow me an' I blow her fuckin' brains all over the tunnel!"

The slime ball had no idea who he was up against was not your average law enforcer.

The goon's hand trembled slightly while he held the gun to Vicky's temple, while he knotted his other hand in her hair. His eyes gaping in total fear they darted rapidly while the goon tried to keep his eyes on everyone.

Against the backdrop of the girls snarling, Mindforce held

wide his arms in the narrow doorway to hold them back. Then turned his full attention to the trembling hood.

The hood's mouth curled in a harsh grimace. The girls fell suddenly silent. Against all the hood's resistance, deliberately slow, Mindforce used his levitation power to turn the gun barrel away from her and straight into the goon's face. Try as he might he couldn't move the gun one fraction of an inch.

"Go ahead asshole!" said Mindforce. "Pull the Fucking trigger now! See if I care!"

Startled out of his socks, the hood released the weapon. It fell sideways to Mindforce's hand.

The girls pounced on him en masse, beating him to a bloody pulp. Like as not, would have killed him too had not Mindforce intervened.

"You hang on to these guys. I gotta find the one that got away."

Four blocks down the tunnel he caught up with Phil. Running like his tail was on fire.

Phil stooped just short of slamming into Mindforce who had landed in the gloom ahead of him. Eyes bulging, Phil drew his pistol from his holster only to have it whisked from his grasp by Mindforce's left hand. Grabbed by the collar with the other hand, Phil found himself flipped around and bobbed like a marionette in less than a heartbeat.

"Uh uh. Not today Phil. It wouldn't have worked anyway. Let's go back to see your friends. Though I doubt they'll see you through all those swollen black eyes."

2:30 PM: Up into the warm afternoon sun, Mindforce led his rag tag caravan. Consisting of twelve hoods shackled together with pieces of old iron railing bent into shape. Plus 986 scruffy, sweaty, dirty but grateful ladies of the evening.

He'd found and kicked open another access door about a hundred yards from where the girls were held captive. The door adjoined a downtown subway station platform, from which he took the girls up the stairs to the street.

Passers by gaped at the spectacle and were told to go get a life by several while the girls paraded up the stairs. Soon, the increasing crowd drew the attention of a few passing patrol cars.

The twelve hoods were taken into custody. Vicky, Diane and a few of the girls went downtown to give their statements. The rest wanted to go home to get cleaned up and would return to sign a complaint.

Charlotte had come out of her stupor and with slight help, managed to walk out under her own power.

Being unnoticed wasn't easy but Mindforce managed to slip away to change so he could come back to retrieve Charlotte.

After she'd come to down there, Mindforce told her he'd had the help of a detective friend in finding them. He told her Jason Parks would be waiting for her on the surface to take her home.

Being only six blocks from Jason's parking garage he opted to walk the short distance to his car and to let her shake out the cobwebs. While walking she explained that she was enrolled at the local college, taking Architecture and Business Administration. Her father made an honest living but after her mother died most of her parent's savings went to pay the bills. There wasn't anything left to pay for college.

Working at menial jobs bought the essentials but at that rate she'd never have anything for tuition. After years of beating her head against the wall, getting nowhere, she gave up her dream. That's when fate stepped in, took a hand and reshuffled the deck.

She'd gone into Chicky's one evening to drown her sorrows. Some John mistook her for one of the usual hookers who hung out there.

She informed him she wasn't for sale and to get lost. Offering her fifty bucks only got him a succinct refusal. When he upped the ante to a hundred she was struck dumb. His reasoning being she was new around here and most likely unused . . . and he wanted her.

Charlotte saw a golden opportunity. She'd have to mortgage her self-esteem but she kept telling herself it was for a good cause.

That the ends justified the means . . . Somehow. Her initial shyness and tentativeness turned the Johns on even more, and they looked for her almost exclusively. Too soon it was business as usual for her; just another night at the flesh factory.

Unfortunately, there were other considerations she hadn't allowed herself to foresee. With all her success and the lack there of from the other hookers, it didn't take long for the pimps to get around to her. If she wanted to work their streets she had to pay their dues.

Compliance being less painful and cheaper than plastic surgeons, she went along with them.

Soon she had the funds needed to start her classes. Once she had her degree it was good-bye hustling Johns.

She took the easy out, telling her father she'd received a scholarship. Since she had classes during the day she said she had a night job to keep herself in clothes and other needs.

Hustling Johns till four or five in the morning left her a few hours for sleep before her first class at 11 AM.

Now she didn't know what to do. She was too scared to work the streets again, but if she didn't, her pimp would surely cut her face for quitting.

"Who's your pimp?" said Jason.

She hesitated, then didn't care. "Silky Malone."

"Ah, yes."

"You know him?"

"Only by reputation. He's a real slick dude thinks he's one bad assed ladies man."

"That's him."

"He's a legend in his own mind." That brought a grin to her glum expression. "Don't concern yourself with him."

"What can you do? He's got a lot of tough friends."

"I've got tougher friends. He won't bother you again."

The reunion with her father was tear filled. Jason stood by quietly while she related the whole sordid affair to her confused, grateful father. Surprised, he understood; he didn't care what she'd done. She was home now and he was willing to forgive and forget.

For both their sakes, Jason hoped those feelings would never wear off. They were talking to each other now. Really talking. Probably for the first time in their lives.

Jason left quietly so they might be alone to get to know each other again.

Jason felt as if a huge weight had been lifted off him. With the safe return of Charlotte to her father the ghost of Carmen was laid to rest; finally. He'd have to make a point to visit Carmen's brother once this was over to see if there wasn't a way to settle their differences.

At his car he decided the sooner he got Silky off Charlotte's back the better it would be.

Silky owned a part interest in an up and coming heavyweight boxer. This time of day he usually sat in the gym watching his boy train.

Parking in the lot behind the gym, Jason looked for a place to change. The alley looked deserted.

Entering the gym from the front, Mindforce ignored everyone's gawking and mumbling. The training room was on the second floor. He walked slowly up the stairs.

Among a row of folding metal chairs by the ring sat the object of his search watching two would bes pretending to box.

Amazed eyes were glued on him while he walked up next to the slickly attired dude with the obligatory preponderance of jewelry.

"Silky Malone?"

"Who wants to know?" he said without looking up.

"Stand up when I'm talking to you, PUNK!" said Mindforce, grabbing Silky's lapels, yanking him to a standing position.

A couple of troglodytes in business suits, standing nearby, reached inside their coats for their courage.

"Get your fucking hands off me!"

"Tell 'em to shoot if they like. The ricochet will only kill you.

Go ahead. Tell 'em to shoot!" He shook the rotten purveyor of female flesh by the collar then said softly. "I dare you."

His bravado unimpressing, Silky mulled it over while staring unwavering into where Mindforce's eyes were behind the lenses.

"Put away the heat boys. Can'tcha see? We're jus' talkin' business."

Silky gave a toothy smile while his goons put away their play toys and stood quietly by.

"Now that's what I like to see. A couple of well behaved Neanderthals you got there Silky. Train 'em yourself?"

Trading dumb looks the two goons likely couldn't understand words of more than one syllable.

"What can I do for you?" said Silky, faking a confident exterior for his audience.

"You got a hooker in your stable known as Charly."

"Who's got any hookers?" he said, grinning, while his goons looked on amused. "Didn't you know? They was all yanked off the streets by the Crime Czar's men."

"Uh uh. I cut 'em loose this afternoon. I even picked up a dozen of the Czar's men as a bonus."

"That's good to hear. You're a fine upstandin' citizen," he said through a toothy grin. "What's it got to do with me?"

"Charly's decided to retire from the business. And you're going to leave her and her family alone."

"Heyyyy! No can do, pal. She's a good little filly; in demand a lot. I don't let that kind out of my control."

"I said. *YOU* and your degenerate people will leave her alone. PAL!" Mindforce said while shaking Silky forcefully.

"And if I don't?"

"I was hoping you'd say that. . . . If you don't . . . you'll have to answer to me."

"Shoot. I been threatened before," he said, feigning indifference. "An' I'm still here."

"Ain't no threat. It's a promise. . . . But I see you need some convincing."

Taking both of Silky's lapels in his right hand, Mindforce lifted him off the floor. Just far enough so that the tips of his toes just kissed the floor.

"Watch."

While Silky dangled like a spastic marionette, Mindforce stepped to the left placed his free hand on the top of the steel ring post, then bent it over double like he was twisting soft taffy.

"Remember, SCUM BAG! What ever harm comes to her or any of her family comes to you. If someone cuts her face, yours is gonna look like hamburger. If she should happen to die, you better make funeral arrangements. From here on out you're going to be her guardian angel."

Releasing his grip, he dropped Silky unceremoniously to the floor. He attempted to get up.

"Stay there in the filth where you belong, you bastard."

"You think you're so damn tough!" said Silky while straightening his suit. "You're bluffin'"

"Am I? You better hope she doesn't get so much as a hangnail, or I'll be all over you like flies on shit. Pal!"

Weighing his options, the wheels churned in his brain.

"All right. All right," he said in a hushed voice. "She's retired, with my blessings. Okay?"

"Sure. Oh. And one more thing."

"What?"

"You've skimmed off probably, shall we say, $40,000 from Charly since she's been hooking for you. Now don't you think that would be a nice retirement gift to her college fund, hmmmm?"

"You're askin' an awful lot," he said, smoothing his lapels.

"I'm letting you off easy. . . . The alternatives ain't worth it."

"I ain't got that kind of money." His biggest lie yet.

"Yes you do. And you'll get it to her by the end of the week."

"No way man!" He glared.

Mindforce yanked him from the floor, dropping him hard on the soles of his feet. "By—the—end—of—the—week!" he bit of, poking a sharp finger into his chest, forcing Silky to step back and stumble onto a metal chair. "You don't, I'll find you and take it from you. Through your nose!"

"I'll write her a damn check."

"You'll give her cash; and no queer dough either."

He meant business and Silky was sure of it. His look was of a man caught between a rock and a hard place. Not sure which was the lesser of the two evils.

"All right! You got what you came for," he said, turning in his seat to avoid Mindforce's glare. "Now. Get out," he said, waving an arm toward the door.

This moment was to good not to stretch out Silky's torment a few seconds more. "I'm going. Don't rush me. But since I don't want any damage suits."

He grabbed the bent ring post and with an effortless motion, returned it to its former position.

The sparring partners in the ring, having stopped to watch the little drama unfold stepped back quickly. Not wanting any part of the goings on. They had some brains after all.

"Don't Forget! Cross me and I'll come looking for you. And you don't want to see me when I'm pissed."

He turned his back on the scum with a smug turn and strode out with a haughty step, pausing just long enough to say "Boo," softly to the two Neanderthals.

In the alley he changed swiftly and headed out for his office.

The traffic, both foot and auto, was heavily laden with people trying to get either to or from work. It was nearly 5:00 when Jason strode through the door to his agency.

Sheila shadowed him to his office, giving him his messages after he sat behind his desk.

"Oh. By the way. Mr. Greenleaf called a few minutes ago. He wanted to thank you again for bringing his daughter home. You didn't tell him what he owed you."

"Send him a bill for two days. No expenses."

"Okay. . . . You know. It's been on the radio all afternoon

how Mindforce rescued all those girls from the old subway tunnels and captured those gangsters as well."

Jason got the distinct impression he was about to be asked a rather pointed question. Beating her to it he gave her his prepared answer.

"Yes. It seems we were on the same case and didn't know it. Though I was only looking for Charlotte, Mindforce was out to rescue them all. We ran into each other down there and compared notes."

"But. How'd you find out she was down there?"

"Every good detective has a few informants."

"Who?"

"I can't say. Revealing your sources tends to make them dry up on you."

That answer satisfied her for the moment while she slowly nodded her head in agreement.

While she returned to her desk Jason swiveled in his chair, placed his feet on the windowsill and gazed out at the encroaching twilight. He reflected on the days event.

He'd managed to stymie the Crime Czar's latest plans. Would this force his hand, make him come out into the open? Would he do something before witnesses so they could nail him?

The clock ticked closer to the time limit. From what he'd tricked out of Alfie, the Crime Czar had only two months left to fulfill the terms of the bet.

Jason wasn't going to wait that long.

They had enough to nail Mr. Big to the wall. When ready, he'd be there to collect on his promise to the little fat man. To be the first to snap the cuffs on him.

The police didn't need his help with the research they were doing. He'd concentrate his efforts on bringing the Crime Czar to justice.

* * * *

CHAPTER FIFTEEN

Fate

He'd been staring out the window, pondering Mindforce's next move for so long, the twilight had drifted into night without notice. He'd only become aware of Sheila after the third series of light raps on his doorjamb.

"Jason?"

"Hmmm? Yes. What is it?"

"Detective Carlson just walked in."

"Vince? What the hell does he want?"

"To see you," he said, walking around Sheila. "You always sit in the dark?"

Jason dropped his feet to the floor, snapped on the desk lamp and glared up at him. All trench coat and fedora.

Vince stuck out his hand. It stayed orphaned. Unmoved, he returned it to his pocket.

"Nice secretary you have there. It's about time you got someone to answer your phone."

"I don't know what I'd do without her," Jason said through clenched teeth.

"Oh. You two guys are going to make me blush. I better get back to my desk where it isn't so deep."

"You do that," said Jason who turned his attention to Vince.

"You haven't been around in months. This a social call or business?"

Vince's demeanor darkened dramatically. "It was gonna be a

little of both. You were seen this afternoon when Mindforce brought all those hookers up from the old subway tunnels."

"So?"

"So. You left with one of the girls I'm told. How're you involved in this?"

"Through you, Vince."

"Come again?"

"Your office didn't have the time to help her father."

"Who?"

"Sid Greenleaf. He had a missing Daughter. Your department was busy. So he came to me."

Sid Greenleaf?" said Vince, scratching his chin. "I remember now. He was upset about his daughter not coming home. You mean she was one of those hookers?"

"Give the man a cigar."

"And he didn't know it?"

"He does now. She confessed it all to him. You might be interested to know she's decided to retire."

"Well, that's one less we have to worry about."

Now it was Jason's turn.

"Since you're here I got a bone to pick with you."

"Why do I get the feeling I'm not going to like this?"

"You shot your big mouth off to Sheila."

"In what way?"

"About my drinking problem!"

"You couldn'ta hid that anyway."

"Maybe so. But Carmen, and what went on in New York was none of her business."

"Sure I told her! She came to me, asking what kind of person you were."

"So, you just spill your guts to whoever asks?"

"You know better. She told me of her desire to work for you. It was my duty to warn her."

"Of What?"

"Of what kind of ASSHOLE you'd become! Of the self-pity

you were wallowing in. Of how you'd tossed a successful career in the dumper. All because of BOOZE!"

"Some friend you are."

"Yeah! And the only one you got in this town! I'd hoped to bring her to her senses. When she insisted, I told her that if she wanted to work here, she better not baby you. Just lay it on the line, and goad you if need be to get the best out of you."

The man was wiser than Jason had given him credit. He sat back in his chair and turned to glare at the thick air hovering over the city.

"I nearly fired her twice," he said, turning around.

"Worst mistake you could have made. She seems to have done wonders."

"Oh?"

"Certainly. I haven't seen your chin in years. Your suit's clean and your eyes aren't various shades of red. I'd guess you haven't had a drink in some time."

"For reasons you'll never know."

That elicited a quizzical look. Jason cut him off before he could ask the uncomfortable questions.

"You know, I felt betrayed again when I found out you told Sheila."

"I'm still your friend. Believe it or not. I just did what I felt I should."

True enough. He'd misjudged Vince. Now Jason had to ask the questions Vince would expect even though he knew he couldn't answer them.

"So. What's the deal with Charlotte?"

"Can't tell you, Buddy. It's top secret. Just got the word this morning from the Commissioner."

"What's so top secret about a bunch of kidnapped hookers being turned loose on the streets. Unless it's bad PR."

"All I can tell you is that something big is going down," he said in a hushed tone. "And if the Commissioner knew I told you that much I'd be in hot water. By the way. How'd you know where to pick her up?"

"Wasn't hard. Mindforce and I ran into each other down there. When we compared notes we found out we were working on the same case, more or less."

"What'd he tell you?"

"Less than you just did. He's tight lipped and all business. He just said he was going to bring them all out and I could pick out the one I wanted. Then he told me to go back up to the surface and stay out of the way. When I saw the gathering crowd on the corner I went for my clients daughter."

"Mindforce didn't hang around long. Did he tell you where he was going or what he was up to?"

"Only that he had business to take care of and that he'd get back to me."

"All right. We've had about five hundred girls come into the station to sign the complaint already. We most likely won't need your client's testimony anyhow. So we'll let it ride."

"You're all heart, Vince."

"You figure that out all by yourself?"

"Hey. I'm a detective."

"Yeah, well. Don't let it go to your head. You'll never get it through the door."

Sheila closed up shop about ten minutes after Vince had gone. There was nothing for Jason to do now but go home, get dinner and go out on evening patrol.

Vince had been correct about one thing even if he didn't know it. Something big was going down. Mr. Big. Tubby was going down for the count, if Jason had anything to say about it.

Tulio must have related all to his boss who must be ready to burst now that all the hookers have been released. All Mindforce had to do was wait.

* * * *

While Mindforce prepares his next move, the Crime Czar contemplates his own plan of attack.

"The plan was perfect!" shouted the Czar, slamming the door to his office. "How the hell did it all go wrong?"

"You couldn't figure on that Mindforce dude gettin' in the way," said Freddy.

"Mindforce! Yes. If not for him I'd be sitting pretty in Mr. Big's office right now."

"So whatta we do now?"

"First we do damage control. Then we eliminate Mindforce. After he's gone the city will be wide open. Free for the taking."

"We still goin' after Mr. Big?"

"Certainly. . . . Only, this time we don't just humiliate him. We're going to torture the shit out of him. Then we'll slowly cut the fat pig's throat."

"But—"

"But what?"

"Nothin'. Nothin'."

"C-mon. Spit it out!"

"No Boss. Whatever you say."

"You're a spineless little weasel, Freddy. But I need you right now. And you better hope I continue to need you."

"W-what about the Syndicate boys?"

"My lawyers will contact them today. The bet's been violated since Mr. Big's been informed of our plans. It's all null and void as far as I'm concerned."

"But, they know who you are. You can't cross them. They'll hunt you down no matter how long it takes."

"You think so? Do they really know who I am?"

"I dunno. You tell me."

"I know you think I'm nuts, but do you really think I'd let them know who I really am?"

The light flickered in Freddy's head. If ever so dimly.

"Ya crossed them."

"Just as they would me."

"Why didn't ya say so?"

"You didn't need to know."

Only slightly nervous when they came in, now Freddy's trembling was nearly noticeable.

"How ya gonna ice Mindforce?"

"I've some demolition boys I'm gonna call in. They'll take care of everything."

"You sure it'll work?"

"If you've a better idea I'd like to hear it now. Otherwise, just shut your yap and pay attention."

"S-sure Boss."

"Once we've got the flying freak out of the way I'll dance on his grave."

"And Mr. Big?"

"The drug heist is still on. Why should I give that fat pig a breather. You got everything ready?"

"Yeah. Raul, Jerry and Frank got it all lined up for tomorrow night. The Sarebo is docking at pier six at 10 o'clock."

"Good."

* * * *

Ten days slipped by, and nothing. Other than the scuffle down on the docks the previous week, the gangs stayed quiet. None of either Mob's men allowed themselves to be conspicuous; a bad sign. This quiet before the storm meant sooner or later all hell would break loose. Police informants either knew nothing or just wouldn't say. No major arrests were made anywhere in the city.

Each side held back to see what the other was up to. Lord help them when one side made up its mind to move.

Tired of waiting, Mindforce refused to wait for that to happen. It was time to make some noise. He made his presence known in every hangout in the city. Letting everyone know he wanted information. No one would talk. Threats of pain and or violence did nothing. The word was out to lay low and clam up.

He'd even paid a visit to his favorite snitch, Leroy. He knew nothing. Freddy remained out of touch.

The city must have swallowed up every big time hood. He had no idea what they were up to but knew it had to be no good.

The hookers were back in action again. In fact, they'd been out the very night after their release—all but one. True to his word, the Commissioner arrested anyone caught soliciting.

The only difference being, the pimps were watching the girls and their johns more closely. Regulars were treated accordingly. Unknowns were told to either take a hike or were escorted to a place of better protection.

All the girls were either carrying cans of pepper spray or packed heat. No chances were being taken by anyone.

The one bright spot: Silky Malone had followed Mindforce's instructions to the letter.

Charlotte dropped by Jason's agency to tell him one of Silky's men hand delivered to her a package containing forty grand in cash with a note saying, "For your tuition, Silky."

Confused, she came to ask his advice.

She earned it; why not keep it? No matter what she'd done. Put the money to good use and keep her nose clean. Her face and health were intact, so use the golden opportunity to make something of herself and not blow it.

Thanking Jason for his help she asked him to thank Mindforce for her if Jason ever saw him again.

SATURDAY MORNING, 6 AM: Flying on morning patrol, Mindforce spotted several police cars parked along the Schuylkill River near the Fairmount Dam. He dropped down to offer his help.

"What's the trouble?" he said to the nearest officer.

"Someone out on an early morning jog called in a floater tangled in some growth near the dam."

"Anything I can do?"

"I don't think so. They're hauling the body into the boat now."

"Mindforce," came the Commissioner's voice from behind.

"Morning, Jake. Looks like a floater."

"Yes. I heard over my radio at home. What brings you here?"

"I was flying over when I saw all the cars. I just dropped in to see if I could be of assistance."

"Probably someone tied one on last night, fell in the river and drowned. I'll alert Missing Persons, see if we get a match."

"HEY!!" shouted one of the men in the boat. "This guy's got bullet holes in 'im!"

"That means we got a homicide and not a simple drowning after all," said the Commissioner.

Ten minutes later the boat reached a spot where they could bring the body ashore.

Walking to the bank, Mindforce and the Commissioner looked on while the corpse was carried ashore where they rolled it over on it's back.

"Alfie Tulio!?" said Mindforce in disgust.

"You sure of that?" said the Commissioner.

"That's him all right. And from the look of him, he's been in the water at least ten days."

"What makes you say that?"

"That's the same outfit he had on when I last saw him."

"He's got three holes in him," said the Coroner when he examined the body. "Probably shot at close range with a large caliber weapon."

The Commissioner took Mindforce's elbow, motioning him to an area more private.

"Don't get me wrong, but I have to ask this question."

"Did I kill him? The answer is NO! . . . Besides, I wouldn't need a gun . . ."

"Good. I believe you. Do you have any idea who did?"

"Only one suspect comes to mind."

"Mr. Big?"

"He tops the list. Tulio's been in and out of his casino. He may have got wise."

"Speaking of the casino. We're just about ready to go. The FBI boys have been watching Quincy's and staked out the tunnels. Our Mr. Big hasn't missed a night. And Judge Bradley was in last Tuesday as we suspected."

"I just wish Judge Mercer had let us tap Bradley's phone."

"You know what he told the DA."

"Not on the word of some masked vigilante! I remember."

"Yeah. Well. I'm not supposed to tell anyone this," said the Commissioner, making sure no one could hear, "but the FBI boys went and did it anyway."

"You're kidding."

"It's true. After they read the DA's file on Bradley and saw him go into Quincy's they hooked him up."

"Did they say why?"

"Only that after they sent an agent into Quincy's to tail him and he was nowhere to be found, it was good enough for them. They said they had a higher power to answer to than some local officials."

"Have they heard anything?"

"I don't know. They let me in on it out of professional courtesy but won't tell me anything. If it goes down bad they want me in the clear."

"Nice of them."

"They did tell me, once a proper arrest is made they'll share any pertinent recordings."

"I'll be on hand when you're ready. I wouldn't miss this for the world."

"We're having a strategy session this morning and I want you there. You're the only one who's seen the casino and how to get in there."

"I'll be there. But first I have some business to attend to."

"I assume you're going to see if Mr. Big knows anything about this."

"That's right."

"I don't have to warn you to be careful not to tip our hand.

About to take to the air, the Commissioner took Mindforce's upper arm in his right hand and warned, "Don't do anything I'll have to arrest you for later."

"That depends on Mr. Big."

7 AM: Approaching the Commerce Building, Mindforce flew in high from the west, taking in a long distance view of the penthouse balcony.

Half expecting to find the balcony empty at this hour he found one occupant. A young woman, leaning on her elbows on the parapet wall. Gazing toward the orange sunrise.

Unseasonably warm for the first week in March, this morning was quite chilly. Dressed only in a floor length nightgown, the crisp, easterly breeze blew through her long brown hair.

Landing noiselessly, fifteen feet behind her, so engrossed in her thoughts she was unaware of his presence.

Not wishing to disturb or startle her, he reached out with his Empathic sense. Studying her he picked up the unmistakable traces of despair and frustration, of envy, and most predominantly, hate.

She stood contemplating a serious move, torn between which of two paths to take. Filled with internal conflict and turmoil to such an extent it relegated her to total inactivity. And one more thing . . . he knew this woman.

"Suicide isn't the answer, Vicky."

She spun around. Startled by the abrupt break in the silence and the fact she was no longer alone. With relief filling her mind, she must have expected someone else.

Her reddened eyes wet, tears trickled down her cheeks, dripping from her chin for some time, staining the front of her translucent gown. Shivering in the chill damp air she paid it no heed.

"Mindforce!?" she croaked. "What're you doing here?"

"That was my first question."

"Didn't I tell you?" she said, pointing to the penthouse. "I've been that bastard's personal floozy for over a year now!"

He came up beside her. She turned, not wishing to face him,

once again toward the warming rays of the rising sun, folding her arms before her, placing them on the wall.

"I know what you're thinking. But it paid the bills."

"Why that little toad?"

"At first it was great. I was off the streets. I didn't have to lie down for every weirdo the pimps brought me. It paid a hell of a lot more money and I had a feeling of importance." This evoked a flood of new tears. "I was able to afford any of the best apartments in town. I really thought I was living the good life. And all I had to do was be on call when the slime bucket wanted some entertainment."

"Sounds like you had it made." He knew better.

"Yeah! I had it made all right; a touch of irony in her voice while she snapped her head around to face her rescuer. "Everything was just fine until he started lending me out to his business partners."

Unable to see through his mask, Mindforce's stance gave away the puzzled look on his face.

"Yeah! That's right! I became a part of everyone of his business deals. 'Be nice to this one,' he'd say. 'Be nice to that one.' Do you have any idea what those BASTARDS were like?"

"I can't imagine." But he had a good idea.

"Well, I'll tell you. There was no degrading stunt, no unnatural act they didn't demand."

"And you couldn't say no?"

"I didn't dare," she said, turning to face the sunrise again. "The Mother Fucker would have crippled me if I had. And I had to pretend I liked what they were doing to me. At least when I was on the streets I could always get my pimp to take care of the scuzballs and keep them away from me. Here, I've got no protection."

"And when you asked to be let go, he refused."

"That's putting it mildly. 'I was his property. To be used as he wished, for as long as he liked.' The only refuge I had was being able to go home to my own apartment. Now I don't even have that!"

"Why?"

"Why!! . . . Why, the man asks," she said, throwing her hands up in disgust while turning toward him. "You should know why!"

"I'm sorry, I—"

"Don't be sorry," she said, tears flowing profusely. "It's the Crime Czar's fault. You couldn't know this, but I was the first girl snagged by him. He must have known I was Mr. Big's main squeeze. They did it to show him up. Since you released me, he's locked me up in here so I can't get out."

"He's holding you prisoner here?!"

"The two weeks in that underground hell hole was a welcome vacation now that I think about it. I thought once we got released I could sneak out of town. But his goons caught me at my apartment just as I was leaving. He said, 'It was for my protection.' *BULL!* He knows I'll skip if I get the chance!"

He knew the answer . . . but asked it anyway. "Do you want me to take you out of here?"

Eyes lighting up, the tears flowed faster. Tears of joy and relief this time.

"Don't tease me. Can you get me out of here?"

"No sooner said than done. Just as soon as I have a few words with that fat tub of lard."

Stepping back to arms length she gazed into his face.

"I really wasn't going to jump."

She only half believed that. Having not actually made up her mind when he landed. Given hope now, she put it in a different perspective.

"How touching," came a voice from the patio door. The unmistakable rasp of Mr. Big.

Flinching, Vicky stepped half behind Mindforce, peeking out at the fat little man with a sense of foreboding, instinctively afraid for her safety.

"What? No goon squad to back you up, Francis!"

"What do I need them for? You're the only one that can get up here. And I couldn't stop you anyway."

"You got that right, tubby. You can't stop me."

"Why don't you go inside like a good little girl, Vicky, while Mindforce and I discuss what he came here for."

"Yes. Do that," Mindforce said, nudging her. "And pack whatever you want to take with you."

"Oh? Is that how it is?" he said softly, like he'd just seen the handwriting on the wall.

Vicky stepped cautiously past the fat little man, then quickly into the penthouse.

"How interesting. You've come to rescue her . . . again."

"That wasn't the original plan. But since I'm here."

"And I suppose you'll take her straight to the police to swear out a complaint."

"To what end? Who's going to take the word of an admitted prostitute over a, so called, respected businessman?"

"She has you as a witness."

Since he was only here to investigate the Tulio murder he didn't want to raise Mr. Big's suspicions. If he did a little acting, laying it on just thick enough, Mr. Big should believe Mindforce and the police were up a blind alley. That they were as inept as Mr. Big thought they were.

He was no idiot. Mr. Big didn't get to where he was by accident. He *might* be subject to overconfidence. Mindforce would use that to his advantage. It may have helped Mr. Big to rise to his lofty position; now it would be his undoing.

He was in deep water and Mindforce was going to hand him a brick.

"You know as well as I do that anything I have to say won't stand up in court. While you, you have hundreds of paid witnesses who'll swear you never laid eyes on the girl before."

"Yes. How true. How true. Isn't it amazing what money and power will get you?"

"You'll slip up one day."

"Not in your lifetime."

Mr. Big laughed up his sleeve at him at the belief in his own invulnerability. Little knowing that this house of cards was, in a few short days, about to fall down around his ears.

"Now. You said you weren't here just to rescue Vicky."

"No. I'm not. I actually came here about a dead body found floating in the river this morning."

"So. What's that got to do with me?"

"So. He was a small time hood named Alfie Tulio."

There was a flicker of recognition.

"So, we know he freelanced a lot. So, we know he was working for someone in town. So, we know, but can't prove yet, that no one gets bumped off in this town without your say so. That's what."

"So, maybe the Crime Czar bumped him off."

"So, he was working for you then?" Even though he knew this to be untrue it might catch him off guard.

"I knew of Tulio. But he never worked for me. I run a respectable business y-know."

"You keep telling me that, Francis. But it ain't never going to be true."

"Your word against mine."

"Did you or one of your men kill him?"

"No."

His *Esper* sense gave nary a tingle. He didn't have Tulio killed and knew nothing about it. If he didn't, who did? No way Mindforce could believe it was just some random act with no bearing on the case.

When last seen, Tulio was in a very agitated state. The bet and the time limit were supposed to be a deep dark secret. Could the Crime Czar have done it? Could he have, in a fit of rage, blown Tulio away? Could he have mistaken the agitation for guilt-ridden fear and believed Tulio had spilled his guts to Mindforce? All things were possible.

"All right, Francis. I can't prove anything right now. But one day I'll nail you."

"Don't hold your breath."

"It may take years," he said, pointing a sharp finger at him.

"But I'll catch you in a mistake and nail your filthy fat ass to the wall."

"Never in a million years." He believed it too.

Having dressed and collected her belongings, Vicky reappeared.

"No one quits me," he said, catching sight of her.

"There's a first time for everything," she shot back.

His attitude abruptly changed. "Ahhh g-wan! Take the slut with you. Cheap tricks like her are a dime a dozen. She can't hurt me. I'll replace her in a half hour. There's plenty of bimbos out there that'd gladly have her place."

Mindforce's *DANGER* sense began tingling since Vicky's reappearance but he ignored it. Now it wouldn't let him.

She'd produced a rather vulgar looking .44 semi-auto pistol from her handbag.

"Stick your head between your legs and kiss your ass good-bye!" she said while slowly pulling back the hammer. "Say hello to Satan for me you Bastard!"

A gesture from Mindforce and the gun flew from Vicky's hand to his. She stared at him incredulously.

"That's not the way we do it."

"NO! Don't stop me!" she said, tears welling up. "He doesn't deserve to live!"

"Neat trick," said Mr. Big. "I'd heard you could do that but didn't believe it."

"Lucky for you I can."

"No way. She wouldn't have squeezed the trigger."

"What makes you so sure?" she said.

He was blatant. "She ain't got what it takes."

"You're wrong! That's why I was out on the terrace this morning when Mindforce showed up. You were right, Mindforce. I was debating throwing myself off the parapet . . . or shooting the bastard through the head while he slept. He didn't know I found where he hid his gun. I've been up all night trying to decide what to do. Or maybe both." She finished with large amounts of despair. Turning, she walked to the parapet to gaze at the ever rising sun.

"See! I told you she didn't have the guts! If she did, she wouldn't have to think about it. She'da just blown me away."

He was trying to sound sure of himself. In truth, his heart rate soared and his fear level leaped to the top when Vicky pointed the gun at his head. He was skilled at not letting people see him sweat but he couldn't be sure she wouldn't pull the trigger.

Mindforce raised the pistol, pointed it at Mr. Big's head, flipped the safety and yanked back the hammer. There was a short sucking sound from the fat man's lips.

"What makes you think I won't shoot you?"

He smirked and calmly stood his ground.

"Don't do it Mindforce," said Vicky. "I was wrong. He's not worth it."

Mr. Big stood cool, not batting an eye.

"You won't do it either cause you're a goody two shoes," he said while calmly lighting a cigar. "Maybe I couldn't be sure of her, but you, you're not built that way."

The fool thought he knew it all.

"Wrong, Francis! I answer to my own sense of values, not what Society dictates. I deal in justice first. It would give me great pleasure to put you out of your fucking misery. That's no more than what filthy, bloodsucking sleaze balls like you deserve. But that would be quick—simple—and pointless. No! I wanna see you squirm before a jury, watching the damning evidence pile higher and higher. I wanna see you sweat while the Judge pronounces sentence on you. I want it to be as slow and as painful as possible. I want to make an example of you to all your friends who live off of other people's misfortune. I want them to know I mean business. Killing you would only make a martyr of you to all the crud that walks the streets. That's why I won't pull the trigger . . . now."

"Get in line. There's a whole police force out there ahead of ya. Waitin' for what ain't gonna happen."

The man's unmitigated gall was amazing. He bore absolute disdain for anyone he thought his inferior. The further amazing part, Mindforce did want to pull the trigger. There was no bluff.

Only those reasons he stated prevented him from committing cold-blooded murder.

He'd been through Southeast Asia. Been on the NYPD for ten years and never used his weapon other than in the course of his duty. Since he'd been a PI, he'd never attempted to fire the damn thing.

Through the fickleness of Fate he'd been given all these powers. Now, on his first big case, he wanted to kill someone just because he despised him and all he stood for.

The pistol felt light in his hand. Cool to the touch. Even through his gauntlet. His grip firm, his finger itched on the trigger. One, small, involuntary twitch and this rotten filth would be history.

Fortunately for Mr. Big, sanity prevailed.

"Just so you don't forget I mean what I say, I'm gonna leave you a little reminder."

Extending his arm to the right he changed his aim from Mr. Big's head straight through the open patio door. Squeezing the trigger in rapid succession he emptied the 15 shot clip into the penthouse living room.

Vicky stood in astonishment, holding her ears, while Mr. Big's jaw fell open, dropping the lit cigar at his feet.

The well-aimed shooting spree took out Mr. Big's TV, stereo, videotape player, speakers and the rest of a few thousand dollars worth of electronic equipment around the room. Satisfied, he squeezed the pistol into a chunk of useless scrap.

"You'll pay for this!"

"You got no witnesses. You didn't see anything did you Vicky?"

"Couldn't, my eyes were closed."

"And nobody knows I'm here. So you got no case," he said while dropping the mangled gun on the patio table. "Besides. This isn't any setback for you. You can replace it out of petty cash. Just look at it as a . . . warning."

"I'm not afraid of you! Not a fucking one of you can touch me!"

"You better be afraid. You and your kind aren't welcome here. Before I'm through, I'm gonna make it too hot for you and any of your Syndicate cronies to hang around."

"All right. You've had your say. Now, take the tramp and beat it!"

"Just remember one thing. I'm gonna nail your fat carcass to the wall before I'm through."

"Yeah. Yeah. So you say."

"Remember. The next time you see me, it just might be to snap the cuffs on and haul your fat ass away."

"You'll never live to see the day!" he yelled after them when they flew off.

Mindforce couldn't help dwelling on what he was prepared to do. He really wanted to send the slime to Hell. What disturbed him most was he didn't give a damn either. He could have, quite calmly, yanked the trigger in the little fat bastard's face, instead of the house.

He'd never had these kind of feelings before or so intense. These empathy powers were still uncontrollable. He could not be sure these feelings were totally his own or that he was absorbing them from those around him.

Was he slowly becoming as bad as the scum around him or was he always this way? Has the greater confidence and the subsequent lack of fear after gaining these powers only released what was always suppressed deep in his psyche?

Was he too close to the problem? Is this just an isolated incident. If he didn't find the answers soon he'd need a shrink.

Wouldn't the papers eat it up. He could see the headlines, "MINDFORCE CONSULTS SHRINK, GOES INTO ANALYSIS!" The Mayor and all his bleeding heart friends would want to run him out of town.

Just what the world needs, a super-hero with mental problems.

No. This was bullshit. He reacted like a rookie cop again. They all held doubts about their resolve. They were warned those doubts would make them indecisive and only get them or someone else killed. If they couldn't cope, they should get out at the start and not waste anyone's time.

Intelligence and resolve got him through then but he didn't know if it could now.

Since he was having second thoughts, maybe he wasn't so crazy after all. Overreaction was normal, or, as normal as one in his position could be.

The city operates and maintains a safe house run by the police. used for key witnesses to keep them safe until they can testify.

Cells in the basement sometimes held prisoners who wouldn't stand a chance anywhere else.

The place was a miniature fortress, though outwardly, it didn't look it. A full-scale assault would be required to breach the building.

He left Vicky here for her own safety. The DA would want her statement in hopes of reinforcing his upcoming case against Mr. Big and his crime family. Afterwards, he hoped they could help her escape the city and the Syndicate.

His good feelings about Charlotte slowly supplanted themselves with lousy ones. Tulio getting killed. He should have suspected; followed him. If he'd saved him he might have testified, but would he? Mindforce couldn't know. It was frustrating.

Vicky emanated apprehension when she came up from the tunnels. He caught it but was more interested in getting Charlotte home. Could he have saved her all those days of grief? He didn't know.

Those urges he'd repressed in the last few weeks gnawed incessantly at his gut again . . .

It was 8 AM when he walked into his office. He hadn't expected to see Sheila there.

He tried to hide the paper bag from her but she was too sharp, quickly chasing him into his office.

"What's in the bag Jason?"

He put it on the desk.

"I think you know."

"Don't do it. You've done so well. Don't blow it."

"You can't know what pressures I've been under."

"Well, tell me."

"I . . . can't"

"What about AA?"

"Don't start on that," he said, pulling the quart of Old Grand Dad from the bag.

She looked at the bottle, then at him. Back and forth several times.

"Don't do it! What's so bad that you'd sink back to the bottom again?"

He was torn inside out. This wasn't going to help. It was a habit. A crutch. A waste of money in more ways than one. He'd feel no different afterwards. The pressures of his failures, of this secret, became more than he wanted to bear. He unscrewed the cap.

"Jason, don't!"

He lifted the bottle. She hurried around the desk and caught his arm, fury in her eyes.

"Don't be a God Damned Fool!"

"Don't worry. This won't affect me in the least."

Her eyes widened. Fury lapsed into the depths of despair. She released his arm.

"All right. Drink yourself into a damn coma for all I care. But don't expect me to watch," she said, stalking off.

"Oh, very good. Reverse psychology. Shame I'm ahead of you."

That stopped her in her tracks. Some part of him hoped it would. She watched while he raised the bottle to his lips. He paused, her eyes darting about the room then back to him. Tipping it up he downed the contents in a matter of seconds.

"Are you Nuts?" she yelled, reaching for the phone and 9-1-1.

He took the phone from her hand, gently laying it back in the cradle.

"That won't be necessary."

"Not necessary!? No one can drink that much alcohol all at once!"

Her eyes gaped at him. Genuine concern engulfed him amid waves of confusion.

He let go of the empty bottle. Against all logic, it didn't fall to the floor. Instead, it flew sideways to the wall, smashing against it. The glass shards refused to fall but flew straight to the trash can. Books flew from the shelves to the floor. Plaques and trophies dropped from their perches. Furniture tipped over, the door opened and closed. Then everything returned to its original position. Sheila stood speechless. The room deafeningly quiet while she groped for her ability to speak.

"You. . . . Jason, you're . . ."

"Fraid so."

She had to sit.

"But, where? How?"

He sat slowly in his chair then began to lay out the whole sordid affair.

What Jason couldn't know was three thousand years ago, far across the galaxy, a star of great magnitude, old when our Sol was new, ended its allotted life span in that most dramatic of all deaths, a Super Nova!

Upon the stars stupendous death the rapidly expanding corona of superheated plasma and intense radiation incinerated the innermost planets, along with any and all life on them; debris hurtling out in all directions at nearly light speed. The outer planets, pelted with flaming hot debris, became subjected to the howling force of the tremendous explosions might.

What planets remained whole, without the attraction of the stars gravity, spun off in various directions to wander aimlessly through the void.

One thousand years later the light of that long dead star reached the Earth. Fulfilling the prophecy, it led three weary Middle Eastern travelers across the desert to a stable behind an inn in a small Judean village.

The physical evidence of that super nova lay nearly two millennia in the distance.

TIME: The present.

PLACE: Deep space.

A peculiarly radioactive meteor, several feet across, a remnant of that long since exploded star concludes its trillions of millions trek across the galaxy. Its course: directly towards Earth.

Whether by Fate, the Gods or the one Supreme Being, it is here; destined to change forever the life of one man . . .

Jason spoke of her mother who'd hired him because the police were overworked. Of how he'd found the cabin five days before her rescue. This revelation raised her eyebrows.

Approaching the cabin cautiously he peered in the window. A habit that, on many occasions, kept him from walking blindly into trouble. He recognized the two men; a couple of convicts who'd escaped from the state prison in Rahway, New Jersey . . .

Out in space the meteor touched the outer reaches of the atmosphere. On its journey through the far reaches of space its progress slowed by the pull of gravity from the planets and star systems it passed near. In all the countless miles since the outset of its travels it had missed colliding with numerous planets, asteroids and other suns. Having reached the Earth it began the final leg on its date with destiny. Rushing headlong through the atmosphere the friction with the air slowed its descent even more. In doing so it heated up and began to burn, leaving a trail of dust, smoke and ash in its wake . . .

Policy dictated he only report to his client the whereabouts of the missing person he'd been hired to find. The client had the responsibility of coaxing the individual home. Policy also dictated he not stick his nose into something he'd later regret. This might be Patty Hearst all over again. Unlikely, for nothing her mother told him about her daughter led him to think Sheila could be that kind of person. In hindsight, having learned of her radical leanings, if he'd known them then he might have leapt to an opposite conclusion. Parents didn't always know everything about their offspring. Their rose colored glasses oft times clouded their vision. More likely she was a hostage though she didn't appear mistreated.

The stainless steel flask in his breast pocket found its way to his hand like it had life. He'd taken several long sips before the taste hit his brain.

Lacking all the facts, he needed to back off and think about this. Clueless parents, he'd experienced in the past, could be misleading. What he wanted now was to regroup and figure out how those two scruffy dudes figured in the scheme of things, and to get out of the cold.

She couldn't elude Jason. Very few had.

. . . The meteorite was halfway through the atmosphere on its journey with fate. Having lost over half its bulk it lost more at an ever-increasing pace . . .

His car lay far in the distance. He groped through the night, down the hill, over rocks and shrubs, lighting a cigarette. A nasty habit he knew, but one he'd had since his tour in the Army. If you didn't have some bad habit when you got there, you sure as hell did when you left. At least his was one of the least debilitating ones.

The car sat hidden off the road behind some boulders and shrubs so that no snoopy cop would see it, and possibly thinking it abandoned, have it towed away.

The evening was crisp and cold. The nearly full moon shone through the gathering clouds. Snow was predicted for later. All he wanted was the warmth of his cars heater.

. . . Three quarters of the way through the atmosphere, ninety percent of its bulk gone, the meteorite sped on.

While pondering all he'd seen of late, Jason's thoughts were interrupted by the uneasy feeling of something, somewhere behind him. This instinct, born and honed during his tour in Southeast Asia, he learned to trust.

Cautiously turning to look, his jaw dropped! His heart fairly stopped; the blood drained from his face leaving him ashen white. There. Hissing and popping, glowing all the colors of the rainbow, streaking straight for him raced the meteorite. Burned down to golf ball size.

For the first time in his life instincts fail him. Instead of ducking or leaping aside he does a 180 and sprints directly away.

Before taking two steps the splinter of interstellar matter slams into the back of Jason's head; shattering bone—penetrating the skull—lodging in the sinus cavity of his brain. The enormous timing of the accident is staggering; all those years—all those miles. If it traveled another hundred feet it would have burned to nothing.

The impact drives Jason through the air and across the ground. Landing on his face he slides to an abrupt stop at the base of a huge hickory tree. Life oozes rapidly from the gaping hole in his skull. Vital signs ebb swiftly.

In a handful of heartbeats it ended. All lay still again. The woods cemetery quiet once more while a human life fast fades from this world . . . all alone. On a cold windy mountaintop an owl hoots softly. The first snowflakes of winter start to fall.

Belief says a persons whole life flashes before their eyes when they approach death. Jason's did with a flourish.

An only child because his mother could not have more, Jason's life was no better or worse than others. He excelled at games, especially Hide and Seek. He always found everyone. This uncanny knack precluded any of his friends escaping his detection.

In high school he excelled at sports; developing into a strong healthy adult. Passing up college, even though offered a scholarship, Jason opted for the Army.

The war, for the USA, was over in Vietnam by the time he got into the service, but there were still mop up chores to be done.

Fresh from OCS he volunteered for a specially trained, covert group, whose mission would be to secretly penetrate into North Vietnam to search for any and all MIAs and POWs. He'd been very successful to say the least. For his efforts, Jason's leadership and valor won him the Distinguished Service Cross.

On the scene were several members of research institutes sticking their collective noses into the psyche of the returning war vet. Jason's *Esper* powers became rated far above normal. This could have explained his abilities in finding people.

After an extended reunion with his family Jason set out for

New York City. He'd spent leave time there with a friend and fell in love with the place.

Since childhood he wanted to be a cop. He earned top honors at the Academy. Assigned to Manhattan, he honed his craft on the streets for three years. Due to his help on a difficult kidnapping case he received an opportunity to join Missing Persons. In all his years there the citations for meritorious service began to pile up.

All good things must end sometime and so it happened with Jason's career. It all fell tragically around his feet after the incident with Carmen.

This prompted Jason's long slow fall from grace. More and more time became spent with his new friends: *Bacardi,* and his *Old Grand Dad.*

At first he drank only after hours and on days off. Soon it became a drink to brace himself in the morning. Then one or two at lunch to ease the afternoons tasks. In time he would sneak drinks whenever life intruded.

In time it became apparent to all save Jason that he had a problem. He would shave irregularly, showing for work in suits he'd passed out in the previous evening. His work suffered so badly he soon ran out of second chances. Only because of his outstanding record was he permitted to resign rather than being summarily dismissed.

Bitter and resentful, he stalked out of New York, returning to Philadelphia. An old friend on the force, Lt. Vince Carlson, pushed to get him hired when he applied. Commissioner Parman, having checked his record, would not place a drunk on the force.

Getting his PI license hadn't been easy. If not for Vince smoothing the way Lord knows where he might have fallen.

He lucked into a dirt-cheap office. Only because the whole block lay scheduled for urban renewal somewhere in the uncertain future and set up shop. He got results but his bad habits hung like anchors on his efficiency. Too soon, out of necessity to stay afloat, he pawned the last remnants of his pride and accepted any sleazy case that would have him. Then the client that would change his life forever walked in the door. Rita.

Here came the ultimate fall, into the waiting arms of Death on a lonely mountaintop in Pennsylvania. Slow—slower—gone. The Grim Reaper, biding his time till the proper moment, moved in to collect his charge now that his heart had stopped beating. . . . Or had it! One beat. Two. Three. Jason's heartbeat, slowly, miraculously increased when it should be dead still. The sliver of meteorite in Jason's brain dissolved and mingled with his blood. Something in the radioactivity or the odd alien minerals kept his heart not only beating but promoted rapid blood restoration.

Jason's heart rate returned to half normal when the eerie and unheard of took place. The large gash in the back of his skull not only stopped bleeding, it was closing; healing itself. Slowly at first, then more rapidly until after a couple of hours it was totally closed. In minutes it would be healed without a trace. He was still comatose . . . but alive.

Within the hour an expedition formed to see if they could find any remnants of the meteorite that had been sighted falling. Mother Nature took her turn with destiny. The light, snow flurries gently falling changed into the Mother of all blizzards; dumping twenty inches of snow in the first hour. Any attempt to find anything, not even Jason or his car, was foiled for several days.

Under three feet of snow he lay comatose for three days, still alive. Near dusk on that day the surface of the snow mound began to crack and rise. From within, rising Frankenstein-like, came the body of Jason. First on all fours, then to his knees while the snow slid off his trench coat. Groggy, head reeling, using a nearby tree for support, Jason made the first feeble attempt to pull himself to his feet. His first two tries ended in pathetic defeat. The third try succeeded. Teetering on rubbery legs he succeeded in maintaining his balance. Forcing his eyes to focus, everything came across as a dull gray blur. His conscious mind nearly blank.

Functioning solely on instinct, hardly knowing where he was

let alone who he was, Jason took the first tentative steps on wobbly legs. Failing miserably, he flopped face first in the snow.

Stumbling, falling, slipping and sliding on the ice and snow covered slope, he made his way in search of his car. Unerringly, if not always upright, he found it right where he left it. Once there he paused, trying to think—trying to clear his head—trying to remember.

He groped in his soggy pockets for his keys. Though greatly disoriented, he somehow knew he needed the keys to make the vehicle work. Memory hazy—logic nonexistent—reflexes down, he hopelessly flooded the engine. No way it would start now. Which in the long run was just as well. He couldn't have driven it far. Not in his condition. Jason got out of the car, closed the door and after resting there propped up by the car for a minute, stumbled and crawled toward the main road.

He staggered along for what seemed like hours or ten minutes. He couldn't tell which; his time sense nonfunctional. Thanks to Lady Luck, a large semi pulled up and stopped next to Jason. The door opened slowly. Reeling, Jason turned haltingly. Vacant eyes stared blankly up into the cab of the truck to a burly looking man who appeared a thousand miles away.

"Well, c-mon!" barked the driver. "If you want a ride, get in."

Jason slowly climbed into the cab, taking the place on the seat. Searching for, then closing the door.

"Where ya headed?"

"Into Philly," mumbled Jason. Somehow knowing that's where he had to be.

"Ya look terrible, bud. And you smell worse." Jason's flask had broken during one of his falls, its contents permeating his clothes. "But I can't leave ya out there to freeze now. Can I? Ya have an accident or something?"

"I-I don't know," Jason slurs. "I remember . . . a bright light . . . pain . . . then nothing."

"Mebbe ya hit your head? Ya want I should drop ya off at a hospital?"

"N-No. Just . . . home."

It was after nine by the time they reached the city. Jason napped in the cab.

"Hey. Bud," says the driver, shaking Jason. "This is as far as I go."

Jason stirs. "Huh? What? . . . O-Okay."

After fumbling with the handle he opens the door on the third try, then slides down to the curb. Jason turns, thanks the driver for his kindness, who again tells him he better seek medical attention. Jason nods obediently then turns to walk away, leaving the door of the truck wide open. The driver shakes his head, mumbles something inaudible then reaches over to close the door.

While the truck pulls away, Jason stares at his surroundings. Despite the dirty piles of plowed snow, everything is familiar somehow. The unerring radar of a drunk instinctively set him on the right path to his apartment a few short blocks to the west. Staggering, slipping and nearly falling over the ice encrusted sidewalk, he makes his way. Luck alone prevented any patrol car from seeing him.

Entering the foyer of his building, Jason couldn't feel his wet coat, frozen stiff from the cold.

"Christ! Sloshed again," mumbled one of the tenants when Jason staggered by, fumbling in his pockets for his keys. "What a waste of humanity."

Contemptuous eyes followed Jason while he made his way into the empty elevator. There was no one to notice him on his trip up to his floor or on the short walk along the corridor to his door. Unable to locate his keys, a practice that occurred all to often, he staggered to the plant stand a few steps away, dug around in the foliage and came up with his emergency key. Hands trembling, he used four tries before he located the keyhole. Without removing his coat he stumbles to his bedroom, collapsing across the mattress; falling into a deep fitful sleep.

* * * *

Fifteen hours later, on a bright, sunny afternoon, the streams of western sunlight begin their slow crawl up Jason's bed and across his face. Blood red eyes creak open to the swirling ceiling overhead.

"Oh, my God. . . . Where am I?" comes out in a cracked whisper.

Getting a grip on his retching senses, Jason forces his legs to slide off the bed, puts his feet on the floor and haltingly pushes himself to a sitting position.

"Ooooo, my head," moans Jason, gently placing his throbbing cranium in his open palms. "Did somebody get the number of the truck? Oh Christ! Feels like my head just ran the marathon . . . barefoot."

Gingerly raising his head from his trembling hands he opens his eyes just a crack; letting in the least amount of light possible. Sluggishly focusing eyes scan the area. Soon, the familiar surroundings of his bedroom become apparent.

"How the hell did I get here? The last thing I remember, was tracking down a runaway in the mountains." Habitual reflex causes him to reach for the ever-present liquor bottle on his night table. Several gulps to calm his nerves, but the hair of this dog had no bite this day.

Running his hands down his coat he discovers he's still soaking wet. "Shit. That musta been some binge."

Head pulsing, he feels the area around the healed over injury. It is still slightly swollen. A few particles of dried blood cling to his fingertips.

"What's this? . . . Oh Shit. I was mugged."

Rolling the dried blood in his fingertips triggers Jason's memory. The graphic realization rushes back to his mind like a flood in Spring. Vivid, like it was just happening, the scene rolls before his eyes. An anguished cry escapes his lips while he throws his arms in front of his face and ducks.

"The meteor! It hit me . . . in the back of the head," he recalls, rubbing the sore spot. "But it's healed already. . . . Oh Fuck! How long have I been out of it? And why ain't I dead?"

From the corner of his red, puffy eye, he captures the electronic clock on the night table. Pulling it close he gapes in awe; hardly believing what he sees. The day and date appearing on the face of the timepiece says Friday. The last he remembered it was Monday. Four days vanished from his life . . . forever.

The only thing the physical at the hospital proved was that he was in fine shape; an anomaly in itself considering his years of alcohol abuse. If asked, he'd have said he belonged in the morgue for this exam, not among the living. He neglected to tell them exactly what kind of accident he'd had. They weren't going to measure him for that cute white jacket with the fashionably long sleeves that tie in the back. All went well until the Doctor called for a blood sample.

"Now that's weird," said the Nurse. "I've never seen a needle break before. It must be defective."

The second attempt ended with a like result. Something strange was going on here. Jason's detective instincts told him he better excuse himself before anyone got too curious.

"Look. You don't need a sample," he said, reaching for his coat. "I've things to do."

"But Sir. We're not finished."

"That's okay," he told her, backing swiftly toward the exit. You've got my name . . . and address. Just send me the bill."

"But Sir," she said, chasing after him.

Walking along the sidewalk in the early twilight he tried to sort out what just happened, not paying any attention to the world around him. When he absentmindedly crossed the street to get to the subway entrance, *DANGER* flashed through his mind like an air raid siren!

The driver of the bus bearing down on him must have been just as dumbfounded as Jason. The pedestrian he should have run down not only leaped to one side he cleared the semi across the street and landed in the park.

This was crazy. Jason was in no mood to sit around and answer a bunch of stupid questions from a gaggle of avid rubberneckers. Fortunately, a cab sat across the court waiting for a fare. He jumped in, telling the cabby there'd be an extra ten in it for him if he got out of there quick.

Jason sat in his apartment for the better part of an hour, watching the sun go down, trying to sift through it all. He chose to run some tests of his own. Certainly, his strength had increased, and he was less susceptible to harm. A stroke of a razor sharp knife on his fingertip proved that. With ever increasing pressure he found he could indeed draw blood, but not for long.

To his utter amazement the wound closed up almost immediately. He could only conclude that somehow the meteorite did this to him.

To test his strength he stacked up all his old barbells. He curled more weight with one arm than anyone could do with two.

Strength and rejuvenation; hundreds of times normal. What else was he capable of?

Dumbfounded, he stares out at the starlit sky. In the upper corner of the window a small spider engrossed him, spinning its web. After several seconds it dawned on him; the spider was over fifteen feet away but he saw it like it were only inches from his nose. Striding to the window he closed the drapes then turned off the lone lamp. Standing in the gloom his eyes perceived more and more until the room looked just like it would just before twilight.

"Fantastic!"

What of the other four senses? He tested his hearing first. The din that accosted his ears damn near took his head off. Even clamping his hands over his ears wouldn't shut it out. All his concentration was needed to shut it out. With careful practice he learned to control the direction and intensity of reception. The newlyweds upstairs were whispering sweet nothings to each other. Didn't they ever get out of bed? The cat down the hall was meowing to get out. He even heard the janitor, two floors down, cursing the tenant for clogging the disposal. Again!

He erred toward caution with the sense of smell, not wishing to take it in all at once. Gradually, different and distinct odors came to him. Harry, down the hall, smoked a particularly pungent cigar. Janice, across the hall, must be going out on an exceptionally heavy date. The perfume she was applying, she once told him, she wore only on special occasions. The odor of gas came from the upper floor; he called the Super to tell him about it.

The city water doesn't have too swift a taste like it is; what with all the purification and chemicals they have to add to make it drinkable. When you concentrate your taste buds to pick them out individually . . . what an awful experience. It took four shots of whiskey to flush the taste from his mouth.

It's incredible what you can feel with an enhanced sense of touch: the ridges in smooth glass, the grain of wood in the coffee table, even your own fingerprints. Practice would develop all his senses.

What of that intangible sense? The so-called sixth sense, ESP. He knew his ratings were high, but how to test them. The deck of cards? Where were they? He'd left them across the room on the coffee table.

His off hand gesture brought results that made him sit down to have a couple of shots. Impossible or not they flew on their own across the room to his hand. Shock dropped them to the floor.

This levitating trick had its limits; forty feet was it. He'd stacked up most of the furniture and found little trouble raising it up close. When he stepped away it became ever more difficult.

Then revelation set in; if he could levitate the furniture . . . why not himself? The initial attempt got him little more than a few tentative inches from the floor. The second attempt thumped his head on the ceiling. Shortly, he was flying around the room. His learning curve and reflexes were developing as swiftly as all his other senses.

The power of flight was intoxicating. He needed more room. The spirit of adventure, something he hadn't felt in years, grabbed him by the collar and ran him up the stairs two at a time to the roof to take one grand flight.

Totally dark now, no one should see him. The air, quite cold, couldn't be felt even though he stood there in his shirtsleeves. The first few flights were but short hops across the roof. Then, after checking the sky, he took off—straight up—fast as he could go.

At night, with the lights reflecting off the recent snowfall, the city shone quite pretty, the filth and trash hidden by the gloom. Soon, he could make right angle turns without slowing and stop on a dime. He even caught one very surprised pigeon with relative ease.

How fast was he? The airport lay twenty miles from where he hovered. The trip took exactly thirty-six seconds by his digital watch, which figured out to about two thousand miles per hour.

Hovering there, *DANGER* flashed through his mind like it did earlier in the day. Whirling to see what could be wrong, he found he'd blundered into the approach pattern of the airport. If he didn't want to be the hood ornament of an approaching 747 he'd better scram, and fast. It missed by several feet. If the pilot saw him he should have the good sense to keep it to himself.

The grand experiment over, it was time to plant his feet firmly back on the ground. He took a leisurely, round about flight, home to not cause further problems with air traffic.

* * * *

This *DANGER* sense had saved his hide twice. He doubted either incident would have been fatal but who needs to take chances.

Sitting in his room he tried to piece together the events of the day. Tossing down a few shots the warm pleasant burn in his throat was missing. These powers could open the door to a great many possibilities and pitfalls. Something absurd revolved in the back of his head.

When he realized what he was thinking he tossed back a quick shot then went to stare out the window.

The dirt-encrusted snow was melting off the dirt-encrusted

city. All manner of evil was having its way out there. No. It wasn't his place or responsibility. He needed another drink.

Getting Sheila away from those hoods was his first priority. Was she still okay? Like it or not, these powers were going to do it for him.

He'd need a disguise. No way he wanted to be recognized doing things no ordinary human could. His life, however bad it had become, was his alone. If the government knew who he was they'd hound him incessantly. He'd be a fugitive. They'd want to control him—try to dissect him—maybe even clone him. Then there would be the alienation of a public that would fear him because he was different rather than understand him. If anything, he learned from the comic books he used to collect, the super-hero never let the public at large know who he is. Super-hero. . . . That's the first time he thought of it that way. Well, he'd only be doing it once. Then it'd be back to business as usual.

The more he flipped through old comic books for ideas the more absurd the whole thing became. If he was going to wear a disguise, why not a flashy one? He knew he'd have to make it himself. Those kind of duds don't come off the rack at K-Mart.

The design was a piece o' cake. Making the thing was one friggin' adventure.

Fortunately, the stores were still open. Finding a pair of tights for the basis of the costume, he shopped for the accessories needed to complete it.

Taking an hour of cutting and sewing on the machine he'd borrowed from old Mrs. Mapes down the hall, he was glad the Army had taught him to sew. His enhanced reflexes allowed him to work at a faster pace than he'd thought possible, catching mistakes before they happened. Shortly after eight thirty he finished.

For better or worse he put it on. Crude at best, it fit well enough. Spandex can be so forgiving. Besides, he'd only be using it once.

He gawked in the mirror. Brother did he go overboard.

This power, this force of mind would later give him his name.

His subconscious must have known already for it prompted him to fashion the emblem on his chest and belt buckle. Gazing at himself he was certain that hit on the head had scrambled his brains.

Using his enhanced hearing to make sure the coast was clear, he sneaked up to the roof. He stood for a few moments taking in the night sky, took a deep breath, got a hold of the butterflies in his stomach, then launched himself northwest into the sky.

He flew at a leisurely pace. Not wanting to cause another sonic boom like he had earlier that evening. Fifteen minutes later he found the spot where he'd left his car. It was still there . . . and so were the keys in the ignition.

"Christ! I must have really been out of it. Well. Let's see if it'll turn over."

It did after some coaxing; much to his relief. Tow trucks were hard to come by way out here at night nor did he relish the idea of having to carry it home. Carry it home? What the hell was he thinking. Absurd? Certainly. But he couldn't resist trying. The remnants of a little kid wouldn't allow it. Being an adult he could pass it off as an experiment. Lifting the car overhead proved easy enough; flying with it wasn't difficult either.

Putting it back on the ground he remembered he always carried a change of clothing in the trunk. Your better drunks always had a change of clothes, just in case. Besides. Before he made a fool of himself in this get up, he'd see what Jason could find out.

Walking up the slope he passed the area where the meteorite struck him; where he lay for three days under the snow; more dead than alive. He shuddered. Again uncertain why the second chance at life. Unnerved by the feeling, if he'd had the bottle in his trunk he could not have resisted it.

Being a little cocky and self-assured he took the straightforward approach. He went right up to the door and knocked. While he approached he'd spotted a kerosene lamp shining in the window. Someone must be up. To his surprise, the girl opened the door. He hadn't seen her face too clearly on his last visit but this was Sheila.

The smell of cooking came to his enhanced nose. They were having a late supper. Too much pepper.

"Are you? . . ." but he never finished the question. He sensed the fear and despair in her mind like it were his own. The two dudes were still here, though he couldn't see them. To sense the tension in one and suspicion in the other was eerie. His senses were overloading with contradictions. He had to get out of there.

"I'm sorry. I'm looking for two priests that are vacationing somewhere in these hills. You're obviously not them, so I'll be on my way. Good night." He excused himself and stepped off the porch.

"That's right!" said Sheila. "I'd forgotten you were there fifteen minutes before Mindforce showed."

She was safe for the moment. The conflicting emotions he caught from them overloaded his senses. There was too much fear and tension in all their minds.

Deja vous only enhanced the overload while he reflexively scanned the night sky for falling objects.

There had to be a way to get closer to the situation. There must. *THERE MUST!* Get a grip. Your senses are overloading.

Without warning, and to his shock, a wraith-like copy of himself rose from within, while his body stood transfixed. Startled, he shouted an unheard "NO!" and the wraith returned to the body.

He gasped and clutched at his chest from fear and confusion. Calming himself, he realized this was his ticket in. They couldn't see or hear him, but he could learn a lot. Provided he could do it again.

Concentrating intently, the wraith appeared like before. Getting a grip on his emotions he willed himself to float toward the cabin; passing through the walls like so much smoke.

Inside, Sheila stood by the stove while the two scruffy looking dudes watched over her.

"That was good," said Ray, fondling the gun in his hand. "One wrong word from you and I'da had ta smoke 'im."

"So, What now," says Sheila. "Why don't you let me go? You've taken everything I have."

"No, no, no. We can't do that," says Lyle. "That was the best thing ever happened to us, your hitchin' a ride from us."

"You knew it once I explained it to ya," said Ray. Then he turned to Sheila. "Since the money ran out, I've sent a letter to your parents. If they wants ya back they has ta pay."

So that's their game. Ransom.

Waves of dizziness and weakness crash over Jason. Instinctively, he knew he must return to his body as swiftly as he could will himself. Returning to the spot where his zombie like body stood the merger of the two forms was not without incident. Upon touching the body with his ghostly hand the wraith was sucked inside. A moment of ill at ease, like the nausea and vertigo you felt after a long binge passed shortly. Apparently, he couldn't stay from the body for more than fifteen minutes. It was unlikely he'd ever want to again.

Time for his alter ego to take over. A swift change at his car, a few featureless gulps on the bottle, a deep breath and he flew toward the cabin.

A dramatic entrance felt like the best approach. Rush in and take them off guard before they had the chance to think. If he had it to do over. . . . She knew the rest.

After which, he flew to his car, changed clothes, then retraced his steps up the path to intercept Sheila running the other way.

After reuniting her with her parents and being he was closer to his office than his apartment, he went there. After firing up the coffee pot to warm the Bacardi he sat to contemplate. He'd debuted and closed after the first act. Of this he was sure. But these powers. . . . Would they eventually fade away. While he had them he would test their potential and limitations. Nothing more.

The rum tasted better than it had in years, but the buzz it brought with it never showed while he stood at the window through the night.

Dawned crept in between the office buildings out there before him. It was Saturday morning. The first Saturday morning in years he could remember seeing the dawn, and not on his way home to crash. He felt good for a change.

What a beautiful sunrise. . . .

* * * *

"So, that's it. Start to finish," said Jason, neglecting to tell her of his Empathy and Wraith abilities. To know that her emotions and feelings were not truly her own matters could be unsettling for her. He didn't want her to always be self conscious around him. "I couldn't tell you, but soon after, I found out I was immune to alcohol."

"So that's why you stopped drinking."

"Uh huh."

"And here I thought it was from my influence."

"Well, I did stop smoking because of you even though that can't hurt me anymore."

"But . . . why this, now?"

"Just pressure. Old habits die hard. I knew it wouldn't work. . . . It doesn't even taste good anymore. It's . . . it's just so difficult to cope. Being busy has helped."

"Christ. What the press has put you through in the last few weeks," she said, coming around to sit on the corner of his desk.

"A month ago I'd have cursed them to the depths of their ugly black hearts. Now. . . . Now I really don't care."

"So, why tell me all this?"

"I don't know. I needed to talk it out with someone. In costume it would be impossible. This way was easier."

He did know why he told her. Because she had an inner strength and an honesty he felt he could count on.

She picked up the broken bottle neck from the trashcan.

"I guess we'll never see this around her again," dropping it back in the can. "Will you be telling your parents?"

"No. I don't want to worry them.

"Your history of alcoholism couldn't have worried them any less."

"Touché. But I think I'll pass for now. I never wanted this. I would have much preferred to remain uninvolved. But . . . after this caper is over . . . Mindforce may never return."

She understood like he knew she would. Though there remained a hint of skepticism.

"I can be your sounding board, but you're still going to need counseling I can't give you."

"After this case. Right now I have no time."

"Okay. Look. I'm hungry. How 'bout I let you buy me breakfast?"

"Sounds great," he said, fishing around in his pockets. "What can we get for $3.59?"

She shook her head, giving him that wry grin. "All right. I'll buy. . . . This time."

* * * *

CHAPTER SIXTEEN

Time to Act!

Breakfast had been enjoyable with Sheila, if short. She understood his having to get to the meeting with the Commissioner and the FBI, telling him to go easy on himself and good luck.

He was glad he'd shared his secret with her. Doing so lifted an enormous burden from his mind. On the other hand, he felt a measure of guilt because his sharing had the reverse effect on her. She was a strong person emotionally. He doubted she wouldn't be able to handle it once the facts all settled in.

Nearing the Commissioner's office he paused outside to peer in the window. He plainly saw Jake and Capt. Quinn, along with one other person he'd never seen before; most likely the FBI agent.

Bowing to whim, he chose an impressive entrance.

Paying attention to some charts on the desk, they were unaware he zipped in at top speed; landing noiselessly.

"Good morning, gentlemen."

Three heads snapped around. Three sets of eyes gaped wide. Three mouths fumbled for words. The Commissioner, being used to this, found his voice first.

"Mindforce. Glad you could make it. How long you been there?"

"About five seconds."

"Well. Now that you're here we can get started. This is Inspector Atkinson of the FBI."

The Inspector looked him over with a distrusting eye while

they shook hands. Mindforce could sense the mental notes the Inspector made in those few seconds.

"I've been looking forward to meeting you. That was an impressive entrance you just made. Ever think of joining the Bureau? We could use a man like you."

The man was absolutely calm, not one to jump to conclusions. There was a half-truth to his words but Mindforce caught the sarcasm in his mind.

"Too dangerous for me," said Mindforce.

"I think you've met Capt. Quinn," said the Commissioner.

"At the press conference two weeks ago."

The Capt., a man of few words, preferred to listen before making judgments. The cop in him was not one to stand for outside interference, but the Commissioner was his boss and he was obliged to bow to his wishes most times. The cynicism rang true and clear. A barrier that Mindforce could see all too well. This made him hesitant to hold out his hand. When he did he made sure the Capt. got a firm grip; being sure to make eye contact.

"What say we get down to business," said the Commissioner. "The DA couldn't make it so we'll have to fill him in later."

"I understand you've seen the inside of the casino and can give us a layout," said the Inspector.

Sketching a rough diagram, Mindforce laid out the position of the secret elevator, the location of the various gaming tables, the bar and Mr. Big's private office with the exit to the abandoned tunnels.

"As you can see, there are only two ways into or out of the casino; the elevator and Mr. Big's private entry. I found no others."

"Did you find out how to work the elevator?" said the Inspector.

"No, I didn't. But it's undoubtedly inside the broom closet. You'll have to find it when you go in."

"When we go in? Aren't you going to be there?" said the Commissioner.

"Yes I will. But I'm going to be underground at the secret entrance when you raid the place."

"Any special reason?"

"Because when you go in from the top flashing the warrants, he'll try to escape out the exit."

"We expect they'll have some sort of warning device," said the Inspector. "That's why we're going to have men stationed in the tunnels."

"That's what I thought. You see, I've promised the little fat man one day I'd be there to snap the cuffs on him."

"Then you did see him this morning." said the Commissioner.

"I did. I've got him believing we don't know anything. He's so sure of himself he won't change his pattern in the least . . . Oh. One thing, Jake."

"What's that?"

"He didn't have Alfie Tulio killed. In fact, he didn't know anything about it."

"You certain?"

"You'll have to trust me on this one."

Mindforce ignored the skepticism washing over from both the Inspector and the Capt. He was beginning to not care what anyone thought. He'd not be around to hear their abuse for long.

"Does he know Tulio worked for the Crime Czar?" said the Capt.

"Doubtful. At least I didn't tell him. I didn't want him to think the Czar knew of the casino."

"Who do you think killed him?"

"Top suspect now . . . I'd say the Czar himself. Or at least he ordered it."

"Kill his own man. Do you suppose they had a falling out?" said the Inspector.

"Could be. He may have believed Tulio squealed on him, or tried to cut a better deal somewhere else."

"Why should he think that?"

"I'd found out about the Czar's bet with the Syndicate. Ten days ago I tracked down Alfie, who I believed to be the Czar's second in command. I told him what I knew about the bet and a few things I'd guessed at. In a fit of anger he told me he was prepared to step in and take over himself if the Czar succeeded."

"And this Tulio could have gone back to warn him."

"Exactly. I expected my scheme to smoke the Czar out into the open where we could nail him directly. At least, that's what I'd hoped for. This whole plot of theirs was supposed to be a secret. Even the Syndicate wasn't talking."

"So, how did you find out?"

"That'll have to remain my secret. All I can say is that I found out by accident while working on something else. Anyway, I assume the Czar must have been so enraged he blew Tulio away."

"Couldn't someone else have done it?" said the Capt., anticipating the Inspector's next question.

"Maybe. But I find it a rather large coincidence to find him dead, ten days later, in the same suit I last saw him in. I'm sure the Coroner's report will show he'd been dead at least that long."

"I put a rush on that report," said the Commissioner, "but I don't expect it until Monday. We know someone tried to weight him down when they dumped him in the river above the dam. We believe the increased flow from the Spring thaw in the mountains may have dislodged the body."

"Have you been able to dig up any proof that Mr. Big actually owns Quincy's?"

"It took some doing," said the Inspector, "but we got it. What a tangled mess."

"How's that?"

"My men waded through a bunch of dummy corporations and businesses that don't exist. The gist is: Quincy's is run by Elf Productions, which is owned by Atlas Entertainment. The Chairman of the Board is the proxy for the chief stockholder, the Westrix Corp., which is owned by one F.A. Bigsby. Your Mr. Big."

"That's a fairly thin connection."

"Maybe so. But it's enough to get me a Federal Warrant to seize all his records to check for possible income tax evasion."

"If you're going to seize his files we'd better coordinate it with the raid on the casino so they don't have a chance to destroy anything."

"That can be arranged. Y-know. There was one curious thing we discovered while investigating Mr. Big's ownership of Quincy's."

"What's that?"

"A group of lawyers was checking into all of Westrix holdings for a third party."

"Who?" said the Commissioner.

"Can't say. We didn't have the manpower or cause to do so."

"Do me a favor? Keep your men on it," said Mindforce.

"Sure. But why?"

"What's up your sleeve, Mindforce?" said the Commissioner.

"It all ties in. I've been convinced the Czar's actions were only a smoke screen."

"To what end?" said the Inspector.

"To keep Mr. Big busy. Drawing his attention elsewhere so that he couldn't see the real plan; to take over the Syndicate real estate holdings. Legally."

"If that's true, the man is insidious, and extremely intelligent," said the Capt.

"And doubly dangerous," said the Commissioner.

"And now that I've blown the lid off, that genius could cross over the thin line to insanity," said Mindforce. "If it hasn't already."

"I'll keep my men on it," said the Inspector. "Where do you expect it to lead?"

"If I'm right . . . straight to the Crime Czar. I doubt these lawyers know who they're really working for. If you dig deep enough, something may turn up."

"I'll do it, but only because it's a good idea."

The Commissioner flashed the Inspector a critical glare. He had no place for such hubris, though he himself had been guilty of it in the past. "Then we're a go for Tuesday. Is everyone agreed?"

The Inspector would have the warrants ready by Tuesday. He and a few of his men, supported by the police, would storm Mr. Big's offices and confiscate all records.

The Commissioner would lead a group of Federal men, along with Capt. Quinn and a select group of officers, on the casino entrance while Mindforce spearheaded the raid through the tunnels.

Together they'd arrest everyone on the premises, herd them into police vans and confiscate all property.

TUESDAY: 9 PM: The last three days couldn't go fast enough for Mindforce. Everything was ready.

Stationed atop the building across from Quincy's with three Federal men, stood Mindforce. When the word came He would drop them off at Mr. Big's penthouse.

The minor player in their quest, Judge Bradley, entered Quincy's as expected fifteen minutes prior.

9:15 PM: Mr. Big passed the first checkpoint in the tunnel. When he passed the second checkpoint, that was the cue to begin the airlift.

9:25 PM: Mr. Big passes the second checkpoint. The airlift to the penthouse begins. The extra duty police under the command of Capt. Quinn are alerted and move out.

9:30 PM: The Federal men are dropped on the patio of the penthouse where they find seclusion and await orders to move in.. Mindforce returns to take up his post in the tunnel.

9:35 PM: Judge Mercer signs the search and arrest warrants.

9:40 PM: The Federal men enter Quincy's one at a time, blending in with the crowd; taking up vantage points around the room.

9:45 PM: Commissioner Parman arrives with the Federal officers and the warrants. He waits out of sight while the troops are deployed.

9:48 PM: All streets are blocked off. The police force is deployed. From now on no one will be allowed to enter or leave the area.

9:52 PM: The Federal men take over the elevators in the Commerce Building and begin their ascent to the offices of Mr. Big.

9:55 PM: Mindforce and the men begin to move in cautiously.

There are electric eyes and surveillance cameras down there that have to be neutralized.

10:01 PM: On word from Mindforce that they are almost in position, Commissioner Parman enters Quincy's and presents search warrants to the manager. All patrons are ordered to remain seated. Telephone lines are cut outside.

10:03 PM: Thanks to the FBI and their high tech gear, all electronics have been neutralized. Mindforce stands at the two way mirror behind Mr. Big's private bar, watching him entertain his guests.

10:04 PM: All hell breaks loose. Someone upstairs has activated the emergency alert system in Mr. Big's office. A bell is sounding and a flashing red light over the door comes to life.

Mindforce watched through the glass while Mr. Big grabbed a few ledgers from the desk, headed for the secret exit and him.

The fat little man gaped, his face draining to ash white when the glass panel slid back and he came face to face with Mindforce.

"Hello, Francis. Fancy meeting you here."

Dropping his ledgers along with his jaw, Mr. Big turned to run. Before he could move an inch, Mindforce produced the handcuffs He brought along and snapped them on Mr. Big's wrists.

"I promised you, the next time you saw me, I might be there to snap on the cuffs. You know your rights as well as I do but there's a gentleman behind me who'll be glad to reintroduce you to them."

He opened his mouth to speak but Mindforce pushed him aside before he could utter a sound, and entered the room.

10:05 PM: Of the eight other people in the room Mr. Big entertained, the four closest to the door yanked it open and ran to try to escape.

To Mindforce's left stood one of Mr. Big's bodyguards. He reached inside his coat for his persuader. Before he could pull the trigger a gesture from Mindforce had it in his hand.

"UH uh. That's a no no."

The others, seeing the futility of it all, began assuming the position against the wall while Feds and Police flooded the room.

10:07 PM: Grabbing the door to the casino Mindforce's *DANGER* sense went off. Something bad waited for anyone trying to enter the casino; only one way to find out.

"You men stay put until I check out what's on the other side of this door." Then he yanked it off its hinges and stepped through.

A shotgun blast exploded from his right. The deadly pellets slowed against his force field, then dropped; rattling around the floor like pearls from a broken necklace. A second blast! The same results.

Mindforce turned his head slowly and deliberately to the right to the shocked bartender still with the sawed off 12 gauge in his grasp. Mindforce looked disdainfully at the pellets still rolling at his feet then back to the dumbfounded bartender.

"Didn't your momma never tell you, you can hurt someone with that thing?" he said while walking the five short paces to the near catatonic bartender, took the weapon from his hands and bent it over double for all to see. Then turned his attention toward the rest of the room.

"I suggest that anyone else who has firearms on them, remove them slowly, put them on the nearest table and step back against the wall."

Several complied without hesitation. Others did so grudgingly. One foolhardy one thought he'd shoot it out. A gesture, and it flew to Mindforce's hand to be disabled. If anyone had thoughts of heroics that quashed them.

10:09 PM: The Commissioner and his men, after finding the controls to the elevator, now entered the casino.

Weapons drawn, they did not expect to find so serene a situation. The Commissioner stood one hand on hip, removed his hat, scratching his head.

"What kept ya?" said Mindforce.

"Did you leave us anything to do?"

"Just the cleanup detail," he said, leaping over the bar.

They met in the center of the room to compare notes.

"Did we get 'im?"

"He's in the back room cooling his heels. And he's not too pleased about the whole thing."

"That's his problem," said the Commissioner, taking in the whole room. "We'd have been here sooner but the manager was playing dumb about where the controls for the elevator were. When I threatened to leak to the Syndicate that he blew the whistle on this place he couldn't have been more helpful."

"Typical."

"Would you get a load of this place. Looks like something from Atlantic City."

Stepping back a pace the Commissioner looked Mindforce straight in the eye. "Y-know. You handled this so well I can't see what you needed us for," he said with a sly grin.

"I guess my reputation preceded me."

"Commissioner," said Capt. Quinn, approaching. "Judge Bradley'd like a word with you."

The Judge, approaching in handcuffs, was not a happy camper.

"Jake! You gonna let them do this to me?"

"What're you doing here, Chuck?"

"Why I . . . I'm working under cover to expose this place!"

"You got any proof of that? Any documentation?"

"Well . . . no! I—"

"Well, I've got a general warrant here to arrest everyone on the premises, pending charges!"

"Well, what about this masked vigilante here? Aren't you going to arrest him? He was here! He came out of the back room!"

"It won't work, Chuck. Mindforce has been working with the FBI and my office on this raid for the past two weeks. He's the one who found the casino in the first place."

Realizing his bluff wasn't going to work, the Judge resorted to baser tactics.

"You can't do this to me, Jake! I'll see you lose your job! I'm still a powerful person in this town! I've got connections!"

"You read this man his rights?" the Commissioner asked of the Sgt. restraining the Judge.

"Yes we have."

"Well get 'im out of my sight before I puke all over his nice expensive shoes."

"You'll be sorry! I've got friends in high places!" The Judge's voice trailed off as he was taken away.

10:16 PM: Confirmation came by radio that all was secure at the Commerce Building and all reports were being seized. One casualty was reported.

From the slot machine area came a mild commotion. One of the officers was having trouble handcuffing one of the patrons. Mindforce and the Commissioner walked over to investigate.

"What's the trouble?" said the Commissioner.

"This man won't leave the slot machine, Sir."

"It's not fair!" cut in the man, imploring the Commissioner and Mindforce.

"What isn't?" said Mindforce.

"I've lost over twenty grand in this place! Now I finally hit this damn machine for the fifty grand payoff and this guy tells me I can't collect because everything's being impounded by the city! It just ain't fair!"

Somehow, Mindforce couldn't bring himself to feel sorry for the man. He and the Commissioner had a good chuckle over it after the man was taken away.

"We've got quite a few known members of the Mob here. Plus a few we thought were on our side," reported Capt. Quinn. "Aside from the Judge, we've also got Senator Belson's aide and the Mayor's secretary."

"The Mayor's not going to be too happy about that," said Mindforce.

"Tough!" said the Commissioner. "Now. Let's go talk to Mr. Big shot."

Led inside the private room, the Commissioner saw Mr. Big sitting quietly if not happily on the sofa. Two agents stood by awaiting orders,

"Nice place you got here," said the Commissioner."

"What? You think this is mine!" he said in his most innocent pose. "You're crazy. I'm just a customer. All you got on me is an illegal gambling charge. My lawyers'll have me outta jail by morning."

"Not hardly, Francis," said Mindforce. "You're going away for a long time."

"No Chance."

"Get 'im outta here!" ordered the Commissioner. "Before I do something I won't regret."

10:40 PM: They were up on the street again. A fine rain had begun to fall, leaving the street glistening in the bath of the streetlights.

The Commissioner pulled up his collar then tugged down on his hat to brace himself against the dampness.

"Hey? How come I'm getting wet and you're still perfectly dry?" said the Commissioner.

"Just a minor bonus from the force field I have," said Mindforce, placing a hand on the Commissioner's shoulder.

Instantly, the field shot out around the Commissioner, shutting out the drizzle.

"Thanks."

"Don't thank me. I didn't know I could do that until just now."

Everyone inside the casino had been placed in the vans and taken downtown.

The restaurant patrons had their IDs checked and noted. All were free to go.

All entrances to Quincy's Nite Spot were in the process of being sealed. Several men were left on guard in the tunnels to prevent anyone from entering via that route. Tomorrow, the casino would be gone over with a fine tooth comb.

10:45 PM: Mindforce was about to leave on his night patrol when Inspector Atkinson arrived.

"Looks like all was successful," he said, getting out of his car. "Any trouble?"

"Not a bit. They went quietly," said the Commissioner. "We heard you had a casualty."

"One of theirs. The man got a little trigger-happy and had to be put down. The few that were left lost their nerve after that and gave us a minimum of fuss."

"Did you recover all the files?" said Mindforce.

"Yep. Got a little hairy though."

"What happened?" said the Commissioner.

"They had a napalm gadget installed in the room. It was wired to several locations in the place. A trip of a switch and we'd have had a vault full of ashes to sift through."

"Sounds like you had your hands full," said Mindforce.

"Nah. Once we neutralized the device it was a piece of cake."

"We're all finished here and were about to leave," said the Commissioner. "You coming back to the office, Mindforce?"

"No. I've still got night patrol to do. I'll drop by tomorrow some time. . . . After all the paperwork is done."

"Thanks a lot, pal."

"I'll be by your office after I check with my men," said the Inspector. "Before you get away Mindforce, I should have something for you soon on those lawyers."

"Good. Whatever you turn up you can give to the Commissioner and I'll pick it up."

"Y-know. I like your style. You sure you don't want to come work for the FBI?"

"Too much red tape," he called down while he flew off into the night sky.

One down and one to go; they were halfway home.

Once the news hit the streets, he was certain the Crime Czar would contact the Syndicate to take over the vacant spot left by Mr. Big. Only, what the Czar didn't know was the Syndicate reneged on the bet a long time ago.

The strangest feeling of doom washed over Mindforce while he flew on patrol. Try as he might, he couldn't shake the feeling of impending disaster. His *Esper* sense, still so very new to him; he hadn't yet learned to read it properly. One lesson he had learned was not to ignore it. Would the final conflict spell the end of the Crime Czar . . . or Mindforce.

* * * *

CHAPTER SEVENTEEN

Final Conflict

The morning papers ran an account on the secret gambling den under Quincy's Nite Spot. They also related the fact that a prominent businessman, a long suspected leader in the underworld, had been arrested in the casino and was being held for questioning pending bail.

They even mentioned Mindforce's presence there but could only speculate on what his contribution was. A lot they knew.

Sheila called Jason at home, early, warning him to ignore it. "Those paragraph factories are only looking for a means to sell their fish wrap. Most honest people know better."

He had no idea how the media learned of the raid. They were there on the scene before they'd finished mopping up. But for the fact the whole block was cordoned off, allowing no one in, they'd have swarmed all over them. Asking all kinds of questions.

The media are most resourceful. Any time a number of official vehicles gather in one spot too long you can bet several reporters will descend like locusts to a wheat field to check it out.

In this day of telephoto lenses and long-range microphones, they don't miss much.

By noon on Wednesday nearly everyone within a hundred miles must have heard or read about the little midtown raid.

One in particular: the Crime Czar. Mindforce believed finding him would be the easy part. He was convinced no one could elude him for long. The web closed tighter all the time. Certainly, the information the FBI was gathering for him would be the final piece to the puzzle.

Sure. The Crime Czar was seen at a couple of the bookie joints that were taken over. Yes. All the men Mindforce captured in connection with the kidnapping of the hookers, fingered the Crime Czar as the mastermind behind it. None ever saw him without his mask. Not one knew who he really was. Thus the dilemma; if he can't be identified he can't be arrested and convicted.

One person knows who the Crime Czar is. One man could identify him as the brains behind it all. Like as not, that one man could confirm who bumped off Alfie Tulio.

He needed Freddy Lester in order to nail the Crime Czar. Freddy was the key. If he could figure it out so could the Crime Czar. He just might try to tie up that loose end before Mindforce could get to him.

Freddy had been summoned to the boarding house. Even now he entered the upstairs office where the Czar waited for him.

"You wanted to see me, Boss," he said upon entering the room.

"Yes. Did you see the morning papers?" he said, shoving his copy across the desk to Freddy.

"Yeah. I did. From what I heard, the FBI had them staked out for weeks."

Retrieving his paper and leaning back in his chair, the Crime Czar added, "You must learn to read more closely. The police were led there by Mindforce."

"How can you be sure, Boss? The papers hardly had anything to say about him. And it wasn't all good."

"Only because they couldn't get close enough to interview him."

"But, what about what the FBI boys said? "Forget about the FBI! They're a bunch of glory mongers! They'll take the credit for anything that goes down the way they want it to. No, no. You can believe Mindforce was the one behind it all."

"If you say so."

"That's what I like about you, Freddy. You're so rock solid in your opinions."

Freddy had no idea he'd just been insulted and the Crime Czar knew it.

"Now. How are the preparations for ridding ourselves of Mindforce progressing?"

"All the explosives are in place. The wiring and all the electronic gear you wanted installed should be ready by this time tomorrow."

"Excellent!" he said, slowly rubbing his gloved hands together while staring blankly upward.

"With Mindforce gone and Mr. Big out of the way, does that mean you take over the city?"

The Crime Czar's demeanor did an abrupt about face. Gnashing his teeth, his eyes turned colder, more sinister than ever. He crumpled the newspaper in his hands, ever tightening his grip, as if trying to strangle it or someone to death.

"NO! It doesn't!"

"But I thought y—"

"You thought wrong! As did I. We've been double-crossed."

"What happened, Boss?"

"I had my agents call them this morning after I heard the news."

"Well, what'd they say?"

"What did they say; the filthy rotten bastards reneged on me 'cause they said I didn't get rid of him! The cops did!" he raved, slamming the paper to the desk.

"Does that mean they're gonna come down here and claim the bet?" Freddy stammered. "I don't like the idea o' having ta take on the whole damn Syndicate."

"They better not try it! I haven't come all this way to stop now!"

"Whata we do then?"

"We go on with our plans. After we eliminate Mindforce, we concentrate on the assholes in New York. I'll show them they can't jerk me around and get away with it. They haven't heard the last of me!"

Freddy listened to the ravings of the Crime Czar, wondering all the while if he was indeed in league with a madman.

Only after the Czar calmed down did they get down to the business at hand.

"You remember the plan?" the Czar asked.

"Yeah. I'm to leave a message with the Commissioner's office to be given to Mindforce. I'm to fess up ta working with you and want to give myself up. But only to him."

"And when we get him in the warehouse, we blow his ass to kingdom come."

"Are you sure he'll walk to the middle of the building where we want him?"

"Don't worry. Once he's in the warehouse he'll check all around until he finds you. And once he's on the spot. . . ."

* * * *

After morning patrol, instead of going to the office, Jason found himself walking the streets of his old neighborhood.

He couldn't shake the feeling of doom all day—of imminent tragedy. Of this he was certain. What? He didn't know.

Good sense urged him to spend the day with his parents. Things were happening so fast he hadn't seen them in a couple of months. He told them this. With no cases pending, he felt he should spend his free time with them.

They were relieved and elated that he had cleaned himself up and was off the booze. He knew not nor had he cared about the anguish they suffered.

They spent the day going over old times; looking over old picture albums. By the time he'd finished one of Mom's special dinners he'd put his silent troubles to rest.

The sense of foreboding remained but now it didn't weigh so heavily. What ever, he was determined to handle it. He felt recharged.

6:30 came all to soon. Taking his leave after extended hugs and kisses and promises to take better care of himself, he changed to Mindforce again. He hoped the Commissioner was still in his office.

Arriving by 7, he found him in but not alone. Inspector Atkinson was with him; embroiled in a heated discussion.

Taking a sitting position on the ledge, Mindforce eavesdropped. What he heard set his blood to boiling.

The Inspector was informing the Commissioner that after he'd checked in with his own superiors, they were prepared to offer immunity to Mr. Big. Immunity and a new identity if he would reveal all he knew about the rackets to a Senate Committee.

With the confiscated records they were sure of an open and shut case against Mr. Big; and he knew it. Held without bail, facing a lengthy stay in the slammer, they felt he was ripe for a deal.

The Commissioner was beside himself. Mindforce echoed, thoroughly protesting any such deal no matter the supposed gains.

The Inspector reminded the Commissioner that his office's authority superseded local jurisdiction in such cases. He was arrested, he reminded, under a Federal warrant and they really didn't need his permission. They could take the prisoner any time they wanted. It would just look better for all concerned if the Commissioner gave his cooperation.

"BULLSHIT, Paul!" said the Commissioner. "You guys are real glory mongers. Why don't you take the keys and let 'im out on the street right now. For all the good it'll do."

"And I agree, Jake." said Mindforce, stepping through the opened window.

"Mindforce," said the two of them, their heads snapping around.

"You'll gain nothing by dealing with him."

"What makes you the expert?" said the Inspector.

"The Hydra has too many heads."

"And what's that supposed to mean?"

"Suppose he does deal with you. All the time he's talking the Syndicate will be acting; if they aren't already. By the time your

Senate Committee is finished, all the bigshot's alibis will be iron
clad. Sure. You'll get a few sacrificial lambs to keep the public
happy but you won't deter the Syndicate one iota!"

"You don't know what y—"

"Let me finish. So, when you've wound up your investigation
you'll have spent untold amounts of taxpayer's money running
around in circles. And you'll have to release Mr. Big because you
made a deal with him. And you can't violate his constitutional
rights. The Justice boys won't stand for that. After he's gotten a
new identity and location he'll get his face changed by a plastic
surgeon who'll die an accidental death. Then Mr. Big will resurface
somewhere else to start his corruption all over again."

Mindforce fumed; he was right and the Inspector knew it. All
their efforts to bring this man to justice would be for nothing.

Scanning the Inspector's emotions, Mindforce knew he
wouldn't win this one either.

He'd been through this before, early in his police career, after
his promotion to Detective. He'd collared a big time rackets boss
after a lengthy search and destroy effort. They made the same deal,
and after all of Jason's efforts to the contrary, he lost. Hopping
mad, he nearly quit the Force.

Called aside, Jason's Captain advised him he'd have to learn to
keep his personal feelings out of it. To work with the system they
had until the people demanded a change. That, or spend a lot of
time beating his head against the wall.

The system never changed; the red tape strangled him. Only
the transfer to Missing Persons kept him from walking away from
it all. From time to time he'd be ordered to help out on one case or
another because of cutbacks or manpower shortages. It was just as
well the force didn't want him. He didn't think he could have
coped. Upon reflection, Carmen was only the straw that broke the
camels back.

Now. Here he was. Facing the same situation again. He still
didn't like it. Maybe he should have shot him.

"That may be true, but I have my orders Too," said the

Inspector to the Commissioner. "When everything's cleared we'll be taking custody of the prisoner and shipping him to Washington."

"So your Senate buddies can find out how much incriminating evidence he wants to spill on their own corruptions first."

"That's uncalled for," said the Inspector. "I could have you arrested for that kind of talk."

"Try it," said Mindforce, stepping forward a pace, the Inspector reaching for his piece while he retreated.

"Easy, Mindforce! Easy," said the Commissioner, placing himself between them. "We're outmaneuvered here. Let it go."

Jake was right. He didn't like it, but he was right.

"Even if you can get him there alive," said Mindforce, the Syndicate knows Mr. Big is aware he was double-crossed. They may take the easy route by shutting his mouth; permanently."

"That's the chance we gotta take. We've done this sort of thing before y-know. We're not novices."

"I'll bet Jimmy Hoffa believed that, too."

"You're pushing it mister."

"Hey! That'll be enough of that," said the Commissioner. "I don't need this in my office."

"We'll take the prisoner as soon as possible," said the Inspector, implying his rank.

"Just like that." said the Commissioner.

"My hands are tied."

"If that's the case. He's yours . . . with my blessings."

"Thanks Jake." There was a complicated pause. "Look. Mindforce. I've got some data here that might help you find your Crime Czar." Reaching into his briefcase he produced two thick folders of Photostats. "Two of my men broke into those lawyers offices the other night and photographed their real estate files. I don't know if it'll help. I haven't looked at any of it."

"Well, we'll just have to sift through them and see if we can make sense of it. . . . Thanks," said Mindforce.

"No problem. Of course you know this is illegally gotten and therefore inadmissible in court."

"If it leads us to the Crime Czar, we'll worry about it later," said the Commissioner.

"I wish you luck."

They spent the better part of four hours sifting through the records. Front to back, back to front; checking against all the known companies in the registry. In the end they came up empty. They were missing something they were sure; but what?

"I think we're up a blind alley, Jake."

"Sure looks that way," he said, yawning and stretching. "Maybe we outta call it a night and tackle it again in the morning."

"You're probably right. It is getting late. I just can't help thinking we're overlooking something."

"Whatever it is it'll still be there in the morning," said the Commissioner, standing up from the desk and slipping on his coat.

"Y-know, I can't help feeling that if I'd followed Tulio that night he'd still be alive . . . and the Crime Czar would be cooling his heels in a cell right now."

"Don't reproach yourself son. You're a damn good *cop* and you did what you thought was right at the time."

"Come again?"

"Does it surprise you I know you're a cop? Or more precisely, an ex-cop."

"What ever gave you that idea?"

"Simple. You talk like a cop. You think and act like a cop, probably a Detective. You know Police procedure too well. But you weren't on the force here. Some big city though: New York—Detroit—Chicago—St. Louis maybe. My gut feeling is you gave it up because you couldn't work with your hands tied. Now that you've acquired these powers you've pushed yourself back into police work because you feel you can make a difference."

"Nice theory, but—"

"But I couldn't be farther from the truth. Yeah. I understand. You don't have to worry. What I believe will remain between us."

Trouble was, except for his being asked to resign, Jake couldn't be more correct, Mindforce mulled while he flew toward home. He was an intelligent man. No doubt about it. He hit the nail on the head.

They'd been in close contact the past few weeks. Allowing him ample opportunity to fit the pieces together. He'd need to be extra careful in the future. Better still, it would be in his best interest to be more aloof from the force, dealing primarily with the Commissioner. He'd sealed Mindforce's fate even if he wasn't yet aware.

Whether he let him in on his little secret would remain to be seen.

The hour loomed late for most everyone, but with the hours Mindforce kept the night was still young. His favorite snitch hadn't had a visit from him in over a week. Home would wait a little longer.

Mindforce scoped out the usual haunts and came up wanting. Strolling through some of the crummiest dives in the city, Leroy was nowhere to be found. Talking to no one, Mindforce just let his presence be felt. Leaving an air of uneasiness in his wake.

A strange breed frequented these joints just one step up from the gutter. With nothing to fear they feared him anyway. The tougher ones made eye contact but none were about to challenge someone they felt they could not best.

Not finding Leroy in his usual habitat wasn't any setback. If he was still in the city he'd have to go home sometime. He'd just wait for him there.

The window to Leroy's apartment wouldn't have held out a ten year old. The ancient locking device was a futile effort and he was inside in seconds.

The room was unchanged—except maybe it was a little filthier.

Searching the room he found, hidden behind the dresser, a cloth sack filed with several watches and some jewelry. Leroy had been busy at his trade. Shame he wouldn't get to fence these.

The clock was half wound and still ticking, so he'd been there within the last eighteen hours. His clothes and meager belongings remained making it unlikely he'd skipped town.

Sooner or later he'd be home and Mindforce would be there to greet him. The wait proved minimal.

2 AM; the sound of a key entered the lock. Mindforce positioned himself behind the door just before it opened. Leroy entered.

"It's about time you got home," said Mindforce, slamming the door behind Leroy.

Startled to find himself not alone, Leroy spun around, pulling his gun from his pocket, pointing it toward the voice.

A gesture and the gun flew to Mindforce's hand.

"Really, Leroy. Must we go through this every time I stop by to pay a visit?" he said, releasing the clip and ejecting the last cartridge in the chamber. "I'm gonna start believing you're unfriendly if this keeps up."

"Mindforce! What chu 'spect man when you bust into a guys home and sneak up on 'im inna dark! A man's got a right to perteck hisself in his own home. It'sa cruel world out there y-know."

"Only because crud like you make it that way," he said, tossing the empty gun to Leroy.

Not in a mood to bandy back and forth with Leroy he got to the heart of the matter. "You seen Freddy Lester lately?"

Prepared for the usual carping, bellyaching and grand run around, Mindforce was surprised at the quick response.

"I-I just left him . . . an hour . . . ago"

"What'd he want?"

"He s-said he couldn't come . . . around the past two weeks . . . because the Crime Czar . . . w-was keeping him busy."

Leroy acted like he were trying to keep his mouth shut but was losing the battle. Mindforce hadn't a clue why.

"Did he say what was keeping him busy?"

"They're . . . they're setting up a-a trap."

Something wasn't kosher here but he was getting results and

since his *Esper* sense was quiet he went on. He knew the answer but asked anyway.

"Who's the trap for?"

"You."

BINGO!

"Me? Where?" he demanded, his earlier premonition of doom recurring.

"D-Don' know"

"When?

"Don' know."

He'd expected someone might try to take him out one day, but never did he expect to be warned by anyone who'd just as soon see it done. There was a simple way to find out why.

"Why tell me all this? You'd love to see me wasted."

"Be-because y-you said I could never . . . lie to . . . y-you."

"What? When was that?"

"T-Two weeks ago. . . . Las' time you was here."

"Oh . . . my . . . God!" escaped his lips in a hushed tone.

"Huh?"

"Nothing . . . nothing."

His memory raced back to that night when he'd held Leroy by his heels off the fire escape. He recalled leaving him in a heap, cowering in the corner. Mindforce had scared him half to death extracting the info he wanted. Now it hit like a ton of bricks. He'd told Leroy, while Leroy was so distraught, not to leave town and that he could never lie to him. Without realizing it, Mindforce placed that suggestion in Leroy's mind; just as he had Benny back in New York.

The hesitation in his voice must have been due to the internal conflict between his secretiveness and Mindforce's mental suggestion forcing him to tell the truth.

He'd forgotten about that power and inadvertently used it on Leroy. He'd have to be careful in the future. Not knowing the range of this power it might one day do more harm than good. Still, that was over two weeks ago. Why hadn't it worn off by now?

"All right, Leroy. I'm finished with you," he said while pulling Leroy's sack of loot into view. "But I'm taking these little trinkets into the Lost and Found Dept. Maybe they can find the rightful owners."

"Hey man! You can't do that!"

"You wanna come down to the station and explain how you got these?" he asked, swinging the sack from the string closure.

"No. . . . But a man's gotta make a livin'!"

"Get a job," he said, making his way to the window.

"Easy for you ta say."

"One last thing. You keep your mouth shut about what you just told me. Got it?" Leroy nodded hesitantly.

Having heard all he needed or at least all he could think to ask, Mindforce left the way he came.

The trap was set. Only, the trappers didn't know the mouse was wise to them. A small advantage but it was better than nothing.

Mindforce had no idea what would be needed to take him out and he was sure he didn't want to find out.

Sleep didn't come easy nor did it visit for long that night. Jason's mind continued to sift through all the records he'd absorbed the past evening. The answer was there somewhere. He just couldn't put a finger on it.

Around 5 AM he drifted off to a fitful sleep, waking only an hour later.

He got to the office at 10, after his morning patrol. Two potential clients were waiting for him.

The first was a parent needing help to find her runaway teenager. The second, a jealous husband wanting someone to follow his wife around to see if she was unfaithful.

Taking the first he declined the latter. Telling him it wasn't his line of work, then steered him to the competition down the street. They'd surely be eager to assist him.

By noon he'd cleared the desk. He told Sheila Mindforce would be busy for a while and he couldn't be sure when he'd return if at all today. He hesitated telling her the truth. Why worry her. Though she likely would anyway.

He arrived at the Commissioner's office in the middle of lunch at his desk.

"Mindforce. Come in. Have some lunch. I ordered way too much."

"Uh, no thanks, Jake," he said, sitting on the corner of the desk. " The hood y-know."

"Sorry."

"No sweat. You been able to make any sense of all the data the Inspector left us?"

"I'm having it fed into the computers now. Maybe it can come up with a pattern."

"I keep thinking we're missing something so simple. Something so obvious we can't see it. But I can't put a finger on it. I hope the computer can."

"Assuming we're not chasing a wild goose here, it's the best chance we have to come up with something quickly."

"We Should—"

A sharp rap on the Commissioners door interrupted them. The Sgt. entered carrying a small envelope.

"What is it?" said the Commissioner.

"I've got a message here addressed to Mindforce in care of you, Sir."

Mindforce took the envelope and read it's contents with chagrin.

On it was:

DEAR MINDFORCE,

I WISH TO TURN MYSELF IN. BUT ONLY TO YOU!

I'VE BEEN WORKING FOR THE CRIME CZAR FOR THE PAST YEAR. HE KILLED MY FRIEND AND MAY KILL ME NEXT.

BE AT THE NORTHEAST CORNER OF VET
STADIUM BY THE TELEPHONES AT 11 O'CLOCK
TONIGHT AND BE ALONE.

FREDDY LESTER

"Where did you get this?" said Mindforce.

"It was hand delivered by a private messenger."

"See if you can catch him before he gets away and bring him to me."

The Sgt. looked around Mindforce to the Commissioner for confirmation. Jake nodded.

"What is it?" said the Commissioner.

"An invitation to a murder."

"A murder! Whose."

"Mine . . . actually," he said, handing the note to Jake.

"That's a pretty wide open spot to attempt a murder."

"True. But it's still a trap to get me, Jake."

"How can you be so sure?"

"I have my sources." Relating the incident with Leroy.

"Can you trust him? After all—"

"I know. He's a small time hood and probably in league with Freddy Lester. But why warn me of a trap if there wasn't one?"

"I don't know but I don't like it."

"I've got other powers besides the ones I've shown."

"Oh? . . . ," said the Commissioner, settling back in his chair.

"Yes. One being a built in lie detector."

"So that's why you're always so sure of your facts."

"Uh huh, but the less known about my powers the less anyone can try to circumvent them."

"Can . . . can you read minds?" he said, half out of curiosity, half in apprehension.

"No. And in some ways I'm glad I can't. But I can tune in on a persons emotions. I just want you to know why I sound like I have inside knowledge."

Somewhat relieved and not really sure why he should, the

Commissioner went on. "Look. How about I have my men surround the place?"

"No. He wants me there alone. Besides, his wanting me by the phones leads me to believe I'll probably get further instructions once I'm there."

"So. We'll tap the phones there."

"You can, for all the good it'll do you."

"Meaning?"

"Meaning they don't want any cops anywhere. You know as well as I do I'll probably get the run around a few times before they tell me where the trap really is."

"You're right. How about a tracer on you somewhere?"

"Might not have enough range." He was deliberately trying to dissuade the Commissioner from having him followed. He couldn't be sure what the trap was but it had to be something big. He didn't want a bunch of police officers dogging his heels and maybe getting killed. If he were to die tonight he'd prefer to do it alone.

"Okay. You handle it your way and I'll stick with the computer. Just keep me informed if you can."

"Will do," he lied. "Hopefully the computer will tell us something before I have to spring the trap."

The Sgt. who'd handed them the letter returned with the messenger.

"Got your man for you, Mindforce. Just before he got into his car."

"Good work, Sgt.," he said, retrieving the note from the Commissioner.

"Who gave you this note to deliver to me?"

"Don't know," he said, shrugging.

"Why Not? Aren't you supposed to keep records?"

"Yeah, we are. But that was slipped under the door before we opened this morning, pinned to a twenty. The note said to deliver it here between noon and one o'clock."

"And you have no idea where it came from?" said the Commissioner.

"Sorry," he said, shrugging again.

"Okay. Thanks," said Mindforce, dismissing the man.

"Whata ya think?" said the Commissioner.

"I think it's a trap."

10:59 PM: northeast corner of Veterans Stadium.

The computer hadn't hit on anything significant yet but there were still a few programs to run.

At exactly 11 PM one of the phones next to Mindforce called attention to itself as he expected. He picked it up on the third ring.

"Talk to me, Freddy."

"No-no. We can't be sure the cops ain't got this line tapped. We know you can fly pretty fast. If you want the Crime Czar, go to the phone on the corner in front of the Art Museum. Be there in 30 seconds or the deal's off."

Freddy hung up without another word. The chase was on as Mindforce hung up his end and took to the air. He arrived at the Art Museum with 10 seconds to spare. He could have been there sooner but he didn't want to cause any low level sonic booms.

The phone on the far end of the array rang right on schedule. He answered it before the first ring had completed.

"What kept ya, Freddy? I've been waiting patiently for your call."

"Good. You made it. Be at the southwest corner of Hunting Park for your next instructions. You got 30 seconds." (click)

He was off like a cannon shot, covering the few miles to Hunting Park in good time. The southwest corner had several phones scattered around it. The one that began to ring stood next to a park bench occupied by a wino sleeping it off. Mindforce lifted it to his ear by the third ring.

"Where to next, Freddy?"

"I was afraid you'd gotten lost."

"Yeah, well, there are a lot of phones here."

"Never mind that. I'm gonna tell you where to meet me."

"It's about time."

"You want the Crime Czar don't ya?"

"More than you know, Ace. But why me? Why not go to the police?"

"I got my reasons."

And Mindforce was well aware of those reasons.

"Now go to the end of Kingsley St. in Manayunk, near the river. You'll see an old abandoned warehouse there. I'll be waiting for you inside. If you're not there in one minute . . . well, you'll never find me." (click)

Now he knew where he would either live or die.

While talking to Freddy, the wino on the bench stirred. Propping himself on one elbow, the wino was none too pleased at being disturbed.

"Hey! Wa-sha big (hic) ideaaaa? Whooo tol' ya (hic) tol' ya you could ushe m-(hic) m-phone?"

There wasn't time to belabor the point. Mindforce had places to go and people to see. Disappearing so fast the old wino blinked his eyes in amazement, then pulled the brown bag from under his coat for another dose of amnesia.

The warehouse was due west of the park, roughly five miles away. No way he'd need a full minute to get there. He'd have time to scout the area before he was expected.

Freddy had said "We" instead of I when he said he knew Mindforce could fly pretty fast. If he didn't know it was a trap, that little slip would surely have put him on his guard.

The whole thing seemed slipshod. They must really have underestimated his intelligence. And though it shouldn't have, it kinda ticked him off. If the Army taught him anything it was never to underestimate your adversary. Always assume he knows as much as you do. To do otherwise could prove fatal.

Nothing outwardly unusual expressed itself with the appearance of the warehouse. It was in a deserted area of the town with only a few lights to illuminate it.

Next to the loading dock, on the street side of the building, was an access door. As expected, it was unlocked.

Some time had passed since he last attempted to release his

ghost. Not since the time in the subway tunnels. He really had had no need of it. Even if it could emerge he wasn't sure he wanted to be out of the body at a time like this. He couldn't be sure how vulnerable it was while the ghost was gone. He shuddered to think what could happen if someone were to find it.

He opened the door—stood there for a couple of seconds—then, for better or worse, went inside. The door closed automatically behind him and latched shut.

He turned instinctively at the sound of the latch closing. Despite the fact there were no lights, his night vision clearly picked up the micro-switches on the door and jamb. The wiring ran off to who knows where.

The installation was fresh. Like as not installed in the last few days. He wasn't supposed to see the setup but they couldn't know that he could see perfectly in the dark. They, because his enhanced hearing picked up the distinct pattern of two heartbeats.

Dusty old carpet rolls leaned against or near the walls; remnants scattered everywhere. Several years of accumulated dust lay upon the floor with hundreds of fresh footprints running off in all directions,

Forty-five feet away stood a wall of crates and cardboard boxes; stacked nearly the full height to the roof.

The wall of boxes just about halved the building, an opening about midway from the left wall to the center. This was obviously where he was expected to go. Since he shouldn't want to disappoint his hosts he proceeded through the opening. Cautiously.

Through the opening, on the other side, lay a corridor some six feet wide. It's boundaries formed of more crates and boxes stacked some fifteen feet high. Dusty carpet remnants lay strewn all about making it necessary to walk across them.

About fifteen feet in the corridor turned right. He negotiated the turn with increased caution.

His quarry were aware he was here; their heartbeats accelerated now that he was getting nearer.

Mindforce stood at the bend in the corridor for several seconds, looking over the situation; weighing his options.

Light from the street lamps outside filtered through the rows of glass block high up on the far wall; giving a faint glow to the crates and boxes high upon the stacks.

The corridor he was expected to traverse lay in the gloom cast from the makeshift walls. They were hiding something from him and without his night vision he'd be as good as blind in this low level of light. At the end of the corridor lay an exit door, a fresh installation of micro-switches upon it.

He must have been making his hosts very impatient while he stood there, not moving.

From an alcove to the left near the door one of them stepped into the dim light at the opposite end of the corridor. It was Freddy Lester. He'd remembered his face from the mug books.

Freddy's heart thumped at twice the normal pace and was increasing. Agitated and apprehensive would be an understatement. Whatever was going to happen would be in this building, very soon.

They stood for several seconds sizing up one another. Mindforce was at a loss to know how Freddy knew he was at the end of the corridor in this ebony gloom. A person with normal vision shouldn't be able to see their hand before their face let alone where he stood.

His unspoken question was answered when he glanced around the parts of the building he could see. Up, in the girders, tucked in the corner sat a miniature surveillance camera, probably infrared too. That's how they knew he was in the corner.

Mindforce broke the silent stalemate first.

"Freddy Lester. At last we meet. Face to face."

"Mindforce! I knew you'd make it." The sweat running down the sides of his face did not go unnoticed.

"Whata ya got for me, Freddy?"

"I-I wanna make a deal."

"What kind of deal?"

"C-Come over here a-and we'll discuss it."

"I can hear you just fine from here."

Their plan was unclear though it was apparent Freddy needed him closer in order to spring the trap. If he stalled a little longer he might learn if the other heartbeat was the Crime Czar and capture them both.

Willing to gamble, Mindforce felt that if they believed he was secured the Crime Czar just might step out into the open to gloat.

"I've got names and addresses written down, with me." Freddy waved them out in front. "You want 'em you gotta come get 'em."

That was a lie! Freddy's emotional pattern and heart rate went through the roof.

With few options and unsure what they were up to he still wanted the Crime Czar and would have to take that chance.

"If this is a double-cross, Freddy, You may live to regret it," he said, hoping to make Freddy reconsider his options.

"Trust me."

The lying serpents tongue should snap off! That statement was supposed to lead the lamb to the slaughter? Freddy was committed to whatever they had in store for Mindforce and convinced they could pull it off. Slowly stepping forward, Mindforce was just as convinced they didn't have a prayer.

His *DANGER* sense hummed in his brain ever since entering the warehouse. He'd been trying to shut it out all the while to no avail. On his fifth step it hit the roof!

Flood lights all around the corridor erupted into life, bathing the area and Mindforce in intense blue white light. At the same time a voice blared out of a half dozen speakers all around him.

"IF YOU WANT TO LIVE BEYOND THE NEXT SECOND, YOU WILL STAND EXACTLY WHERE YOU ARE, MINDFORCE!"

Disoriented for a couple of seconds from the sudden brightness and the loud voice he was not so confused he didn't heed the advice.

"All right. You got me for now. I'm standing still," he shouted in no particular direction. "What now?"

"VERY GOOD. . . . UNDER THE CARPET BENEATH

YOUR FEET IS A PRESSURE SENSITIVE PAD. I'M ASSURED THAT WITHIN TWO MILLISECONDS AFTER YOU STEP OFF THAT PAD THE DETONATOR WE'VE RIGGED WILL SET OFF THE EXPLOSIVES ALL AROUND YOU."

The layers of dust and damp moldy carpeting had helped mask the smell of the explosives he now sensed. He kicked himself for not checking closer. Had he heeded his *DANGER* sense instead of trying to shut it out his nose would have alerted him as it now did. What would they have done if he'd floated over instead of walking? There was no telling now.

The Czar was insidious. Mindforce had underestimated his guile. Genius or madman? He opted for the latter.

"IF YOU'LL LOOK AROUND YOU, THERE ARE THREE TONS OF EXPLOSIVES IN ALL THOSE CRATES."

Great! One move and he'd kill all of them . . . and take out half the block in the process.

"You won't get away with this."

"YOU WON'T BE ALIVE TO FIND OUT."

"How do you know the police aren't on their way here right now?" he said, half hoping the computer had come up with something.

"LET THEM COME. I'VE GOT YOU NOW. WHEN THEY BREAK IN HERE THEY CAN HAVE THE RESPONSIBILITY FOR BLOWING YOU TO KINGDOM COME.

"ON THE DOORS INTO THE BUILDING ARE A SERIES OF MICRO-SWITCHES. ONCE I LEAVE AND THE DOORS CLOSE BEHIND ME, IF ANYONE SHOULD TRY TO OPEN ONE OF THEM, THE DETONATOR WILL AUTOMATICALLY EXPLODE."

"You're a madman."

"THAT'S YOU'RE OPINION."

"Why kill innocent people just to get me?"

"TO SHOW EVERYONE I MEAN BUSINESS."

"Tell me something. What's to prevent me from stepping off this pad now and taking you two with me?"

"BECAUSE A GOODY-TWO-SHOES LIKE YOU WOULDN'T DELIBERATELY TAKE A LIFE."

"Self defense."

"GO AHEAD. STEP OFF THEN."

Sweat cascaded from Freddy. His heart thumped like a trip hammer. He was unsure what Mindforce might do but Mindforce wasn't. The Czar had him. He couldn't do it; wouldn't do it. The Czar called his bluff and won.

"NOW. AFTER I'VE GOTTEN SAFELY AWAY YOU CAN STEP OFF THE PAD AND PUT YOURSELF OUT OF YOUR MISERY. OR, YOU CAN WAIT FOR SOMEONE TO COME SNOOPING AROUND AND DO IT FOR YOU. OF COURSE, THAT MIGHT TAKE SEVERAL INNOCENT PEOPLE WITH YOU. THE CHOICE IS YOURS. BUT YOU WON'T HAVE TOO LONG TO FRET OVER YOUR DECISION BECAUSE I'M SETTING A TIMER THAT WILL DETONATE THE EXPLOSIVES IN THIRTY MINUTES. NOW, ON THE OFF CHANCE THAT YOU MIGHT BE JUST FAST ENOUGH TO FLY OFF THE PAD OUT OF HERE AHEAD OF THE EXPLOSION, I'M GOING TO LEAVE FREDDY HERE TO KEEP YOU COMPANY."

Freddy, who had been standing nervously, went ashen faced in horror. Abject fear emanated from him while he turned to his right. He attempted to speak while his hand darted into his coat. Nothing came forth because the Crime Czar stepped from the alcove striking Freddy upon the head with an iron pipe.

He fell into a heap at the Crime Czar's feet, then dragged back into the alcove and beyond.

What could he do? Mindforce was helpless. Compelled to stay rooted to the spot. Out of levitation range, he was unable to halt the stunning blow.

A million scenarios raced through his head and were rejected. Whatever, someone had to die here tonight.

If he moved he'd kill them all. Maybe he could fly out fast enough and save himself, but there would never be enough time to find Freddy and get them both out. No way he could leave the man behind whether he deserved it or not. They were doomed in thirty minutes or less if he couldn't come up with an answer to this dilemma.

His brain accelerated. How the hell could he have let this happen. Could he come up with the solution before the timer ran out or someone entered the building. And there was no way to warn them before they tried. He kicked himself for his cavalier attitude. He should have worn some sort of wire. At least anyone who might come to his rescue could be forewarned.

The Crime Czar returned seconds later from where ever he left Freddy; still alive since he could detect his heartbeat somewhere back behind the crates. Their only hope lay in whether Freddy could come to in time to halt the countdown, and only if he weren't tied up, and if no one entered the building first. Too many ifs to bet your life on. Now he hoped the computer had drawn a blank.

The Crime Czar took a long look at Mindforce, gave a contemptuous salute and without speaking, walked to the exit behind him. Pausing at the door he took one last look. Mindforce seethed; certain the Crime Czar must be smirking under that mask.

Out of range of his empathy powers he couldn't read the Czar's emotions. He could only guess. Elation? Self-satisfaction? Feelings of Superiority? Lord only knew. The Czar nodded one last sanctimonious salute then turned to go.

When the Czar placed his hand on the exit bar and gave it a shove the world as Mindforce knew it lit up like an Atomic Blast with the thunderous roar of ground zero!!. . . . . . .

4:37 AM: AMID THE WRECKAGE.

The police computer did finally crack the code. The Commissioner and a few of his top men, along with the local police, were converging on the scene when the blast lit up the sky.

Lady Luck had come along for the ride because they were just five blocks away when the warehouse roof leaped into the night sky on a tail of fire and debris. Burning chunks of roof, carpeting and boxes showered down on the area like a July 4th display. Hunks of glass and concrete block hurtled through the air, bashing into and smashing everything in their path. Several pieces ricocheted off the Commissioner's car; smashing a headlight, denting the roof and hood and cracking the bulletproof windshield. If they'd been on the scene they surely would not have survived.

It took a little over an hour and a half for the firefighters to bring the blaze under control. Most everything had been blasted away from the warehouse. A lot of their work was now tied up in putting out secondary fires ignited by the burning debris launched from the site. Fortunately, most of the flaming missiles landed in the river. Very little of the remnants remained in the warehouse to burn.

Now they methodically searched through the still smoldering, steaming piles of rubble for the remains of anyone unlucky enough to be caught in the blast. Especially Mindforce, who they were sure had been lured here.

"Do you think he was in there when it went up?" said Lt. Carlson to the Commissioner while they stood at the edge of the rubble where the east wall of the warehouse once stood.

"God, I hope not! But . . . this is where he was obviously led."

"How can you be sure?"

"If he wasn't then where is he? A blast of this size would have brought him here to see if he could help."

"Yeah. Looks like you're right. . . . How long do you want to keep the men out here?"

"As long as it takes to comb every square inch of this place, and every place within five blocks of here. The blast could have thrown his body anywhere. If we don't find him here we'll drag the river as well."

The bodies of Freddy Lester and the Crime Czar had been found an hour earlier. Leading the Commissioner and his men to wonder what the hell had gone wrong. Due to the heat and blast the bodies had been rendered unrecognizable. They were found near what had been the west wall, at the edge of the search area.

They slowly worked their way across, diligently searching under everything.

Somewhere near the middle of the wreckage one of the men came across the object of their search.

"I've found him, Sir!" called out one of the men. "The body's half buried under one of the girders."

The Commissioner, Lt. Carlson and a half dozen other workmen rapidly worked their way to the spot where the body lay. At the depression in the ruble the Commissioner found the rescue worker kneeling over the exposed parts of the body where he had lifted some loose rubble. The right arm, hip and leg were clearly visible.

"Damn!" said the Commissioner. "I was hoping he'd gotten out of here."

"We'll get some equipment in here to get these girders off him." said the Lt.

"What a waste. If only he—"

The Commissioner caught his breath as the body twitched.

"Must be an involuntary reflex," said the Lt. "No way he—"

"HEY!" said the workman crouched near the body. "This man is still alive!"

"ALIVE! Well let's get this shit off him!" said the Commissioner.

The rescue workers frantically but carefully hastened to remove the rubble from the body of Mindforce while the Paramedics grabbed their equipment and hurried in. A dozen men put their backs into lifting the girder off him.

"Wait!" said one of the Paramedics. "He's got a hunk of metal from the girder sticking through his left shoulder. We lift this off him we're going to yank it out."

"Do it," said the Commissioner after due consideration. "I want him outta there."

"Wait," said the Paramedic. "You could do more harm than good if you do that."

"Noted. I'll take the heat for it. Now let's get this off him."

"We still should wait and cut the piece free of the girder first."

"With what? A hacksaw would take to long."

I've a diamond tipped power saw for such things," said a rescue worker."

No good," said the Commissioner. "There's no room to work down there. One slip and you slice his throat."

"What about an acetylene torch?"

"And then you fry him. No. We pull this thing off him and deal with it later."

The first recollections Mindforce had after the blast were of being lifted by several arms—of direct pressure on a searing pain in his shoulder—and of faraway voices barking orders.

"Carefully now. Lift him gently . . . , get that stretcher over here . . . , and see if you can get BP and heart rate . . . get that oxygen on him."

In a semiconscious, twilight world, he was aware of being carried, drifting in and out of reality.

Someone tugged at his mask, evoking an instinctive reaction. His right arm shot out, catching his assailant under the right armpit, holding him forcibly at bay.

"OW! WOWWOW! He's got a grip like a vise!" said the Paramedic.

"It's all right son. Let him go. We won't take off your mask," said the reassuring voice of the Commissioner. "Give him the oxygen mask and let him do what he wants."

Mindforce took the mask in his good hand and clamped it over his face, inhaling deeply.

"This man is incredible," said the Paramedic. "He should be dead, yet here he is. Even in this state his BP is perfect. And his heart and lung action is twice as good as ours. And look at this! This is incredible!"

Even as they had carried him from the debris and began to work on him the bleeding had stopped. They stood there agape while the wound in his shoulder began to close; healing itself. Within fifteen minutes it was closed completely. Another hour or so and you'd never know it was there but for the bloodstains around it.

Becoming more aware of his surroundings, he made his first feeble attempts at sitting up.

"Careful, son," said the Commissioner. "Maybe you ought to lie back down for a little while."

"OOOOH. Did anyone get the number of that truck?" Mindforce said to no one in particular, cradling his head in his hands.

"Take it easy. You're still with us. Thank God. Do you feel up to telling me what happened?"

In among the verbal tests the Paramedics were trying to give him, along with the poking and prodding, he explained what transpired from the first phone call at the stadium to when the Crime Czar attempted to leave.

" . . . and the last thing I remember was diving for the floor."

"What do you think happened? He obviously hadn't intended to blow himself up."

"You got me, Jake," he said, rising to his feet on shaky knees then thought better of it. "Something obviously went wrong." He sat down on the tailgate of the Paramedic's van.

"Something probably did," said the head of the Bomb Squad who approached from the wreckage.

"How's that?" said Mindforce.

"Well. It's more like some *BODY* went wrong rather than some *THING.*"

"Lay it out for us," said the Commissioner. "And hold on to the technical mumbo jumbo."

"From the description Mindforce gave of the equipment and what my men were lucky to dig up, we feel this Crime Czar himself was to blame."

"You mean he inadvertently set off the charge?" said Mindforce.

"Looks that way."

"But how could such a thing happen?" said the Commissioner before Mindforce could.

"Mindforce, you said that the Crime Czar had set the timer for thirty minutes?"

"So?"

"So. We were fortunate to find most of that timer in the rubble while we were digging them out. From what we found of it we were able to establish its manufacture. It's a digital timer. A highly expensive but very tricky and deceiving little unit."

"Which means?"

"Which means, that in setting the timer for thirty minutes he may have unknowingly set it for thirty seconds instead. It's a dangerous little unit and the smart ones stay clear of it for that reason."

"What a stupid waste."

"The fact that you got down on the floor and that the blast went primarily straight up may have been what enabled you to escape getting killed."

"He tried to kill you and Freddy but ended up destroying himself in the process," said the Commissioner.

"That's the part that doesn't make sense. The man didn't seem that stupid to me. His moves were all so finely calculated."

"But he was pompous and arrogant."

"And maybe overconfident as well," said Mindforce, rubbing the back of his head. "We may never know who he was now."

"Say! You never told me how you knew to come to this place."

"The computer finally coughed up the answer. We were getting nowhere with it until we asked it to look for similarities among the data. This warehouse, the boarding house up the street and the buildings around it were supposedly purchased by four different parties, all on the same day. Checking further we learned that those for fictitious parties all had the same address."

"Where was that?"

"Would you believe it? A Post Office box downtown. That was good enough for us. At least it was worth checking. If we'd been three minutes sooner they'd have needed a lot more body bags."

"And the Czar would have gotten a lot more than he wanted; getting rid of me and you at the same time."

"Maybe that's what he was hoping for?"

"Well, Jake. If you've no further need of me I'll be on my way," said Mindforce, standing up.

"Whoa. Wait a minute. Don't you think you should go to the hospital to get checked out?"

"There's nothing they can do for me," he said, not wanting to be placed under the microscope and looked up every orifice until he was eligible for Social Security. "No thanks. I'll pass this time around."

"Talk some sense into this man," said the Commissioner to the Paramedics while they packed up to leave.

"There's no real need," said one of them. "With those recuperative powers of his all he needs is a little rest. Besides, we can't make him go if he doesn't want to. The man is amazing. We should be in as good a shape as he's in right now."

Rubbing the back of his neck and shaking his head, the Commissioner turned back to Mindforce. "You got any other abilities you'd like to tell me about?"

"Sorry Jake. Some things are just gonna have to stay a mystery for awhile."

"All right. Get out of here. I guess we can clean up the mess without you."

After shaking hands, Mindforce took off into the early morning sky; the rising sun giving a pale pink glow to the eastern horizon.

He'd gambled with his life this night and come out on top. He'd been lucky. Very lucky. Again.

With this case closed he wouldn't be taking those chances again. Mindforce would be hanging up his costume for good. He'd made up his mind long before the blast. Innocent people could have lost their lives here tonight and almost did because he existed.

The public will think he died in that blast even though Jake and a few others knew different. Mindforce could be a force for good but he'd always be a target. Too tempting a target. One that could only get the wrong people hurt.

After reaching home to scrub off the grime and down a pot of coffee he stared at his tattered costume in the mirror before pulling it off, shaking his head in disbelief. His hair hung in a shock before his face where the top of his hood had been ripped off. His chin protruded through another hole. Fortunately, the main parts were intact, preventing anyone from recognizing him.

After showering he stood at his window, sipping coffee, watching the sun rise high and bright over the city, glinting off of every cornice. The rising sun never looked so good as it did since he'd been sober.

His costume, all dirty, blood stained and torn, hung from a hook on the kitchen door. Tonight, under cover of darkness, he'd drop it into the city incinerator and Mindforce would be gone for good. The Phoenix would remain in his ashes this time.

The phone rang. He wanted to ignore it but it might be Sheila. If she'd heard the early morning news she'd be worried . . .

* * * *

EPILOGUE:

From the Private Files of Jason Parks

The Crime Czar and his lieutenants were gone. And with his demise, his entire empire collapsed completely. It's minions scattered back into the rat holes where they'd come from. No one would rise to claim the throne.

Mr. Big had made it to the nations capital; even now, trying to make the Senate Committee believe he was a victim of circumstance.

Vicky escaped New York City with the Justice Dept's help and dissolved into the ether of the nation.

Charlotte Greenleaf returned to college full time. She vowed to stay away from the sordid life. Though she would occasionally drop into Chicky's to see her friends.

All those caught that night in the illegal gambling casino were frantically trying to make deals with the Prosecutor's Office. Judge Bradley would be disbarred and probably do time for his misconduct. Reviewing all his cases would cost the city a fortune. The Mayor vowed to plug all the leaks in City Hall and spearhead an investigation into corruption in city politics.

Lightfingers Leroy remained at his stock and trade. While he remained a reliable snitch the Commissioner might not have him arrested.

It was doubtful the true identity of the Crime Czar would ever be known. The body was burned so severely that no dental characteristics or fingerprints could be determined.

The only thing that distinguished his body from Freddy's were bits of leather gloves clinging to the charred hands and parts of the black hood stuck to the back of the head. DNA testing could not prove anything as well.

Only Alfie Tulio and Freddy knew who he really was, and they were beyond questioning.

The Crime Czar never dealt with his lawyers face to face; only through Tulio and Lester it was later learned. Not even a sample of his handwriting could be turned up.

The boarding house was gone over with a fine tooth comb. Not even so much as a partial print could be located.

The other buildings on the block were searched. The basement of one turned out to be an arsenal of various weapons stolen over a year ago from a shipment that was earmarked for the Philadelphia Police Dept.

The trail of the Crime Czar and his dummy corporations turned cold, ending at that downtown P.O. Box. He'd covered his trail so well the search for his identity would be given up as more pressing matters needed attention.

The Crime Czar had been a tactical genius. But, for one fatal second, he was the dumbest man on Earth!

Jason Parks

* * * *

This done there was but one thing left to do. Fulfill a promise made to a good friend.

"Hi. My name is Jason . . . and I'm an . . . *Alcoholic.*"

THE END

Printed in the United States
848800001B